The Bowli

The Coulter Confessions Part 1

By

J P Hidcote

J P Hidcote was born in South Wales and was educated in Scotland and England. After an early career working in the building industry he joined the Civil Service and spent several years working in various departments including the DHSS where he worked at every level from interviewing Benefit claimants to engaging with cabinet ministers. He subsequently became an IT Project Manager in the Finance sector specialising in Internet and Telecommunications. The Bowling Five is the first of a series of novels based around the career of Edwin Coulter in the British Intelligence Services from the 1980's to the turn of the century.

The moral right of J P Hidcote to be identified as the author of this work has been asserted in accordance with the Copyright, Designs and Patents Act 1988

All rights reserved. No part of this publication may be reproduced, stored in a retrieval system, or transmitted in any form by any means, electronic, mechanical, photocopying, recording, or otherwise without the prior permission of the copyright owner or the publisher of this book.

All characters in this book are fictitious, and any resemblance to actual persons living or dead, is purely coincidental.

Chapter 1	5
Chapter 2	11
Chapter 3	14
Chapter 4	21
Chapter 5	26
Chapter 6	33
Chapter 7	38
Chapter 8	43
Chapter 9	52
Chapter 10	60
Chapter 11	67
Chapter 12	69
Chapter 13	76
Chapter 14	87
Chapter 15	96
Chapter 16	99
Chapter 17	102
Chapter 18	110
Chapter 19	126
Chapter 20	133
Chapter 21	139
Chapter 22	143
Chapter 23	146
Chapter 24	152
Chapter 25	166
Chapter 26	174
Chapter 27	177
Chapter 28	186
Chapter 29	193
Chapter 30	200

Chapter 1

Outside the window a sad gloom descended. Headlights began to cast shadows across the ceiling. I put down my cigarette and picked up the case file again. Its subject Sean Farren, Labourer, Herbert-Star Construction was by all accounts a very bad boy and a conundrum. Farren was an educated man with an English degree who had somehow got a job carrying a shovel on a building site. Not unusual for students on a summer holiday but a trifle unusual in October 1983.

Farren had been taken on by the Site Agent Bob Stewart an old pal from Strathclyde University. Farren was part of a group of Stewart's buddies who were slumming it on that soggy building site in Dumbarton. Again not suspicious in itself as managers had some leeway in recruitment and signing their pals was often a defence mechanism in the building game ensuring that the Site Agent had someone trustworthy to back them up if things got nasty with the sub contractors or the union.

The problem with Farren was that he was on the Economic League's blacklist as a suspected republican agitator. A self confessed IRA sympathiser he was not afraid of shooting his mouth off about British atrocities on the streets of Derry and Belfast. He was a well known figure on Hunger Strike marches and a regular at Celtic Park. In addition he had a girlfriend in CND who was known to camp outside Faslane Submarine Base. Again not unusual in Glasgow a city packed with similar types who never did anything more serious than generate hot air and annoy Rangers supporting colleagues and neighbours.

Farren's problem was much worse; his oldest brother had been caught assembling bombs in his Drumchapel flat. A well known local madman Paddy Farren and a friend Kevin Kennedy had decided to strike against the British state by blowing up the Scottish Office in Edinburgh. To achieve this they stole explosives while they were working at the Cruachan power station as tunnellers. Each Friday they went home with some gelignite or a time pencil in their sandwich bags. They were eventually undone by their fundamental idiocy, regaling anyone who listen about how they would change things forever "Wi wan big bang!" Drumchapel locals let the cops know and for weeks Farren's house was under constant surveillance. Meanwhile at Cruachan the Site clerk noticed that his gelignite supply was diminishing rapidly. After a quick investigation he guessed that Farren and Kennedy were the prime suspects as each time they drew explosives out of the store, they did very little blasting.

A quick call to Strathclyde Police prompted a Saturday morning raid on Farren's flat. The two would be terrorists lay in a drunken stupor in the living room surrounded by bundles of gelignite and maps of Edinburgh. The trial was short but covered in sensational style by the *Daily Record*.

It was therefore no wonder that Sean Farren had subsequently struggled to get a decent job.

He was further undone by Bob Stewart's boss Walter McGlashan, Herbert-Star Construction's Contract Manager, Grand master of the Airdrie Orange Lodge and a committed Freemason. Walter wasn't keen on any "Fenians" working for his company never mind one with a bomber brother. Every time an Irish name cropped up on his list of employees he referred it to his Economic League contact for investigation. Farren's name matched with his brother's and he had an entry of his own for his republican activism and links to CND. There was a footnote suggesting that Farren was actively recruiting a new Active Service Unit to finish his brother's plan. McGlashan it appeared had called his Masonic friend Inspector Chic Gordon of Glasgow Special Branch who referred it to my unit for investigation.

We generally filed such reports in the B1N as utter nonsense but the Government was afraid that Scotland was in danger of becoming the launch-pad for an IRA campaign after the Hunger strikes of 1981 had polarised public opinion on Northern Ireland. I was asked to analyse the reports and investigate whether Farren had any real contact with the IRA High Command.

Fed up and thoroughly bored, I stubbed my ciggie out on the gray government issue desk, slowly creating another brown burn on the imitation formica. Twenty years worth of burns had given the desk a pattern redolent of ocelot fur. The tea in my enamel mug was cold. I got up and carried the cup to the alcove that masqueraded as our kitchen. "Make me one while you are up, Feathers" drawled Simcox from the Fraud desk. I turned on the tap and shuddered as the trombone sound of the airlock reverberated across the office. "Best cut down on those mushy peas" muttered Simcox.

I ignored him and continued to fill the kettle, a Morphy Richards sixties classic that was caked with limescale from the hard water. The brown flex was frayed and looked ready to go up in smoke at any time. It matched the brown colour scheme of our comfort free office, three desks surrounded by walls of filing cabinets. A clerical Rourkes Drift; where we defended the mother country against her many foes.

As the kettle bubbled I spooned tea into the big galvanised teapot, big enough to slake the thirst of a regiment. The kettle clicked and I poured the boiling water into the cavernous pot.

I flicked two spoonfuls of sugar into each cup followed by half an inch of evaporated milk. Soldier's tea for soldiers, was Simcox's mantra. I picked up the pot and swirled it around. Opened the lid and stirred it with a spoon. Mashing the tea as my boss John Foster would say. I poured the tea slowly through our strainer which had turned a mahogany brown after years without a good wash. The amber liquid, the colour of IPA filled the cups turning beige as it met the evaporated milk. My mother a genteel lady would have been revolted by the sickly sweet brew. Fortunately I had developed a taste for it in the OTC so it was no ordeal to drink it several times a day.

Head down I sloped across to Simcox's desk. Thankfully he didn't look up. I carefully positioned the cup between the pile of manila files on the fat buffoon's desk whilst trying hard not to retch at the strange odour of sweat and day old brylcream that emanated from his corpulent presence.

"Many thanks, old boy" followed a slurp of tea.

I turned and walked slowly back to my desk.

Resigned I moved to the second page of Farren's file. Evidence statements collected from Farren's colleagues about the nascent Active Service Unit the villain was forming. A list of employees at the site, split into witnesses and suspects. Strangely all of the witnesses seemed to be staunch Scots Prestbyterians, despite 60% of the men on the site possessing Irish names like John Murphy, Pat Logue and John O'Brien.

Most of the statements from the labourers implied that Farren and his Fenian pals gathered in quiet corners and stopped talking when a strangers came anywhere near them. Nobody had actually heard anything except the General Foreman Rueben Snodgrass. The investigating officer had helpfully documented Snodgrass' personal history:

Name – Rueben Snodgrass
Age – 52
Educated – Airdrie Academy
Family –
- Son of Buchanan Snodgrass, miner
- Married to Jean McGlashan(sister of Walter McGlashan)
- 5 children (3 sons and 2 daughters)
- Mason(member of Airdrie St Andrews)
- Lambeg drummer for the William Jackson LOL
- Sergeant, Highland Light Infantry (1948 – 1960)
    - Served in Malaya, Cyprus and Kenya
- Joined Herbert-Star as a bricklayer after leaving the army rising to GF when his brother in law became the Contracts Manager
- A keen hunter and fisherman

A solid citizen who could be trusted was the copper's message. Snodgrass claimed that his suspicions developed when he realised Farren was engaging the drain layers in complex discussions as they worked. The drainlayers worked for a gangmaster called Pat Rogan who recruited solely from Glasgow's Donegal diaspora. Donegal Ireland's most northernly county had opted to join the Irish

Free State in 1921 rather than the Six counties of Ulster in the Northern Irish state. This cut the Donegal people off from their main economic centre and titular capital of Londonderry. Emigration to Glasgow had always been fluid but since the war had been one way. As a result most of the Irish in Glasgow were of Donegal extraction. A clannish bunch Donegal people tended to prefer their own company to that of Irish from the more southerly counties.

Snodgrass' experience in the colonial bush wars had taught him to be wary when the natives started talking fancy among themselves rather than the usual banter about drink and football. He tried to get his colleague, Franz Zuck, the Polish assistant site agent and General Foreman to help monitor the conversations but Zuck, a Free Polish Army veteran, had given him short shrift. Two years in a Soviet Gulag after he escaped from the Nazi's had made him deeply suspicious of anyone trying to inform on his fellow man.

Snodgrass did find an ally in Hughie MacGregor a Rangers supporting labourer who took great pleasure in winding up his Irish colleagues. MacGregor claimed that Farren's group consisted of five other men from Rogan's outfit:

- Joe Gallagher
- Tommy Wilson
- Francie O'Brien
- Charley Flood
- Henry Walker

Gallagher was a septuagenarian from Dunfanaghy, Donegal. A broad powerful man despite his years, he was better known for his Guinness consumption than any desire for Irish unification. Wilson was also a grandfather who had been in Scotland since the 1940s. O'Brien was in his late forties, he came from the Gaeltacht village of Gortahork, Donegal. A man filled with bitterness against the brother who stole the family farm from him by staying at home. Walker was a family man in his 40's from the Lagan area of East Donegal, a gambler with no obvious political leanings. Flood from Moville in Northern Donegal had been a watchman in the Singer sewing machine factory until the giant industrial complex closed and left Clydebank a post industrial ghetto.

A strange bunch of would be terrorists though they did fit the profile of the Birmingham bombers. It was hard to see them having any common ground with an intellectual smart arse like Sean Farren.

I rubbed my eyes and tried to stay awake by counting the cracks in the ceiling and the number of flies on the flypaper. A fat bluebottle that had been hovering around for days had finally succumbed to the lure of the sticky paper. His wings buzzed furiously as he tried to pull himself free. I wondered how it felt to have fallen into a trap through your own stupidity.

Snodgrass also identified another potential member of the gang. James Herrity a 16 year old YTS trainee Civil Engineer who joined the site in September on a placement from Glasgow College of Building & Printing. Herrity spent his working days with John Coleman the site engineer and a graduate engineer Andrew Logan from Forres. As quasi management they took their breaks in the same room as Snodgrass. Snodgrass described Herrity as a quiet individual with an "unsettling" feel about him. I pressed the play button on the cassette recorder and listened to the recording of Snodgrass giving his statement:

"He is not openly offensive but someone who smiles with his mouth not his eyes. Ye can talk tae him but ye get the feel that he judges you and laughs at yer jokes because he feels he has tae. Underneath I suspect he is a bit of a fenian hothead, but works hard to keep it in check. Wan time I made some cracks about sorting out the Tims at the next Parade when he was making his concrete test cubes in the container shed. He half growled at me. Ah telt him tae behave or he'd get a boot in the baws. He lifted the tamping bar out of the test cube and half stepped towards me, wi a red mist in his eyes. Luckily I stepped back and said ah was only joking or he wid hae split ma skull wi it. After a couple of seconds he was back in control but ah made sure I wisnae alone wi him again and made sure I kept any talk about the lodge to a minimum. A dangerous boy!"

"After that I noticed that he was a lot mair chatty wi Farren and the other Paddies. If he was doon a drain track wi the levelling staff they wid be bantering away. Once he came back up he would be Mister Silent again. He never said much to Coleman or Logan, just the occasional yes/no maybe sort of stuff. Overall I thought he was just a psycho ned like a lot of folk fae Paisley."

"Then wan day I spotted Farren, Gallagher, Flood, Herrity, O'Brien, Walker and wee Wilson standing by a stack o' 18 inch pipes. I slipped behind the pipes and heard Farren talking about making changes. O'Brien said it was about time something was done. Gallagher said the man is a bloody dictator, time for a revolution. Herrity asked Farren when was he planning it for. Farren said the 23rd would be D-day. The visit was scheduled for then, if we are in position then we can ambush him before he gets settled. Herrity said it was a big step, was it worth the risk. Farren said we can't change things without taking action. If you guys are with me I will do the deed. Walker said we need to get our positions sorted out to avoid any crossfire. Wilson said he would be the rearguard and watch yer backs. Farren said this was what needed to be done if they followed his plan it would work and thanked them for their courage."

"I knew then that they were up to no good, I asked Derek Craig the site clerk what was happening on the 23rd. "oh the Royal Visit, you mean. Prince Charles is visiting the whisky bond." I looked out at the pile of pipes, through the site fence at the Ballantines Whisky sign."

"I called Walter and told him that he was right to be suspicious aboot Farren, he was planning an attack on Prince Charles. Walter told me tae calm doon and then he called you guys."

"Since then I have got wee Hughie to work beside Farren every day. This has broken up the group. They haven't said anything else suspicious but Hughie has seen them in the boozer together in the toon."

I pressed the pause button on the cassette recorder and looked out at the London traffic. This was either a masterpiece of investigation or the ranting of bigot. I couldn't tell which and neither could the cops who had referred the case to us instead of arresting the suspects.

The clock reached five. Simcox put on his fawn raincoat and hat and said "Hometime Feathers" before stumbling out the door. I closed the file pulled on my tweed overcoat, turned off the light with the brown switch and walked out into the dingy corridor. I joined the stream of colleagues heading for the Circle line.

Chapter 2

I got off at Kings Cross and fought my way through the crowds to the Northern Line. A very attractive blonde smiled at me but I couldn't get close enough to speak to her. The Clapham South train arrived and I clambered in. Trapped between a Greek's armpit and an Indian woman's head, I had to stand all the way. Almost retching I leapt out of the train at Clapham South and made my way up the near vertical escalator. As I neared the top, the sweet fresh air swept across my face and the nausea began to recede. London is a vile place at rush hour.

I crossed the road, walked past the hospital and turned right down Rubberwood Road. I wandered into the gate of No.25, put my Yale key in the lock turned it and stepped in. The smell of cinnamon spiced lamb and onions drifted out from the kitchen. Ahmed must be making his Moroccan stew again. I turned right and started to climb the stairs Pedro, the Spanish student, opened his bedroom door and said "Hello Felipe". I nodded and said "hi", before opening my room, mortice lock first (two turns) and then the yale.

Inside my room looked the same. Brown pre war mahogany wardrobe, a utility style chest of drawers and an iron framed double bed. The carpet's blue and yellow swirls contrasted violently with the tangerine walls. I closed the curtains in the bay window and sat down. I would give Ahmed half an hour to finish his dinner before I went down to the kitchen.

I turned on the radio, it was the evening news. The fallout from the Russians shooting down a South Korean airliner continued. Reagan was outraged, his ICBM sized sabre rattling furiously. This was the kind of event I joined the service for. The boys on the Russian and American desks would be working 24 hr days. Deciphering secret messages from the world's pinch points and pumping out executive briefings. They would be running contingency planning exercises, maybe even turning on the heating in the secret bunkers. One thing for sure was that they would be having loads of fun.

Meanwhile, on the Counter Terrorism Scotland desk we have to analyse notes from numbskull informers about gangs of crazed navvies. Still if I keep plugging away, Foster has promised me a transfer to the Turkish team which will be more interesting and provide the chance of some exotic trips to Istanbul. I could smell the spices from here, well I could certainly smell Ahmed's dinner; it was time to eat.

I couldn't face the kitchen. The smell of other people's food makes me bilious and there is always the risk that Ahmed will still be there intent on regaling me with his world view, America is Satan, Islam will rise again etc. It doesn't get any more interesting. I put my coat back on and skipped down the stairs.

At the end of the road I turned right and started heading for Balham. I stopped outside Marino's Italian café. Ignoring the fish and chip counter, I decided to sit down and try the Italian food. The waitress, a voluptuous woman of about 40 with blue black hair brought me a menu and asked if I wanted a drink. I ordered a glass of Soave, it was foul; but I don't really enjoy any kind of wine.

The menu offered Spaghetti Bolognese, Spaghetti Carbonara, lasagne, cannelloni, Florentine steak and some seafood concoctions. I ordered the lasagne, wholesome and easy to eat. I hate twirling spaghetti on spoons. A young couple on a date were in the corner directly opposite. She was stroking his hand and laughing as her beau told her a tale about a passenger on his bus. She was pretty with curly red hair and very blue eyes. I smiled at her but she ignored me. Most of the other diners were middle-aged couples out for some kind of celebratory dinner. Most of the men wore suits or blazers.

My lasagne arrived accompanied by some limp flat lettuce and an anaemic tomato, I ignored the attempted salad. The lasagne was surprisingly tasty; the creamy cheese sauce went well with the tomato and mince sauce. I wolfed it down. It made the wine taste passable. The waitress cleared away my plate and said "You must be starving, would you like a dessert menu?" and pressed a plastic sheet with pictures of ice cream sundaes into my hand. I noticed that she wore no wedding ring. Smiling I replied "I will have the knickerbocker glory". She smiled back and said the banana split was her favourite. I suggested we should share one sometime. "Oh you are awful" she laughed in the style of Dick Emery.

After a couple of minutes she came back with a Rum baba, a doughnut style bun full of cream that smelt of some kind of alcohol. "I am afraid, the knickerbockers have run out and we don't have any bananas so I brought you one of these instead". Thanking her, I wolfed down the greasy mess in a couple of spoonfuls. It didn't taste too bad really. "God you are hungry" she remarked as she took away my dessert bowl. "Would you like coffee?"

"Of course, white with 2 sugars" I said.

The coffee came back scalding hot from the espresso machine. I let it cool and looked round the room most people were waiting for their desserts. Eating alone was certainly faster, no breaks for conversation. I counted the raffia coated wine bottles and the old fishing nets. The place probably hadn't been decorated since 1958. I half expected Cliff and the Shadows to burst out of the toilet singing 'The Young Ones'.

I looked down at the coffee and realised that I had drank it without even tasting it. The waitress picked up my cup and said "Finished?"

I looked up and said "Yes, can I have the bill please?"

She came back 5 minutes later with a bill for 6 quid. I almost choked. I didn't remember walking into the Ritz. Thank God I didn't have a starter or some Garlic bread. The waitress stood beside me her purse open; I pulled six pound notes and a fifty pence piece out of my pocket. She gave me a big lascivious smile and said "it was always a pleasure to serve a proper gent". I smiled and stood up. Her plump figure seemed very alluring. I almost asked her out until I realised she had escorted me to the door and gently pushed me out of it. Before I could say anything, the door closed behind me and she turned to serve another customer. Feeling a little discomfited by such an overt rejection. I wandered along the street aimlessly it was nearly 9 o'clock. I had two choices go to a pub for an hour or go home.

Feeling a little alcoholised from the wine and the Rum Baba which had cost a ridiculous £2. I turned and wandered home. As I entered the hall I could hear Ahmed chanting in Arabic. I stomped up the stairs as loudly as possibly in the vain hope of shutting him up. In my room again, I took off my clothes and folded them on the chair. I decided that my life needed some excitement. At tomorrows case review, I would suggest that I go up to Scotland to interview Snodgrass and have a look at Farren and his gang. After Mountbatten, any threat to the Royal family was taken extra seriously, even if I suspected it was all fantasy on Snodgrass' part.

Chapter 3

The dreadful Westclox alarm exploded in my ear at 7am. I rolled over and turned on the radio. Bryan Redhead started explaining why the world was a dangerous place. Apparently Saddam Hussein was the only barrier to religious fundamentalism in the Middle East; the West missed Sadat. A year on from the Sabra and Shatilla massacre Lebanon remained a political basket case. Reagan was on the verge of nuking Russia. I zoned it out as I washed my face at the basin in the corner. I squeezed some Ultrabrite onto my toothbrush then remembered I hadn't shaved. I wet my face again, rubbed the soap stick across my chin. I slowly whipped up the lather with my hog bristle brush. Maybe I need to move to shaving foam; it looks much easier. I picked my razor up from the basin. The water was lukewarm, this as going to hurt. The first stroke down my cheek was fine. I tried an upstroke on my neck but gave up when the pain started. I decided to concentrate on down strokes. After five minutes I was finished. I looked in the mirror, no cuts but I had missed a few bits. Several cautious strokes later I was finished but my face was stinging. I rinsed my face in cold water and rubbed in some Tzar aftershave. I pulled on my clothes, tied my tie in a half Windsor and combed my hair into its fifties side parting.

I never liked long hair and have been much happier in the last few years as short hair has come back into fashion. In the right light I look a bit like a blond Dirk Bogarde, at least that's what mum says.

In the kitchen I pulled my little Hovis loaf out of the cupboard and popped two slices into the toaster. I filled the kettle and put it on front left ring of the stove. The gas lit after a couple of attempts. Alsager, the older man who lived on the top floor, bustled into the kitchen.

"Morning, Phil" he whispered in his hoarse West Country burr.

"Morning Adrian, sleep well?"

"Not bad, finished reading Seven Pillars last night. Lawrence was a strange man; very clever but very strange."

"So they say. I prefer to think of the film version, much more fun"

"Not much fact though. Look out your toast is burning"

I spun round and extracted two charred slices from the toaster. I opened the marmalade and spread it on the toast. The roar of the kettle whistle woke me with a start.

"That's louder than a Portsmouth foghorn" growled Alsager

I spooned Nescafe into my cup, added two sugars and some milk then poured in the boiling water.

I ate my breakfast in silence as Alsager fussed around trying to poach an egg. It always ended up a dreadful mess but he insisted on doing it every Tuesday.

I strode up to the station and descended to the depths of hell on the rickety escalator. I got to the platform just as the warm oily smell of an approaching Northern line train began to build up; slowly increasing to a throbbing violent climax when the train burst out of the tunnel.

The doors opened with the usual crack and a few desperadoes were ejected. God knows what they work at round here. I pushed my way in carefully nudging a tall thin African man out of the way. He apologised to me in a deep sonorous voice,

"I am awfully sorry, not used to crowds like this"

I smiled and worked my way deeper into the carriage. It was standing room only as usual. The Italian woman was on the train again, hooray! I stood opposite her, trying desperately to catch her eye. Her brown hair was thick and lustrous. Her lips were bright red as usual and her business suit was beautifully tailored. She must work in fashion or PR; definitely no average worker this girl. Her black stilettos gleamed at the end of her long slim legs. She calmly turned the pages of her copy of la Repubblica. The headline seemed to be about some terrorist or mafia atrocity. The Italian PM was going to resign or the government was going to fall. The usual tosh, I waited for her to look up. Maybe today we might speak. My palms began to sweat; her station was getting closer. She folded her paper and put it carefully into her black patent leather briefcase. She stood up directly opposite me. My heart started beating like a drum. I smiled. She smiled.

"Excuse me" she whispered in a seductive voice.

I stepped aside and let her get off the train.

"See you tomorrow" she giggled as she stepped on to the platform.

"Same time, same place" I stuttered. She waved and disappeared into the crowd.

My stop appeared. I exited the train in a trance, pushed along by the human train until I was on the Circle line platform. Two stops whizzed by. I pushed my way on to the platform behind a tall red head. Long legs and Titian curls; a spectacular site and a real treat in the morning. Through the barrier she went left; I went right. I dawdled along to the office counting good looking girls. I reached 30 by the time I got to the office. A record!

My heart sank when I found myself outside the brown brick façade of the department. On the wall there was still a sign for the National General Insurance Company. I was never sure if they had ever existed. Ernie the commissionaire nodded to me as I walked in. He was the epitome of High security, British style; a geriatric ex marine with a preposterous uniform. The white sash made him look like a South American dictator.

I took the stairs, tiring but a lot safer than the lift which would have been old in the 1920's. Sweating a little, I reached our office just before Simcox. I hung up my coat, filled the kettle and checked the in-tray for the early mail; nothing interesting, just a bundle of typing full of the usual mix of spelling mistakes and bad page alignment. We would be better off doing it ourselves. The kettle boiled, I made the tea and opened today's can of evaporated milk. I put a cup on Simcox's desk and sat down. I had the department meeting in half an hour. To wangle a trip to Scotland I needed to talk up the Farren threat. My creative writing skills were required.

Case review

Subject – Suspected ASU, Dunbartonshire

Source – Tip off from established informant. Police statements from informant and supporting witnesses. Suspects under observation.

Threat – Suspects are believed to be planning an assault on HRH PoW during visit to Ballantines Whisky Bond on 23rd October.

Mitigation – Field trip to Glasgow for liaison/verification sessions with Strathclyde Police. Surveillance of suspects and arrest if necessary.

Status – Amber

A masterpiece! Old Foster was terrified of having to deal with another Royal getting bumped off. So just repeating the bigoted, rambling theories of the likes of Snodgrass in the right manner, with the slightest hint of a genuine threat was going to get me a week in a nice Glasgow hotel.

At 9.45 I pulled the papers together and strolled along to the conference room. The oak table looked like it had been in use since Victoria's day. I sat down on one of the plastic chairs, very uncomfortable as usual.

Foster coughed and said "Good Morning everyone. Trust you slept well. The first item on the agenda is the NUM in South Yorkshire, Peter please give us your update."

Peter Leach shuffled his papers and began a long diatribe on the nefarious nature of Arthur Scargill and his plans for world domination. I drew a Stuka on my pad bombing a tank.

Foster asked Leach some questions and told him that No 10 wanted 24 hour surveillance of the NUM leadership. Big changes in the mining industry were in the pipeline that would be crucial for the future of the economy. The NUM had to be kept under control. "We are relying on you Peter."

"On to item 2, Philip please fill us in on this Irish terror cell in Scotland. Is it another one of these hoaxes?"

"Not sure John. It could be one of these Celtic/Rangers things but I am not sure. The men involved are the low key types like the Birmingham and Guildford outfits. No obvious connection to PIRA command but definitely Paddies. The main witness served in Kenya, Malaya and Cyprus so he has an experienced eye for terrorist types. He has kept them under surveillance and from his findings there is a strong possibility that they are planning an attack on Prince Charles when he visits Dumbarton on the 23rd."

Foster's lumpy face turned a touching shade of coral. "Good lord we can't have that. How sure are you that they are after the Prince? "

"The site is next door to the whisky plant that His Royal Highness will visit on the 23rd and the lead informant has heard the suspects planning activity on the 23rd. They only talk dates when they think they are alone."

"What action do you propose? Shall we get Special Branch to bring them in for questioning?"

"No, I think it needs a softer approach. I would like to spend some time in Glasgow speaking to the witnesses and observing the suspects before we do anything. That may give us a chance of tracing their PIRA contacts. If we draw a blank then just to make sure, I will get the company to split them up so that they can't try anything against the Prince on the 23rd."

"Good thinking, Philip. Speak to Marjorie about your travel and accommodation. We can't take any risks with the heir to the throne. Now Simcox, what's this about Guinness and dodgy stock market deals?"

Simcox launched into his usual blather about insider trading and market manipulation. I glazed over. The man had the most tedious job imaginable. What danger to the UK national security did city traders present? I couldn't understand why the department even had a fraud section. As long as the City made money Britain stayed rich. My father could never understand why governments were so obsessed with keeping the northern industries going. I could see him in his green tweed suit standing by the mantelpiece regaling the room "Hotbeds of bloody commies with no idea of how to do a day's work. If we shut down the mines and the steel industry the country would be much better off. They haven't made money for years." I had to agree, there seemed to be little point in manufacturing these days.

"Right Philip, tread carefully with this Irish murder gang. Don't spook them and for god's sake don't make a fool of yourself by rushing in. It could be a hoax, a bundle of rumour and supposition." I blushed a little and tried to hide the fact that I was miles away.

"Don't worry John my focus is on making sure of the facts. I will send you a report every day. With a bit of luck it turns out to be nothing. The last thing we want is another attack on the Royals."

Foster nodded appreciatively. He liked people to re-affirm his opinions.

I wandered back to the office feeling smug. Simcox had beaten me back.

"Well Feathers, you wangled yourself a jaunt to jolly Jocko land. Watch out they don't eat you. Fellow like you with an Oxbridge accent will go down like a lead balloon with the Glasgow cops. They don't like the English and they especially despise upper class English."

"Thanks for the tip, Simcox. I didn't know you cared"

"I don't but I do care about the reputation of the department. The last thing I want is for the Gorbals wide boys to make a complete fool out of you. They love gossip our Police friends. Anything goes wrong and every chief constable in the country will cast it up to the man upstairs. Before we know it, the cops will stop communicating with us and we will be forced to beg them to share information."

"Calm down old boy!! I'm going up there to follow up on the leads they have provided this is no Don Quixote exercise. I didn't make it up. The cops wouldn't have reported it if they thought it was a load of rubbish."

"Maybe, but it sounds flimsy to me. Don't jump to conclusions. Careful measured analysis is our game. Catch the crooks before they commit the crime is our motto."

I looked at his florid face. Something had wound him up. Probably jealous that Foster never lets him have a jolly to a tax haven like the Cayman Islands or Monaco. I couldn't understand why he thought I would balls up things in Glasgow. I was only going to interview the witnesses and sit in on some surveillance. Maybe I would get a chance to sample the Glasgow nightlife. Simcox was probably worried that I would get done in by a Glasgow Razor gang.

Headlines like "Spy slashed in Sauchiehall Street" were probably crossing his mind.

Simcox shook his head turned and went back to his desk, muttering to himself. I sat down and opened my rolodex. Marjorie Gault was on 34218. I dialled her number.

"Hello, Philip Featherstonehaugh from the Counter Terrorism – Scotland here. I need to book some travel and accommodation in Glasgow"

"Hi Philip, John told me you would be in touch. I have booked you a room in the Lorne on Sauchiehall Street and a ticket on tonight's Glasgow sleeper. If you pop down after 2pm I will have the ticket ready. "

Majorie had a warm chocolate voice that slithered over you lulling you into a wonderful restful state. Unfortunately she was about ninety and probably worked here during the Great War.

"Marjorie you are a star, this place would collapse without you." I simpered

"See you at two, Philip"

The woman was all work, no time for would be charmers. All her love was saved for some fifties James Bond who probably disappeared behind the Iron Curtain a generation ago.

I called Inspector Gordon in Glasgow and told him him I would be in Glasgow tomorrow morning. He said he was based at Cranstonhill CID on Argyle Street. I told him I would be there at 9.45. He agreed to set up interviews with Snodgrass and McGlashan in the afternoon.

I packed the papers into my attaché case and prepared to go home early to pack. I popped out to Sid's Café for lunch. A massive salt beef and gherkin sandwich left me feeling bilious as I ascended the stairs to collect my train ticket. Marjorie's cauliflower topped head bobbed up as I approached everyone else steadfastly ignored me; all steadfast adherents of the need to know principle.

"Hello Philip, best pack some warm underwear Scotland can be rather chilly at this time of year. Your tickets are in the envelope along with directions to the hotel. John has approved an imprest of £200 to cover the hotel and any expenses. We booked you in for 4 days bed and breakfast. Let us know if you need to stay any longer and we will arrange for a top up from the Glasgow office. If you can sign and date it at the bottom, you will be ready to go."

I signed the yellow top sheet and handed it back to Marjorie. She tore off the yellow and blue copies and gave me the pink bottom copy. I opened the envelope and counted ten twenty pound notes. The travel warrant was hand written in Marjorie's impeccable copperplate.

"Thanks Marjorie, you are a model of efficiency"

She smiled coyly and said "Have a lovely trip and be careful"

"Don't worry; getting some rest on the sleeper will be the hardest part"

Sensing my time was up, I said cheerio and carefully backed out of the room before her colleagues began to hiss their disapproval! They had limited time for field staff who lingered in their sanctum.

I skipped back to my desk incredulous that not only was I getting four days away from my desk; I would have masses of money to spend. This was the James Bond lifestyle I joined up for.

I picked up my case, locked my pen, pencil, ruler, stapler and hole punch in my desk. They would disappear if I left them unattended for 4 days; the place was full of thieves. I locked other papers in temp filing cabinet.

"Cheerio Simcox, see you next week"

"Bye Feathers, remember to pack your toothbrush and don't let the Jocks make a fool out of you."

"No chance old boy"

"Bollocks" Simcox snorted as I went out the door.

Chapter 4

I felt like I was walking on air all the way to the tube platform. My positive mood was not even affected by the dread announcement:

"Eastbound Services have been suspended due to a Security incident at Euston Square"

I hopped on to the West bound train instead and stayed on until Embankment. The train was full of tourists. A group of gorgeous blonde honey tanned Americans got on at Bayswater and sat opposite me until Westminster. I smiled at them and listened to their inane sightseeing conversations. London Bridge, Big Ben, Harrods they loved old London town. I wished they would shut up and start loving me. An afternoon in my bedsit would give them a real happy memory of London. Sadly the lure of Big Ben was too strong and they skipped off at Westminster, one of them gave me a very warm smile.

At Embankment after the usual 20 mile hike I clambered onto the Northern line for the grimy journey to Clapham South. The train was empty except for a few vagrant types. No one spoke or even moved.

At Clapham South I hopped off and hoped I wouldn't get the 'Bends' as the escalator pulled me up to the surface. The cold fresh air seared my face as we neared the top. It was always so warm on the Northern line, permanently sub-tropical, especially if you were wearing your overcoat. Ecstatic to be back on the surface, I walked briskly across the road and was halfway down Rubberwood Road in no time.

The hallway still stank of my housemates woeful cooking. I took the stairs two at a time and carefully opened my door. No sign of forced entry, no-one rifling through my papers, just silence. Funny how the bad guys always know when Bond has been assigned to a new mission: in real life no-one cares. Though I knew that I would run a mile if a mad 'Provo' accosted me.

I pulled my brown plastic suitcase out of the wardrobe and began to pack. 1 blue suit, 1 tweed jacket, five shirts, 6 pairs of underpants, 6 pairs of socks, toilet bag, 1 pair of pyjamas, 1 pair of brown shoes, 2 ties, 1 pair of jeans, 1 pair of slacks, 1 v-neck jumper. Essentially all the clothes I owned.

Mission accomplished I lay on the bed and read this week's '*2000AD*'. Dredd was fighting some kind of block war, Nemesis was overthrowing some bad guys and Rogue Trooper was killing everyone he met. Ace! I would need to get some reading material for the train. The WH Smiths at Euston would be closed by the time I got there. I decided to pop down to the second hand bookshop in Balham.

Work travel gave you loads of free time. It was great to be out of the office in the afternoon.

The bookshop was full of books in no real order. I picked a couple of cheap ones, *"The Long Pursuit"* by John Cleary and *"The Last Parallel"* by Martin Russ. The old ponce who ran the shop looked me up and down and said

"That will be a quid, me duck". I handed him a pound note picked up the books and left without speaking. Nobody calls me a duck.

I wandered aimlessly for a while until I was hungry. The chippy had just opened so I bought myself cod and chips and a can of cola. I raced back to the house, grabbed a plate from the kitchen cupboard and mismatched cutlery from the drawer. The knife had a mother of pearl style handle and the fork was heavy mock silver decorated with flowers.

The fish and chips were their usual disappointing selves; dry fish in soggy batter and a high volume of overcooked chips. Nonetheless it beat cooking and washing a load of pots. The clock struck 6. I had four hours to kill until I could get on the sleeper.

I washed the plate and threw the empty can in the bin. The house was still empty, a good time to leave before my flatmates returned in various states of post work despair and frequent drunkenness. I had no interest in explaining that I would be going on a business trip.

I climbed the stairs two at a time. Opened my door, packed my books into my case and made sure the window was locked and the radio unplugged before I locked the door. I carefully went down the stairs, opened the door and stepped out. I locked the front door and headed off to the tube. No one on the street, no curtains twitching, I had got away without being noticed. Excellent!

The tube station was quiet, just me and an old African heading for town. The train roared into the station. I let him get on first then walked to the next carriage which was virtually empty. At the far end an Asian family babbled in an incomprehensible tongue taking no notice of me.

People came and went as we chugged towards Euston. I barely noticed them, hypnotised by the motion and the noise. Suddenly we rolled into Euston. I jolted awake and stepped off the train remembering to pick up my case. A sudden sinking feeling swept across me; did I leave my tickets on the dressing table? They weren't in the inside pocket of my overcoat. I started to panic then remembered they were in my jacket pocket. The cold sweat started to recede.

I walked over to the left luggage lockers and popped my case into locker 27. Luggage free I decided to go to the Gaumont cinema down Euston Road. '*An Officer and a Gentleman'* was on. I bought a hotdog and a coke and settled in.

It was a hokum film, Richard Gere was a thug who joined the US Navy, took some stick from the drill sergeant and pulled a local girl. By the end however I quite fancied getting a navy uniform to see if it really worked with the women.

I wandered out of the cinema behind a blonde and her boyfriend, her legs tapered into perfectly defined ankles, accentuated by her 5 inch red stilettos. I walked behind them towards the station, transfixed by the ripples in her calf muscles. I strode past them in the station concourse just to see her face. What a disappointment! Thin hard nose and chin! Not my type at all. I left them to head for their train and ambled over to the left luggage lockers. I was relieved to see that mine was still intact; no-one had been round with a crowbar or a lockpick. I took the case out and headed for my platform. It was buzzing. Stewards were waiting at each carriage to guide passengers to their cabins. I showed the fellow at carriage H my ticket.

"Good evening sir. You are in cabin 7; looks like you will be on your own. The buffet car is in coach J and the bar will open at 11.45. We get into Glasgow Central around 7am. Shall I call you for breakfast at say 6.30?"

I said thanks that would be lovely and shut the door to my cabin. It could only be described as snug and blue-gray in colour with the exception of the sheets and pillows which were off white and embroidered with the British Rail logo. There were two bunks on the right, a wash basin under the window: a luggage shelf on the left and a couple of hooks for coats.

I sat down on the bottom bunk and looked at my watch. It was 10.55. Fifty minutes until the bar opened. I locked the door and stretched out on the bunk, I pulled the string above my head and the reading light came on. I got up and opened my case, I pulled out *"The Long Pursuit"* because it had the most racy cover; a big guy firing a gun while holding on to a scantily clad woman.

Hoping for some erotica I started reading. It was set in Singapore as the Japs were about to take the city. An American drifter hooked up with a disparate group of civilians and some British soldiers in order to escape from the city. There was lots of tension in the group but they were working together to escape by boat. My dad had escaped from Dunkirk in 1940. So I had imagined a lot of this kind of stuff happening to him, but he never really told me anything other than the bare facts. Retreated from Arras, managed to avoid being in the rearguard, joined a queue in the harbour dodged some bombs and climbed up the side of a destroyer which took him home. He didn't do emotion or drama; he could have been describing a trip to the park. He spent the rest of the war in Canada and South Africa training colonial recruits and got home in 1946 without firing another shot.

A steady rattle woke me up, the light was on I was fully clothed. I felt awful. I checked my watch, it was 12.20. I considered going to bed but decided to try the bar. Hoping for a stranger on a train experience, a lone heiress seeking a handsome man would do. I stepped out into the corridor and headed for carriage J. Any thoughts of a passionate brief encounter evaporated when I entered the bar. Three Scots were arguing in the corner about politics. Two business men sat contemplating their Gin and tonics and an old man in a raincoat lay snoring with a half pint glass in his hand.

I strode up to the bar and asked for a pint of bitter. The barman said he had no draught beer but did have some bottles of Whitbread. I bought one for 70p and sat down in the corner nearest the door. I poured half of the bottle into my pint glass and took a long drink. The beer was fairly pleasant; pale ale I think.

I looked across at the Scotsmen. One was small fat and bald. The other was extremely tall, vaguely like Plug from *'The Beano'*. The third was younger, heavy set with thick dark hair. They were fairly well educated but pretty hard line socialists. Every second sentence featured the words 'Thatcher' or 'Tories' plus an expletive. The baldie also had a deep hatred for Jim Callaghan and Michael Foot.

The business men drank up and left probably bored senseless by the drone of the Scots. I drank up and left too before they tried to engage me in conversation. They seemed to be regular customers; the barman cleared their table and brought them drinks automatically every 15 minutes but ignored everyone else. Plug from *'The Beano'* seemed to be arguing for an independent Scotland when I stood up. The other two didn't seem to be in full agreement.

Glad to escape before I was asked to provide an English view, I strolled back to my cabin bouncing against the walls of the corridor. The train was swaying like a cross channel ferry. I tried looking out of the window but I had no idea where we were. Back in my cabin I brushed my teeth, popped out to the toilet and had to wait for Plug to come out. He towered over me as he edged past heading back to the bar. The smell was awful; he must have been eating curry. Almost gassed, I stuck my head out of the window when I got out. We still seemed to somewhere between North London and Watford. This was a slow train. The cold damp air washed across my face, occasionally we passed a house with a light on. God knows what they were doing at this hour; the TV was finished for hours. Insomniacs or crazed readers!

I staggered back to my cabin suddenly very tired. I locked the cabin door and took my clothes off. I climbed into bed, turned out the light and tried to sleep despite the noise of the wind whistling down the corridor. A loud Scots voice appeared outside my door. The steward's West Country brogue responded. I listened to their muffled voices as the steward seemed to be gamely helping the Jock to bed in the adjacent cabin. The door closed and loud snoring began to reverberate through the wall shortly after. I rolled over and faced the wall, 1.30am: five hours to breakfast.

At several points during the night I dozed off before being jolted awake as we arrived in some station. At 3.30 we appeared to be in Lancashire. After Carlisle I fell into a deep sleep before I was woken up by the steward banging on my door. I stumbled out of bed and opened the door.

"Breakfast sir; milk and sugar, butter and marmalade?"

I said yes and he gave me a tray with a cup of tea, a jug of milk two sugar cubes, a plate with two slices of toast a pat of butter and marmalade, a knife and a spoon. I said thanks and he banged on the next cabin door;

"Glasgow sir time to rise and shine!" He winked at me and said "He never makes his breakfast" and moved on to the next door. I sat on my bed and ate the toast and drank the tea. A loud bang was followed by a loud Scots scream. The snorer sounded as if he had fallen out of bed.

I put the tray on the floor and brushed my teeth. I put my clothes back on and went to the toilet. Thankfully it was fresher than last night. I stepped out to meet Plug in his paisley pattern pyjamas. He looked like he had a major hangover. I edged past him, he said nothing. I heard him sit down then headed back to my cabin to avoid listening to him playing the porcelain trombone.

Chapter 5

The train rolled to a halt in a large Victorian station. We were on platform 11; crowds of commuters were already arriving in the city. I asked the steward if there was a café or somewhere I could kill time in until 9am. He laughed and said there might be a Henry Healy sandwich shop on Renfield Street that opens around half eight but generally nothing else until nine.

Dismayed I wandered over to the John Menzies newsagent and spent the hour reading comics and magazines. *'The Victor'* cover story was about a Highlander who won a Military Medal for fighting his way to Dunkirk alone after he got split up from his unit. Alf Tupper was working on an oil rig as a welder when he got a late call up for the Olympics and had to row his way to Aberdeen in a dinghy because the helicopters couldn't fly in the fog. He then bummed a ride on a Fish train to London and stank of fish on his flight to the games. What a man!! In the *'Battle'*, Charley Bourne was fighting in the trenches against the Germans and his chinless officers as usual.

At nine I pushed my way through the crowds to the taxi rank. There was about ten in front of me in the queue a combination of old ladies with cases and some very poor looking people who looked as if they should be getting the bus.

Eventually I got a cab, the lardball driver nodded when I climbed in but said nothing.

"Cranstonhill Police station please I said."

"Aye nae bother, there is a closer wan if ye need tae report a robbery."

"Its ok I have an appointment there."

"Ur ye a lawyer?"

"No."

"Ye're no a polis, too rich n too smeirt lookin tae be wan o them"

"My company has dealings with the Glasgow force."

"Ah git it noo ye're gonnae sell them something, plenty o dosh they bams, only growth industry in this toon is crime these days an the polis ur the biggest crooks o the lot!"

"Very true."

"Watch yir bag when ye'r in there. They're are aw thieving bams!"

"I will do."

"If yer here fer a few days ye can use oor nummer on this caird an we'll tak ye aboot tae yir ither customers. The buses in this toon ur crap, ye'll git naewhere fast."

"Thanks that will be very useful."

"Here ye ur, that'll be two fifty."

"Here's three pounds, keep the change."

"Thanks, mind an call us if ye need a taxi."

"Bye."

Cranstonhill police station was an ugly grey two storey concrete edifice. I went into the reception. A grey haired veteran ignored me as I stood at the desk.

"Hello" I said.

"With ye in a minute" he replied.

I waited.

"I have an appointment."

"Just a minute!"

He folded his *Daily Record* and looked at me.

"Ok what can we do for you?"

"I have an appointment."

"So you said, who with?"

"Inspector Chic Gordon!"

"Oh aye is this tae dae wi the stabbing in Byres Road?"

"No!"

"I didnae think so, are you the new procurator?"

"No!"

"I know noo you're the guy that Chic arrested in the park toilets, bad business that."

"I am not!!!, listen tell Inspector Gordon that Philip Featherstonehaugh from Counter Terrorism Scotland is here to see him."

"Aw right whit did ye say yir name wis?"

"Philip Featherstonehaugh!"

"Ok I see yir name on the list Mr Fanshaw, I've made ye up a temporary pass."

I looked at the cardboard pass and fumed.

"You have spelt my name wrong!"

"Have I? F-a-n-s-h-a-w, is there an e at the end or something?"

"No it is spelt F-e-a-t-h-e-r-s-t-o-n-e-h-a-u-g-h!"

"Jesus are you some kind o foreigner. I have never come across sich a strange spelling o a simple name. There isnae enough room on the caird fer that so ye'll jist huv tae be Fanshaw."

I felt like grabbing the old fool by the hair and smashing his face repeatedly on the counter but Simcox's warning came back to me, don't let them make a fool of you. I smiled and said;

"Not a problem, I know you chaps struggle with the more complex aspects of the English language. Please call Inspector Gordon now as we have a lot of work to do."

"Yes sir, apologies for the misunderstanding. We poor Jocks don't have the education of you English."

He picked up his phone while still staring at me.

"Hi Chic that English ponce is here to see you. I'll tell him to take a seat."

"Chic will be down in five minutes, once he finishes his roll and sausage. Take a seat."

I sat down on a green leatherette bench that ran the length of the back wall. The walls had a lot of puerile graffiti. Tongs ya bass!, Up the RA!, celticFC, RFC No Surrender, FTP, FTQ plus innumerable names and declarations of love.

At 10am a man in a grey suit about, 5'7 with greying, receding curly hair and a reddish moustache appeared from the door behind the reception. The old fool turned to him and whispered something before pointing at me.

I stood up and approached the desk.

"Please sit down Mr Fanshaw" said the old git.

"Is this Inspector Gordon?"

"Aye but I need to speak to him first on another matter, please sit down!"

Gordon smiled at me and continued speaking to the old git

Defeated I sat down

They rambled on about football and politics for another 10 minutes. I hummed "Jerusalem" and "Swing Low sweet Chariot". Gordon smiled and appeared to be suppressing laughter. The old git eventually ran out of chat. Gordon opened the counter and stepped over to me with his hand extended.

"Hello Philip, Chic Gordon, how was the trip?"

"Hello, journey was good but a little long."

Gordon's grip was over strong and emphasised the hard, scaly texture of his hand. Not a welcoming handshake.

"Follow me, I'll take you up to our office."

I stepped through the counter and looked over to the troll who had defended it so eagerly.

"Thanks for all your help."

He shot me a derisive look and went back to reading the paper.

Once we had left the reception and the fire door had closed behind us. Gordon turned to me and said

"Don't mind old Jackie. He doesn't like the English."

"Oh! I thought he was auditioning for receptionist of the year!"

Gordon laughed and said "Aye, he wus a bit nicer than usual, must have been trying to copy your accent."

He led me into a dingy office with grey walls and dismal brown plastic furniture. A stocky balding man sat at a desk in the corner.

"Phil this is Davie Farrell, he has been running the surveillance on the Dumbarton site."

Farrell said hello and made as if to speak further but Gordon dragged me off before any words came out.

We entered another equally dingy office but with just a desk, two chairs and a couple of filing cabinets; obviously Gordon's lair.

"Sit down Phil."

I sat down and waited for Gordon to speak.

"Now you are here we can have a proper chat about this nonsense in Dumbarton. I don't want to waste any more of my time on it than is absolutely necessary. It is a fairy story dreamt up by a couple of blue nosed tosspots. I hope once you have a look at the suspects and speak to McGlashan, Snodgrass and McGregor you will agree that there is no Royal assassination plot. The Micks are just getting shafted by Snodgrass for some reason."

"I agree that it is unlikely to be all true but I think that with Farren's family history we have to carry out a thorough investigation. They might be on the edge of something. We do suspect that Glasgow is where the PIRA store a lot of the weaponry for their mainland campaigns. There is a chance these guys are PIRA couriers or quartermasters."

"That is stretching things a little, what makes you believe they are connected?"

"The group dynamic described by Snodgrass fits our profile for a nascent active service unit. Members with no criminal records but a shared bond, in this case they are all from Donegal. A very clannish county!"

"Aye well half of this city is from Donegal and they haven't got anything to do with the IRA. Snodgrass and McGlashan are a pair of loyalist bigots out to cause trouble. I have spent years trying to stop their kind kicking off riots with their provocative behaviour. Have you ever been to an Orange Walk? I have and it is not pretty. Snodgrass plays the Lambeg drum for his outfit; look at this picture of him."

Gordon pulled a photograph from a file on his desk and thrust it into my hand. The picture was off a heavyset man wearing a black suit and a bowler hat playing a huge drum as he walked past a baying mob outside a church.

"That was taken this year outside a Catholic church in Coatbridge. The Orange bastards play outside it when the Catholic's kids are having their first communion. It is blatant provocation designed to generate trouble. The Catholics are stupid enough to get wound up and start a riot when this happens. It makes policing this town a torture. I wish they would all fuck off back to Ireland, every single green and orange bastard of them."

I was taken aback by the vehemence of Gordon's speech. "We need to validate or disprove Snodgrass's theories. When public order is at stake surely we have to act dispassionately and not ignore information because we find the source distasteful. As a loyalist, surely Snodgrass would do all he can to protect the royals hence the speed with which he reported this theory."

"Maybe but I can't get away from the fact that he has a track record of making false allegations against Irish people."

"This one sounds real with some substance. These guys are definitely planning something."

"Aye but what? They could be planning a big bevvy session, a trip to a fitba match or maybe to give Snodgrass a kicking."

"I don't think so, the evidence hints at something more sinister surely."

"Aye Snodgrass' evidence does but nobody else's. Zuck thinks Snodgrass is talking shite."

"Are we going out to the site today?"

"Yes when Davie finishes contacting the overnight teams we'll head out there."

"Overnight teams?"

"Yes we have been watching these guys night and day."

"Why?"

"Just in case the blue noses are right. Do you want a coffee?"

"Yes that would be lovely."

"The kettle's over there; help yourself. I'll be back shortly, make yourself comfortable."

Gordon had left the room before I could respond. I checked the kettle. There was enough water for a few cups. I flicked the switch and an orange light came on, followed by a roar that was as loud as a jet engine. I popped a spoonful of Maxwell House coffee into a royal wedding mug that looked slightly cleaner than the rest. Gordon probably kept it for female guests. Someone had drawn a moustache on Princess Diana. I sniffed the milk bottle, it seemed fresh, so I poured some into the cup. The kettle reached a hurricane force crescendo and thankfully switched itself off. I made the coffee and sat down.

As I relaxed I realised that I was exhausted, the sleeper should be called the no sleeper. I couldn't work Gordon out, he despised Snodgrass but he had committed a huge amount of resource to the surveillance. Following these guys day and night seemed excessive. Especially as I agreed totally with Gordon's analysis but hoped to fabricate something vaguely interesting to justify my trip. Maybe there was some real evidence after all. The coffee was rather bitter, I always preferred Nescafe even the powdered version. I contemplated reading Gordon's file but I was sure he would share it with me when he returned. No point in ruining the surprise.

I wondered what to do with my case. It was too early to check into the hotel and I really didn't want to leave it here in Gordon's office. Too many thieves around, cops and crooks have the same mentality. I was hoping that Gordon would drop me off at the hotel after we had been to Dumbarton.

I was just getting comfortable doing nothing when Gordon and Farrell came in.

Chapter 6

"Right lets bring Phil up to date, said Gordon. We have been following these guys day and night for the past week and running background checks on them. Farren seems a bit dodgy but not the bogeyman Snodgrass thinks he is. The labourers are all pretty non-descript guys whose abiding passion is for Guinness. Young Herrity though has an interesting background. His old man was a mercenary who went missing in Rhodesia in 1976. Johnny Herrity was one of the 'Wild Geese'.

"What? Do you mean he was in that Richard Burton film?"

"No I mean he was one of the crazies who destabilised the Congo in the 60s along with Mad Mike Hoare. There is some suggestion that he was involved with the IRA in the forties before getting into the mercenary game in East Africa and Iraq in the 1950's. He was a sergeant in Hoare's outfit. After the Congo he worked in the building trade for a while before he joined up with his old pals again in Oman in 1971. He went to Rhodesia in 74 and was allegedly killed north of Salisbury during a gun battle with ZANU guerillas in September 76. There is however some suggestion that Herrity senior helped to plan the botched Seychelles coup in 78, impressive feat for a dead guy. Neighbours reported him havering on about his contacts with Amin, Kenyatta, Lumumba and Nkomo. There is a rumour that he arranged the assassination of Mboya in Kenya."

"After the father's death/disappearance the family sunk into poverty. Mother on widow's pension, Herrity and his siblings turned a bit dysfunctional. Nothing serious, just fights at school and in the street. Underage drinking and some vandalism. There is no evidence that they were ever arrested or did anything serious but we were aware of them, thanks to some very diligent neighbours who felt the need to keep us updated."

"Interesting but what is the significance to this investigation?"

"Well there is a suggestion that Herrity senior had a sideline in smuggling guns to the IRA. He had a cousin who was a steward on the QE2 who by all accounts smuggled weapons in on every cruise especially the transatlantic one."

"If he died seven years ago, his son would have been no more than eight at the time so he is unlikely to have taken up the family business."

"No but old man Herrity had plenty of brothers and other relatives, some of them appear to have known Paddy Farren and Kevin Kennedy. Anyway we are not convinced that John Herrity is dead, no body was sent back to the UK and there was no funeral in Rhodesia. If he was killed, he appears to have ended up as hyena bait. There are suspicions among the Herrity's neighbours that the family have a source of income other than the mother's widow's pension. The children are well dressed and the house is well furnished. The mother is deemed a nice woman but a bit stuck up. The kids don't fit in well in their neighbourhood, Foxhill. It's a typical council scheme full of manual workers and the unemployable. Not a good place to be an outsider. Young Herrity and his brothers went to the local schools and appear to have been fairly bright but prone to violent outbursts. The suggestion is that James Herrity was the victim of some attempted bullying at secondary school, as a reasonably quiet lad he seems to have put up with it for a while, then systematically turned on his attackers. There was some blood spilt and some older boys got badly beaten. After that he was left alone feared but probably even more ostracised than before."

"Again interesting story; bullied kid from odd family snaps and turns on bullies but where is the IRA connection?"

"Well the one thing young Herrity is keen to talk about is a united Ireland. One friend, Derek Greene told his mother when he asked Herrity if he would ever consider joining the IRA; he said "Yes" without a moment's hesitation. The boy was shocked and his mother was very happy to pass this on when we made some discrete enquiries. The other point is that Mrs Herrity has some dubious connections too. Since her husband disappeared they have taken to spending the school holiday's with her sister at her farm on the Donegal – Tyrone border. The sister's husband, John Henry McGill is well known to the security forces."

"Ok this sounds positive, what's the story?"

"Mr McGill has been an active IRA man since the 1930's. His father apparently hid in a ditch in Co Derry with the Irish Prime Minister's dad for a year during the Irish War of Independence while on the run from the British Army. After the war was over they were smuggled into Donegal in a dungcart. They settled in the Laggan area of Donegal and started raiding towns in Northern Ireland. When the Irish Civil War kicked off, they took up arms for the IRA against the Irish Free State. They hooked up with a group of southerners led by a man called Charlie Daly and roamed about Donegal having fire-fights with the Free State army and trying to keep raiding into Ulster. Daly and some of the gang were eventually captured by the Free Staters and shot at a place called Drumboe. These guys are now Republican martyrs, with marches every year to commemorate their deaths. Somehow, McGill's old man and the Prime Minister's dad escaped and survived to fight another day.

McGill's father brought him up to be a diehard enemy of Britain. He was a drill sergeant for years training IRA volunteers throughout the 30's, 40's and 50's. He spied on British bases in Northern Ireland for the Germans throughout WWII.

He was apparently involved with the bombing campaigns in the forties, having mastered the art of producing cheap home made explosives."

"So Herrity's been spending his summers within this man's house? He sounds like the guy from 'The Eagle has Landed'."

"Yes, there is a suggestion that Jack Higgins may have based the character Devlin on John Henry McGill."

"Is he still active in Republican politics?"

"McGill is the head of the Donegal brigade. The RUC believe his farm is the rendezvous for smuggling and raiding into the North. He ferries men and equipment across the River Foyle in a coracle to waiting cars that take the operatives to their targets."

I couldn't believe it, there was a chance we had stumbled into something really big.

"So do you think Herrity is the intermediary between Farren and the IRA command?"

"It's possible, that is why we have put so much work into this. The others are nobodies but this kid is connected to the heart of the Republican movement. I also think his father is not dead and may be here in Glasgow running this show."

"The problem is that you don't have any hard evidence to back this up, do you?"

"No, it is all circumstantial guesswork and theory."

"So where do we go from here?"

"I think we interview McGlashan, Snodgrass and Zuck and let you have a look at the suspects."

"How are we going to this?"

"We'll do a site visit on the pretext that there has been some pilfering and speak to them in the site hut."

"Isn't there a risk that this will spook the Paddies?"

"No the night-watchman has reported a few attempted break-ins so I think we can justify the local CID popping by."

"Ok, anything else in your file I should know about?"

"No take it with you and you can read it at your leisure. The surveillance reports are dry as dust. The biographies of the rest are pretty dull compared to young Herrity. There a few entertaining shots of Snodgrass and McGlashan in their regalia."

I picked up the file and said "When are we heading to Dumbarton?"

Gordon looked at Farrell. Farrell's forehead wrinkled then he said, "Ok Ah'll drive, follow me."

We walked across to a brown fire door with a green and white exit sign which led to a grim stairwell with flaking paint and a faint oily smell which ended with a door to a dingy underground car park. Farrell walked over to a white Cortina that had seen better days. He opened the boot and said, "Pit yur case in here Phil."

I did as I was bid, throwing the case on top of some old wellingtons and a tool bag.

Farrell opened the rear passenger door and nodded for me to get in. I climbed in and almost fell through the seat. There was no padding in it at all. Gordon opened the passenger door and it almost came off in his hand. Farrell grabbed the door and said, "Git in Chic, ah'll shut it."

He then lifted the door up and slammed it shut. When Farrell climbed into driver's seat it felt as if the suspension had collapsed. Gordon turned round and said "Davie is a big Columbo fan. He thinks all detectives should drive wrecks."

I laughed, and Farrell muttered something that sounded extremely vulgar but I couldn't tell what.

The engine roared into life sounding like a Lancaster bomber limping home from the Dresden raid.

We pulled out on the road. After passing through a couple of junctions, Gordon pointed out an impressive red sandstone building in a park, Kelvingrove Museum, then another large building, Kelvin Hall. Before long we passed a hospital, the Western. Soon we were travelling down a lively shopping street, Dumbarton Road, Partick. It seemed that he was determined to identify everything I looked at.

Each street seemed to be in a different district, Scotstoun, Yoker, Clydebank, Dalmuir, Old Kilpatrick, Bowling. By now I could see the Clyde on my left. The car felt like it would collapse at any time. I felt like I was sitting on the axle, every bump went through my vertebrae.

Gordon resumed his tour guide impression, "Dumbuck; home of the world's greatest racing driver."

"Who is that?"

"Jackie Stewart of course!"

"Really does he still live here?"

"No chance, he buggered off to Switzerland as soon as he made some money."

We turned left at a junction that gave us a choice between Dumbarton and some exotic place called Crianlarich.

"On yer left is Dumbarton Rock."

I looked up to see a huge volcanic plug, with a castle on top.

"That used tae be the capital of Scotland."

"Really when was that?"

"Aboot a thoosan year ago" said Farrell dryly.

We passed some dismal shops before turning right under a railway bridge. This took us into a suburban road lined with bungalows on one side and council houses on the other. We passed the entry to Ballantines Distillery before turning into a building site entrance.

Chapter 7

We were here. My heart started to beat furiously. I didn't usually get anywhere near suspects. I could hear the trainer saying that calmness is key to successful interviews; professional detachment allows for effective observation; focus on the task use your nervousness to slow things down. Above all listen and take notes. Don't talk unless you have to.

I looked around; we had stopped in a gravelled area in front of a container full of tools and a workbench. A young man stood at the bench wearing yellow oilskin trousers and a donkey jacket. He appeared to be cleaning some tools. Somewhat ugly he had a big nose, sharp jaw line and plenty of acne. The ubiquitous yellow helmet sat on his head, tufts of greasy black hair poked out underneath the white frame of the helmet.

"I see you have spotted young Master Herrity, Gordon whispered in my ear. Let's get out before he catches us looking at him."

I stepped out and found my foot sinking into the muddy gravel. My shoes would be ruined. A huge broad shouldered man over six feet approached us. He wore a white helmet and a black anorak, blue trousers and wellingtons with green toecaps. "Can I help you he asked in a very foreign accent?" This was obviously Mr Zuck.

"Hi, I'm Inspector Gordon, and this is my colleagues Farrell and Philips. We would like to speak to Mr McGlashan."

"Valter is no here, ye can speak to the agent Bob Stewart."

"No that won't be necessary, is Mr Snodgrass available?"

"Aye Ruby is in the hut."

"Good we'll go and see him. Are you Mr Zuck?"

"Aye, why?"

"We would like to speak to you after we speak to Mr Snodgrass."

"Really, vat about."

"Nothing too important. We will come and get you."

The big man looked hard at Gordon. I got the impression that he would happily wring the little cop's neck.

"Is about Ruby and his tale telling, no?"

"Possibly."

"He talks rubbish. He tells lies all the time. He only work here cos he Walter's man."

"Ok, let's not have the discussion here. We will come and get you."

"No, too dangerous you could fall in one of the manholes or get hit by a machine. Tell Ruby to come and get me. He is in the first hut with Coleman." The big man stomped off shouting at a group of oilskin clad labourers. Who immediately stopped leaning on their shovels and sprang into action. Herr Zuck was a formidable character.

There were four portakabins. One was the toilet. The other three housed the site offices and what looked like a mess/changing room. We stepped into the first site office. Snodgrass was standing at the far end discussing the plans with a thin, brown haired man in a blue anorak. This must be Coleman the Site Engineer.

Snodgrass looked up and said "Who are you?"

"Inspector Gordon, Strathclyde Police."

"Aw right. John I need to speak to these guys aboot the attempted thefts, can ye leave us be fur a while."

"Sure no problem Ruby."

Coleman spoke with a slight Welsh accent. He smiled as he passed us.

"Take a seat Inspector. What's your colleagues names?"

"Sergeant Farrell and DC Philips."

He shook hands with me and Farrell. It was like shaking hands with King Kong. My hand looked like a toy in his. I don't think he bothered giving me the Masonic handshake for fear of doing me a permanent injury.

Gordon opened the discussion. "Mr Snodgrass we have been investigating the concerns you raised a couple of weeks ago. Have there been any other events that you feel may have been of significance since we last spoke?"

I looked at Snodgrass, he was almost as big as Zuck but narrower shouldered. An uglier version of John Wayne would be how my mother would describe him. He had greying gingery fair hair combed in a side parting. The skin on his face had a weathered, waxy texture. His main features were a square jaw, a long bulbous nose and curiously bulging eyes. He wore a white shirt with a pale blue stripe, a dark blue tie with some sort of crest on it. Over the shirt was a dark blue zipper cardigan with a vaguely Icelandic pattern. He wore dark blue terylene trousers and black Unilever wellingtons.

"Naw nothing obvious. We huv been keeping an eye oan them but they huvnae said onythin else about the Royal stuff. They hae jist bin working. I think they know ahm keeping an eye oan them."

"Doesn't that worry you?"

"Naw, they widnae blow an operation jist to take me oot."

"Why do you think that?"

"Ah know terrorists, they huv wan track minds. They won't brek fae a plan unless somebody high up tells them tae stoap. In Malaya and Kenya we could watch folk day and night and they would still try and go through wi thur stupit plans. Only efterwurds when they git caught do they start taking revenge on the folks that turned them in. This bunch think ahm stupit like Zuck and they can pull the wull oer ma eyes and kid oan they ur just a bunch o labourers. I can tell they are at it."

"We have been watching them too but we have no evidence of anything untoward. They seem like a bunch of average men not terrorists."

"That bunch of murdering b's in Birmingham were jist ordnery workies as well."

"True, but if every group of Irishmen were planning to plant bombs and assassinate Royalty, Britain would be on her knees. We have no solid evidence to arrest these men other than your allegations, which as I am sure you are aware would not stand up in court."

"You calling me a liar?"

"No I am just stating a fact, hearsay and circumstantial evidence would not support a conviction. We need to have real evidence of a crime being planned or committed. You don't know what they are planning on the 23rd, all you heard was that they were going to do something on that date. You put 2 and 2 together and came up with 8. It's a hunch and nothing else."

Snodgrass stared at Gordon, his mouth opened but nothing came out. The brute was near apoplexic but unable to find the words to respond. His hands balled into fists, he gritted his teeth. His craggy jaw jutted out further. He eventually said in a low voice, "Nae wonder the fenians huv been able to kill and maim thousands fur the last 15 years if basturds like you are turning a blind eye tae it. Are you a fenian yersel Mr Gordon?"

Gordon looked at him coldly and spoke in an emotion free voice. "Mr Snodgrass, my religious convictions are nothing to do with you or this case. The issue is that all we have as evidence is a rather dramatic tale that cynics would suggest was cooked up by you and Mr McGlashan from your own anti-Irish prejudices. I have a folder in my office with around 30 similar reports from Mr McGlashan dating back to the 1960s, none of which turned out to have any substance. A competent lawyer might suggest that you and Mr McGlashan had some form in the 'cooking up' of slanderous fairy stories about Irish Catholics being terrorists and criminals. Why is it that you are the only one who hears these deadly conversations about assassination plots?"

"Ah'm no gonnae sit here and take this crap fae you ya wee nyaff."

"Oh what are you going to do Mr Snodgrass?"

"Ah'll have a word wi yer superiors and git ye pit in yer place. Yer nuthin but a jumped up fenian sympathiser, yer a disgrace tae the Scottish Police!"

I couldn't believe it. The man was as thick and pig headed as I suspected. I looked at Gordon. He was staring at Snodgrass.

"Are you threatening me, Mr Snodgrass? Who are you going to complain to?"

"Ah know ra Chief Constable and a couple o superintendents very well. A coupla words wi them an you're toast."

"I presume that you are acquainted with these gents through the Masons. Give me your hand."

Gordon offered Snodgrass his hand. Reluctantly Snodgrass shook his hand. Gordon looked at him intently, Snodgrass seemed to shrink as the handshake went on.

"Do you want to continue with threatening me, Mr Snodgrass?"

"Naw ah wus out of order, didnae mean it. Ye put on ma guard, ah wusnae thinking straight. I must apologise to you sir."

"No problem, I think we are finished with you. Please ask Mr Zuck to come in."

A beaten man Snodgrass stood up slowly; he seemed to have aged and lost much of his vigour since the handshake. Gordon had a strong grip but he was no superman. Snodgrass had received a very strong Masonic message. Gordon must be some kind of Third Degree Master. Certainly scary enough to shut a thug like Snodgrass up.

"You can go now Mr Snodgrass said Gordon. Don't forget to send Zuck in."

"Thanks, I'll do that now" said a dazed Snodgrass.

As Snodgrass left the portacabin, Gordon turned to Farrell, who promptly burst into laughter.

Gordon smiled and said "Shut up you Fenian bastard!"

I was confused. Gordon looked at me and said, "What's your problem?"

"What just happened?"

"Nothing much! I just sorted out our friend Snodgrass and made sure he backs off the investigation. The last thing we need is him dropping his size 14s into the proceedings. He is a thick, obnoxious twat who does more harm than good. I don't need him wandering about playing secret agents."

"I see, you went at him pretty hard and then played the Masonic card. It seemed like overkill."

"Maybe to you spooks who are obsessed with subtlety but mark my words when you fight a bull like our Rueben you don't go out there with just your warrant card as a cape. A cop needs a full range of tools."

At that Zuck appeared.

Chapter 8

"You wanted to speak to me?"

"Yes Mr Zuck, please sit down. You have already given us a statement on the allegations Mr McGlashan has raised."

"Aye, as I told you Ruby and Vattie are talking crap. These guys are obsessed with putting Catholics down."

"You are a Catholic yourself, do they cause problems for you?"

"Aye they make my life difficult but not because of religion, because of race, I am foreign so they hate me. I transfer out of here next week and Ruby will take over full time as General Foreman. He has been here only 3 week yet he has caused nothink but trouble. All of the labourers hate him. Some are going to complain to the union. I am amaze hat Ruby has lived so long. I always expect someone to hit him with a shovel the way he talks to people especially the Irish."

"There is bad blood between Mr Snodgrass and the Irish?"

"Oh yes, he shouts at them every day like they can do nothink right. I been here 6 months with no trouble. Ruby is a dud. He cause so much trouble no bastard does any work. The minute he turn his back they stop working and call him bastard."

"He is an abrasive character by the sounds of it."

"Like fuckin sandpaper!"

"As you know Mr Snodgrass has alleged that certain Irish labourers are planning a terrorist attack."

"Listen it is bollocks, the only person they want to kill is Ruby. I am surprised no one has hit him with a hammer or sprayed him with diesel like they did at Inverkip."

"What was the story about the diesel?"

"Ruby wound up a squad of brickies from Easterhouse on a site in Inverkip, told them their walls not plumb. They beat him up and emptied a barrel of diesel on him and threatened to set him on fire. After that is when he developed his eye problem, what they call it something like Bells palsy."

"Eye problem?" I looked at Farrell he was notetaking ferociously. Gordon's eyebrows were raised at this depiction of attempted murder.

"You know the bug eyes he has, well that started after the Inverkip thing. Some kind of nerve thing brought on by stress I think. They say he couldn't close his eyes for weeks. He was off work for months, had to wear eyepatch in bed apparently."

"Did the guys who beat him up get prosecuted?"

"Na they just got sacked. I think Vattie probably put a bad word in about them, probably haven't worked since."

"Were they Irish?"

"No they were Rangers men like him. You don't get many Irish tradesmen in this country you know."

"I see. What is your background Mr Zuck, just for our records."

"Zuck sat back in his chair and looked at Gordon. What do you need to know, I am no terrorist."

"Oh just your age, place of birth, arrival in UK, current immigration status, family background."

"Ok you want my life story. I was born in Danzig in 1920, it was a free city then between Germany and Poland; had been German for centuries but after First World War, Poland was a free country again. My father came from Galicia originally which had been part of the Austrian empire. He moved to Danzig after the First World War to get away from the Russkies, thought his fellow Poles would be better rulers.

Danzig was a beautiful city and I had a happy childhood until Hitler invaded. I went east to join the Polish army on 2nd September. My family stayed in Danzig. See this picture."

He took a small black and white picture from his wallet and laid it on the table in front of us. It was of two dark haired young men and a teenage girl.

"I am the one on the left, the other two are my brother and sister. It was taken in July 1939. I never saw any of my family again. Some say they were killed in the fight for the city, others say they died in a labour camp. All I know is I never saw or heard of them again after I got the train east. That picture is all I have of them."

I shifted uncomfortably afraid that the old guy would start crying. Farrell was still note taking dedicatedly. Gordon seemed fascinated.

"I got to an Army depot near Warsaw, got given a rifle and some bullets, no training. We marched to meet the Germans but couldn't get near them because of the endless columns of refugees. Our officer, I think he was a chemist from a place called Totcyn. His father had been in the Austrian army in the first war. He spoke to a telegraph operator who told him the Russkies had invaded from the east and the Germans were crushing everything in their path. He turned us around and we marched south toward the Hungarian border. There were fewer refugees and no Stukas attacking constantly. We ran into a Russian advance party that we managed to ambush. We were so proud to have finally struck back at our enemies. They say pride comes before a fall; well it is true you know.

The next day we woke up surrounded by Ivans. They took our guns, robbed us and put us on a cattle train full of other Polish prisoners and sent us east. The officers were taken separately. I think our officer ended up at Katyn Wood, anyways I never saw or heard of him again.

After days on the train with no food or water we ended up in a labour camp somewhere in Russia. I was there for nearly two years. It was freezing cold in the winter with only rags to wear, hot and humid in the summer with all the time nothing but crap like fish-head soup for food. All we did was break stones and dig holes all day. Hundreds died of starvation and fever.

Then one day Stalin decided to let us go. We got uniforms, taught how to soldier then got put on trains to Iran. The British picked us up and I ended up based in Crieff. I fought in Italy, France and Germany. Killed as many Germans as I could! When the war ended I came back to Crieff and married my girlfriend, she was from Drymen. We have been there ever since. I have two kids; a son and a daughter, and three grandsons. I was a DP for 20 years then my wife persuaded me to get British passport. No point in dreaming about going home to Danzig, now the commies call it Gdansk. Nobody there would know me anyway."

He stopped looked at us and said; "That good enough for you records? Anything you didn't already know?"

"No Mr Zuck it was very useful. You have had some life."

"I have had a life that has been very happy and quiet for nearly forty years in this country. 1939 – 1941 was a horrible time. But after that I enjoyed every minute of my time in the British Army, always good fun chasing the jerries. I am not part of any plot to kill royalty, this country saved my life."

"No-one suggested you were involved in any plot. We just need to investigate Mr Snodgrass' allegations."

"Well I know nothing about that. It is just a stupid story Ruby made up. He does it all the time. I met many Ivans just like him in the labour camp, never happy except when he can make it bad for someone. Ruby is evil scum."

"Steady on Mr Zuck, no need to get heated up. What about the men Snodgrass has identified as potential suspects?"

"Tell me their names."

"Ok please give your view of each one. We'll start with Sean Farren."

"Clever but useless as a labourer! Thinks he is the shop steward sometimes, always moaning; mainly though he not any good at the job. Only here because he is Jim's pal just like we have Jim's brother Duncan and his two pals from Dundee."

"Joe Gallagher."

"Old man but 10 times the worker Farren is, strong and tireless. He is much older than me you know. Never talks about politics just what is in the papers. No way he is a terrorist."

"Tommy Wilson."

"About my age, has a son who is a doctor at the Southern General in Glasgow. He is very proud of his son; again not a political man!"

"Francie O'Brien."

"A bit of a drunk, always seems hungover and angry but a good worker. He causes no trouble. Just talks about farming and Ireland."

"Charley Flood."

"Flood is a bum who spends all his money on horses that run slow. I feel sorry for his wife, all his money goes to the bookie. A fool who wouldn't be trusted, the last man I would plan a raid with."

"Henry Walker."

"Nice man but like Farren, not used to heavy outdoor work. Gallagher does twice the work Walker does. Walker is always complaining about his ulcer, never seems fit and well."

"James Herrity."

"Seems a nice kid, clever, should still be at school, like all these Irish they can't escape school fast enough. He works hard and listens when you talk. He is quiet but talkative enough when you actually speak to him about things other than work. I showed him how to break stones with the sledgehammer the other day you know. I taught him how to find the grain so that you can split a rock with a couple of hits. Thanks to Stalin I have had plenty of practice."

"Do these men seem to be close as a group? Snodgrass says they stick together and exclude others from their conversations."

"Ja they stick together cos they hate Ruby. The only time I hear them talking it is about what a bastard Ruby is! Sometimes they call him worse names than that. I heard that Farren was going to complain to the union about Ruby. Farren calls Ruby Hitler behind his back, its funny. When Ruby walks past, Farren goosesteps behind him doing the Hitler salute. It's very funny sometimes. Ruby never notices, he is a bit deaf."

"What about MacGregor is he trustworthy?"

"Hughie is a crook. I think he is the one who has been stealing from the site. He sucks up to Ruby for protection. I don't trust him at all. He comes in regularly with a bashed in face claiming his brother in laws beat him up. I think he gets caught thieving."

"So not a reliable witness in your opinion?"

"Hughie couldn't spell reliable!"

"Thanks Mr Zuck I think we have covered everything."

"Do you want to speak to Bob Stewart?"

"No I don't think that would be wise bearing in mind his closeness to Farren."

"He will ask why no one spoke to him, he is the boss after all. He will wonder why you spend all this time with me and Ruby but no go near him."

"Ok I will discuss the thefts with him as a courtesy. You can go now."

Zuck, got up and nodded to us before leaving the portakabin.

I looked at Gordon and Farrell and asked, "Well how did that go?

Farrell shrugged

Gordon stood up and stretched his arms and back then said "It was good. We sorted out Snodgrass and had a decent chat with Zuck. A crazy Polish bear if I ever saw one. He seems decent and fairly honest unlike our Ruby. I still think the terrorist stuff is crap as does Zuck. It could be that Snodgrass is using the terrorist allegations to get his retaliation in first if he thinks Farren is going to complain to the union."

"Possibly, but he is taking a risk. As Zuck said he has pushed people to the limit before and paid the price. If a gang of navvies beat the crap out of me and threatened to set me on fire I would think twice about deliberately winding folks up again."

"They don't sound like a murder gang to me. Most of them seem to be bloody useless, which is probably why Snodgrass is always on their backs."

Farrell added that "Jim Cannon's guys say the surveillance is mind numbingly boring. Gallagher, O'Brien, Flood and Wilson get hammered every night on the way home. When they get home they tend to sleep it off in front of the telly and go to bed.

Walker goes home, has tea with his wife and does the garden or some DIY. Farren and Herrity go home to their mammies for tea and go out with their pals for bevy sessions on Fridays and Saturdays.

They don't all socialise together. Herrity only sees the rest of them at work. He gets a lift in with Coleman every day so he has no opportunity to go bevvying with the old Micks. He is also only here Tuesday to Thursday. He is at the Building and Printing College off George Sq on Monday's and Friday's which restricts his time with them even further."

We looked at each other. This case really did seem to be a total waste of time.

Gordon said "I know what we are all thinking but we need to make absolutely sure that nothing untoward happens during the Royal visit. It is unlikely but we can't afford to take any risks."

"What are you going to say to Stewart?"

"Just some crap about break-ins and rumours that an organised crime gang are targeting building sites. Come on lets go an see him now."

We went into the adjoining portakabin. The first room was the site office a small dapper man wearing a blue v-neck jersey, a white shirt and a blue and red striped tie sat at the desk. His hair was swept back in waves like David Niven, he even had a 40s film star's moustache.

"Hello, Inspector Gordon, Strathclyde Police, may we speak to Mr Stewart?"

The dapper man raised his head, smiled and said, "He's through there, no need to knock."

We walked into the next office. Stewart was sitting at his desk poring over some technical drawings. He was a red haired man of medium build and a fierce orange moustache.

"Mr Stewart, Inspector Gordon, Strathclyde Police and this ugly pair are my colleagues Sergeant Farrell and DC Philips."

Stewart got up and shook Gordon's hand. I noted no sign of any Masonic activity this time.

"Hallo Inspector, are you here about the break-ins Barney reported?"

Farrell spoke, "Yes Mr Stewart we are following up Mr McIlwraith's reports. We think there may be a link with a series of similar burglaries in Glasgow. It looks like it might be an organised operation with possibly some insider knowledge."

"Really you think one of our guys is casing the joint for a gang?"

"Yes that is exactly what we are looking at, do you have some suspicions? Are you able to give us a name?"

"Well I don't want to get into trouble but the site has been pretty unsettled since one guy joined us."

We all stiffened, what was he going to tell us?

Farrell nodded and said "Are you prepared to give us the name of the individual in question? You can rely on our discretion."

Stewart squirmed a little, "I don't have any direct evidence but the team have told me that they are very concerned about Hughie MacGregor. He listens into their conversations and few of them have almost caught him searching through their clothes in the mess room. He has always claimed he was looking for his fags or his socks or something. Nobody trusts him except Snodgrass the new GF and that is only because they have worked together before I think. Overall his was the first name I thought of when Barney reported the break-ins."

I see, said Farrell. "We will put him under surveillance and let you know if you need to take action. Mr Snodgrass and Mr Zuck didn't mention Mr MacGregor when we spoke to them."

"Aye well that sums them up. They are cut from the same cloth, both wanna be Hitlers constantly ranting and raving at the workers. Nobody would confide in either of them. A few of the labourers are old uni pals of mine, they keep me informed on what is actually happening. I actually asked for Zuck to be replaced weeks ago because the labourers were going to complain to the union about him. They say he acts like they are slave labourers in a Nazi death camp. Unfortunately he is being replaced by Ruby "fucking" Snodgrass the biggest most bigoted arsehole in the company. It's a nightmare. Now I can't take any action against MacGregor because Snodgrass would block it. He is responsible for managing the men."

"Sounds like you have a tough job on your hands said Gordon. Are there any other issues or tensions on site that you think we should know about?"

Stewart scratched his head, "No, I think that's it. I feel better having actually talked about it. As I can't really discuss Snodgrass with anyone except maybe Jim Beattie the Group Director and I only see him once a month. McGlashan should be the man to sort it out but he and Snodgrass are related so I am stuck with him."

"Thanks very much Mr Stewart this has been very useful. We won't take up any more of your time. We will be in touch regarding the points you have raised. In the meantime if anything else occurs to you please give me a call on this number."

"Certainly, thank you Inspector, bye." We nodded to Stewart and shuffled out the door. He stood looking after us staring at Gordon's card.

Gordon stopped and looked out across the site. It was a maze of holes in the ground, waist high brickwork, half finished manholes, piles of red clay pipes and even bigger piles of large concrete pipes. A JCB and a tracked digger appeared to be digging large holes at opposite corners of the site. Herrity climbed out of one hole carrying what looked like a giant ruler.

"What is Herrity doing?" I asked.

"He is carrying the levelling staff "said Farrell.

"What does it do?"

"I don't really know, measures the depth of holes maybe. All I know is he spends his days waving it back and forward while Coleman looks at him through a telescope mounted on a tripod. Other times he knocks in pegs for Coleman and hammers nails into the top of them then Coleman looks at them using his theodolite which looks like a different type of telescope on a tripod."

"Sounds thrilling, not much of a job!"

"Keeps him off the streets" said Gordon. "Herrity is a trainee engineer so hopefully he is learning something. Here comes Zuck again. Let's get out of here. We all climbed into Farrell's car and were just about to leave when Zuck tapped on the window."

"You have good chat with Stewart? Inspector?"

"Oh yes very useful, we didn't mention the other issue."

"Good cos he would not be happy to hear his pals being bad-mouthed. He already hates Ruby. He would kill him if he thought Ruby was trying to get his pals arrested."

"Don't worry, as you have said this is a storm in a teacup. We will have it closed in no-time."

"That would be good."

"We really must go, bye now."

With that Gordon wound up the window and Farrell drove off.

I looked back and saw Zuck standing at the gate watching us. I could have sworn he was memorising the number plate.

Chapter 9

Farrell said "I must put this old bus in for a re-spray. Old Zuck seems very interested in her."

"Aye what a creepy bunch they were" said Gordon. "I wouldn't trust any of them as far as I could throw them."

"So ye don't trust Zuck or Snodgrass at all then!" laughed Farrell

"No I do not. I can't make my mind up on which of those two is the dodgiest. As for Stewart; he seemed to be intent on dropping both of them into something."

"A classic disinformation technique" I said, "it was very popular with Soviet moles in the 50's and 60's. Expose your colleagues as crooks or traitors and divert suspicion away from yourself. Stewart is probably the Kim Philby at the heart of this operation."

"Maybe or he is just a man sick of working with total gits like Zuck. Zuck is hiding something, I know it" said Gordon. "He recited his personal history like he had read it in a book."

"Maybe he has been interrogated so often it feels like a book. Displaced Persons were closely monitored during the Cold War."

"Aye but he was just too slick and too open. Not the behaviour of an innocent man. People forget things they get the order wrong, they complain about reciting ancient history. They don't pump out their life story like an adventure novel. Also he was behaving very oddly when we left. Why was he so concerned about Stewart not finding out that Snodgrass had informed on his mates? It doesn't make sense!"

"Especially as Stewart clearly can't stand him" added Davie. "It was a strange thing to do unless he was trying to mix things up, and get us to focus on Stewart."

"Possibly, but why? Unless he is hiding something! Davie, get Melanie to do a full background check on our Mr Zuck."

"Will do boss" said Farrell. "Shall we catch up with Jim Cannon over lunch?"

"Good idea, tell him to meet us at the Shimla Tandoori."

Farrell picked up his radio. "Golf 6 calling Golf 17, over." The radio crackled and then a croaky voice bellowed "Golf 17 here, go ahead Golf 6, over."

"Golf 17 meet us at the Curry house, over."

"Understood, see you in 5 Golf 6, over."

"Thanks Golf 17, Golf 6, out."

Farrell pulled into the carpark of a small shopping precinct. He jumped out and waved at huge man as wide as he was tall with receding black hair and a greying moustache.

"Spitting image of Cannon fae the telly, eh?" said Farrell

I was lost for a moment until I remembered the American detective series from the early 70s starring William Conrad. Jim Cannon was indeed like a clone, I wondered if he had gorged himself deliberately to look like his hero.

"I thought it was the real Cannon" I said.

Gordon shook the big man's hand and pointed to me saying, "This is Phil from the Secret Service."

Cannon looked at me, "Scrawny looking James Bond, mair Roger Moore than Sean Connery!" He offered me his hand and smiled "Hello Phil how did ye enjoy meeting that bunch of bampots at Herbert Starr?"

"They were a bit odd."

"Yup, odd like two left feet or a three legged horse."

We had stopped outside a shabby restaurant with lurid red and gold curtains and a big sign saying Shimla Tandoori over an image of Himalayan Peaks. Cannon pushed the door open and walked in followed by Gordon. Farrell nodded to me and I followed Gordon. Farrell turned around and surveyed the street before following me.

"Hi can we have a table for four?" the big man asked the waiter.

The waiter smiled and said "Follow me."

He led us to a table in the darkest corner of the restaurant. "Can I get you some drinks?"

"Aye four pints of coke" said Cannon.

"No problem, I will come back for your order."

"Ta."

"He realised we were cops and put us here so that we don't spoil his business. Naebody wants four cops sitting in their front window. Bad advert, deters the neds!"

"Too true" said Farrell. "I'm having the lamb rogan josh and pilau rice wi pakora tae start, what about you Jim?"

"Onion bhaji then chicken biryani for me."

Gordon said "I want the pakora then beef madras and boiled rice, what about you Phil?"

I looked at the menu no bhuna or dansac here just curry, biryani, rogan josh and korma. "I'll have the onion bhaji and the lamb madras with a naan bread" I said.

The waiter re-appeared with the drinks. He was a solidly built man with thick black hair and an impressive moustache. He wore a white shirt with a red bow tie, a black waistcoat and black trousers. His notebook and pen looked tiny in his fat fingers. "What would you like to order?"

Cannon yet again ordered for all of us, he must have some kind of father syndrome.

"Boiled or fried rice?"

"Wan boiled and two fried plus a naan bread, ta."

"Thank you, enjoy your lunch."

As the waiter moved off to serve a group of pensioners who had arrived to take advantage of the £2 set lunch for OAP's Cannon grinned and said "Nice guy, did ah get it right?"

Farrell said "Naw I think ye got Phil and Chic's orders mixed up."

"Never mind it aw tastes the same."

"Jim's our memory man, he is always testing himself" chuckled Farrell.

"Jim, give Phil a rundown of the surveillance highlights" interjected the ever businesslike Gordon.

"Where do I start? The truth is there isn't much to tell. They are a bunch of boring arseholes. None of them have any hobbies, don't seem to be members of any clubs. They work and drink and that's about it. The old guys and Farren go to mass on Sundays but at different churches. Even there they don't obviously engage with anyone socially or otherwise. They are the most solitary bunch I have come across. The Herrity's aren't too well regarded by their neighbours, the old man was always bumming his load about Africa and the Middle East and how big a hero he was. Most folk think he did a runner from his wife and the Rhodesia story was just a tale the missus made up. No-one likes her, too snooty. Herrity and his two brothers seem to be dull characters who are not great mixers.

For the past couple of days I have been watching the site. Zuck wanders about shouting and swearing at the workies. Snodgrass shouts at them from a distance. Stewart never leaves his office. The workies wander around smoking fags and occasionally doing some work. Herrity and Coleman are in and out of holes all day measuring and knocking in pegs and playing with their telescopes. It is one of the dullest jobs ever!"

"Yet when you interview Snodgrass, Stewart and Zuck you feel like there is something very dodgy going on" Gordon commented.

"Absolutely, one of them is bent but I can't work out who or what they are hiding."

"Do you think they could be in on the assassination plot?"

"Naw I think that is bollocks. One of those guys has done something very bad and is shitting himself that we are on to him."

Gordon said "Jim I totally agree. I wouldn't even be surprised if Zuck and Snodgrass have both been up to no good. I am going to get Melanie to do a full check on Zuck. Phil can you help with this, your outfit's records must have loads on foreigners like Zuck."

"Yes but they could be classified if he has been involved in anything significant."

"Aye but get us what ye can. Davie and Jim will introduce you to Melanie later on."

At that the starters arrived. They were nearly identical with the same bright pink dips and some wilted lettuce and tomato.

I tasted mine it could have been a bhaji or a pakora but it tasted good especially with the lurid sauce. Gordon wolfed his down as did Farrell, Cannon on the other hand ate his very delicately with a knife and fork.

When Cannon finished a little waiter appeared and cleared the table of the starter plates. The first waiter appeared with a large trestle table packed with serving dishes. He gave each one of us a plate.

"Lamb madras?"

I said "That's me".

He passed me a stainless steel disk full of meaty chunks and thick brown gravy with a strong aroma of spices. He then passed the biryani to Cannon, the rogan josh to Farrell and the Beef madras to Gordon. All four meals looked delicious. The waiter put down two plates of yellow and red rice, one plate of white boiled rice and a plate with a huge naan bread.

"Have a nice lunch" said the waiter.

I started shovelling the food into my mouth barely tasting it.

Cannon looked at me and laughed, "You'll regret that the Madras is very strong here."

I tore off a strip of naan bread and mopped up some curry sauce. It tasted great. I was midway through chewing a very tasty piece of lamb when the chilli started to burn. I felt like my mouth was on fire. I swallowed the meat and washed it down with most of the pint of cola.

"Is it a little bitty strong?" Cannon asked

"Yes" I replied in a very squeaky voice.

Gordon laughed, "Hope ye don't die. They'll send James Bond to find your killer."

"Aye ah kin jist see Commander Bond blowing this place tae bits" Farrell laughed spraying us with his mouthful of yellow rice.

"Phil look what ye've done" gasped Cannon as he wiped the rice off his tie.

"Thanks for your concern but unfortunately I feel a lot better."

"Dae ye no like rice?" asked Farrell as I dipped a piece of naan into the sauce.

"Not really, it's all right but it seems to fill me up too quickly."

"Ah love it!" said Cannon as he practically licked his plate clean

"So we can see!" said Gordon.

Plates emptied, the younger waiter cleared the table and brought us the dessert menu. It was ice cream or more ice cream. I asked for a black coffee. My compatriots stared at the menu musing over the relative qualities of strawberry or chocolate or vanilla before all deciding they couldn't be bothered and asked for coffee as well.

After the coffee arrived, we sat back feeling that unsettling bloated feeling that lunch time curries always leave. Always the same uncertain question; is it going to stay down or am I going to taste it all night. No-one spoke for a couple of minutes.

Gordon drank his coffee and leaned forward. His madras must have moved to a more comfortable location

"This afternoon Jim, follow Zuck and see if he goes straight hame. I wouldn't be surprised if he does something unusual."

"Ok boss, all the way to Drymen?"

"Aye, don't stay all night if he goes straight back for his tea. Just want to see if he makes any calls from call boxes or visits anybody on his way. Phil and Davie; we'll go and see Wattie McGlashan at his office. Then we'll drop Phil at his hotel. Where did they book you in?"

"The Lorne on Sauchiehall Street."

"Oh that's no distance from the station, no problem getting in tomorrow morning, just a ten minute walk."

"Can we have the bill please?" Gordon shouted at the waiters.

The older man turned looked at us then walked to the till and brought back a bill on a saucer with four mints.

"Sixteen quid, that's not bad" said Gordon, "4 pound each."

I reached into my pocket but Gordon had already put a 20 pound note on the plate and asked the waiter for a receipt for £18. The waiter grabbed the money and skipped back with the receipt and £2 change.

"Many thanks, sir" he said as we left.

Gordon carefully pocketed his recceipt, obviously a man who knew how to work the expenses system.

"See ya guys" said Cannon and walked back to his car.

We clambered back into Farrell's boneshaker and headed back to Glasgow. We took the low road close to the castle and the river. At the turning for the castle, Gordon pointed to a little fish and chip shop, "Ma Pastramis the best chippy in Dunbartonshire. Buy a fish supper in there and you get a fish the length of your arm."

"Lovely!" I said trying not to think of food as the curry gurgled within me. "Why did we come this way?"

"In case old Zuck was watching for us up at the site. We don't want him to think we are taking this too seriously" said Gordon.

"Sounds sensible" I said while loosening my belt. I felt like I was going to explode.

Farrell burped loudly and groaned "That curry isnae sitting very well, how about you two?"

"Feeling a bit bloated" I said.

"These might help" said Gordon as he tossed me his pack of indigestion tablets.

"Thanks" I said and popped a couple into my mouth.

I passed the tablets back to Gordon who took out a couple and gave them to Farrell.

We sat in silence as Farrell wove his way through the mid afternoon traffic. Occasionally Farrell complained about the number of cars on the road which seemed strange to me as the place was almost empty by London standards.

Soon we were back in Glasgow passing the Kelvin Hall. As we passed a large hotel on the right, Gordon said, "There's your digs."

The Lorne looked pretty impressive; I started to look forward to my stay.

We continued along Sauchiehall Street then turned left and started to go up hill through a maze of tenements. We eventually reached a very impressive series of crescents with huge ornate tenements. We pulled up outside 80 Park Circus, the gleaming brass sign outside said Herbert – Starr Construction (Scotland) Ltd part of the Osprey Group in huge letters with a big brass bird of prey with a fish in it's beak above the word Osprey.

"Obviously a company with plenty of cash" said Farrell. "Shall we go in?"

"Definitely, it will be interesting to see what the little bigot has to say" said Gordon.

"Ah bet he starts talking aboot 'tims and tattie munching fenians' plotting agin his company."

"He surely cannae be as thick as Snodgrass and manage to work here."

I looked at them and felt bemused. They seemed to dismiss the idea of the assassination plot as bigoted ramblings yet we were investigating it furiously. It was very odd; I felt I was missing something.

Chapter 10

We climbed the steps to the polished black door and pushed it open. Inside there was a very opulent atmosphere. The entry hall was floored in black and white marble with a large reception desk to the right; six chairs and a teak coffee table facing an ornate fireplace to the left. Above the mantelpiece was a huge gold framed mirror. Above our heads there was a twenty bulb crystal chandelier dangling from a blue ceiling with white decorative plasterwork. The centrepiece was a Gone with the Wind staircase covered with a crème shag pile carpet. The shag pile was so deep it looked like polar bear fur.

At the reception desk, a middle aged woman in a bright blue uniform with piped yellow lapels and a yellow scarf looked at us with something close to disgust. Her spectacles sat on top of her gingery red shampoo and set. Gordon looked at her but didn't speak.

Eventually she asked in an authoritative voice, "Gentlemen, can I help you?"

"Yes" said Gordon, "We would like to speak to Mr McGlashan, Walter McGlashan."

"Do you have an appointment?"

"No"

"I'm afraid Mr McGlashan is a very busy man who does not have time to deal with speculative callers."

"Oh we are not speculative callers", Gordon smiled. "You could say that Mr McGlashan invited us."

"Really, if that is the case then why don't you have an appointment?"

Tired with the charade, Gordon stepped closer to the desk looked straight into her eyes, took out his warrant card and said "Tell Mr McGlashan that Inspector Charles Gordon is here to see him about the issues he reported at the Dumbarton site. I have no doubt he will make time in his little diary for us. Please give him a ring now."

She stared back at him then decided to concede. "Of course please take a seat."

We remained standing at the desk until she picked up the phone.

"Hello Jean, we have some policemen at the reception that want to speak to Walter. Names, oh it's an Inspector Charles Gordon and some colleagues."

I looked at Gordon and said "I'm glad it's not just me that has issues with receptionists."

He smiled and growled "Snooty cow!!" under his breath.

"Inspector Gordon! Mr McGlashan's secretary Jean will collect you shortly."

"Oh thank you" said Gordon obsequiously.

"Please take seat gentlemen."

"No thanks we'll stand!"

"If you must!"

Gordon was doing his best to antagonise the woman, though she did deserve it. There was a real attitude problem among receptionists in this town. Must be union rules; treat strangers like shit.

"Inspector Gordon" said a broad Ulster voice.

I turned to see a small middle aged woman with short gray hair and thick glasses. She wore a red polo neck, a gray skirt and beige sandals which matched her tights. Clearly Herbert-Starr didn't go in for glamorous secretaries. Farrell shook his head and frowned at me. He was thinking the same thing.

"Hello I presume you are Jean" said Gordon.

"Yes Jean Gregg, Mr McGlashan can see you now, I'll take you down to him."

Farrell tutted! We were going downstairs. So we were not going to get a chance to walk on the ridiculous stair carpet.

Jean led us past the reception desk and through the door behind the desk to the post room; which was remarkably tidy, they had either sorted their afternoon post or they hadn't collected it yet. Jean led us out into a dull, badly lit crème corridor past numerous small offices. At the end of the corridor we entered the stairwell and Jean led us down three flights to another even more dimly lit corridor. The third door on the left had McGlashan's name on a brass nameplate.

Jean opened the door and we entered the outer office, Jean sat down at her desk and waved us into the next office.

McGlashan was sitting at his desk clearly waiting for us. He was a small man with a grey German helmet haircut and glasses with thick frames like Henry Kissinger, a square chin and a thin lipped mouth that had a semi-permanent sneer. He was wearing a grey plaid suit, a dark blue shirt and a tie with red, black and silver stripes.

"Inspector Gordon please sit down" he said without standing up or offering his hand.

Gordon and Farrell sat down in the chairs opposite McGlashan's desk. I pulled a chair across from the conference table and sat down beside Farrell.

"Mr McGlashan, we would like to discuss your report of a possible assassination plot against the Prince of Wales by staff at your Dumbarton site."

"I know you do. I have just spoken to Ruby. I want you to know that I regard your behaviour as totally out of order. Ruby was made to feel like a criminal for acting as a concerned and loyal citizen. Have no doubt that I will be reporting this to the Chief Constable and as for your fancy handshakes: I am not quite as gullible as my brother in law."

Farrell smiled.

Gordon sat back in his chair, yawned and said "Oh Dear, I best start planning a new career."

"You are damn right! I am not going to let this lie. You guys are all for letting the crooks run wild. My view is prevention is always better than the cure. I am not prepared to risk a hair on the royal's heads yet you seem intent on letting these fenians kill somebody afore you take any action. I want them arrested and off my site by tomorrow."

"Arrested for what exactly?"

"For planning to kill Prince Charles!"

"According to you and Mr Snodgrass maybe but there is no other evidence to support this allegation. We can't arrest people just on the suspicion of a couple of people no matter how influential they may or may not be."

"You have plenty of evidence from Ruby, he heard them planning it."

"All we have is hearsay and circumstantial evidence and it has to be said very little of it is in the least bit incriminating. No-one has actually seen or heard these men do anything remotely threatening. What we do have is a very thick folder of similarly flimsy allegations raised by your good self over the past 20 years. The only real case we have is against you for wasting police time."

The little man wasn't going to take this lying down. Very calmly he said "Listen you are not going to get away with insulting me like you did with Ruby. I will speak to the Chief Constable himself this afternoon and get you disciplined because you clearly have it in for me."

"I am sure the Chief Constable enjoys your little chats but I have a sneaking suspicion he doesn't go round sacking Inspectors on your say so."

"They say pride comes before a fall Inspector. Prepare yourself as you are going to be brought down to earth with a bump."

"Mr McGlashan you are not the first person to try and rattle me with alleged connections to the top of the force. Though you and Mr Snodgrass are novel in that at the moment you are not being charged with anything yet you feel the need to play the big brother card. Do you have any reason to feel so guilty?"

"Not at all I have done nothing: except pass you information on a potential crime."

"Information we have acted on and fortunately found nothing to suggest that it was anything other than a potential crime. I am at a loss to understand why you and Mr Snodgrass both felt the need to attack me when I explained this to you. This is the behaviour of men who have something to hide, not what I would expect of innocent pillars of the community like yourself and Mr Snodgrass. Why are you reacting so aggressively?"

"Your manner is condescending and you don't seem to be taking us seriously."

"We are taking you very seriously. The suspects are being subjected to 24 hour surveillance, to avoid spooking them we need you and Mr Snodgrass to back off and not antagonise them. We don't need enthusiastic amateurs ballsing up the investigation."

"We're trying to help..."

"Sometimes we don't need help; we need space to work without distractions getting in the way. You can help though."

"How, let me know what you want and it will be done."

"We need to break up the group dynamic ahead of the 23rd. I want you to put some of these guys out of harm's way."

"Are you asking me to kill somebody?"

I looked at Farrell, he smiled back knowingly. We were both thinking that McGlashan read too many crime novels.

Unperturbed Gordon smiled and said, "Nothing quite so drastic. I just want you to transfer Farren to another site away from his sidekicks. Can you do that?"

"It's difficult because he is not a permanent worker; Stewart brought him in for the Dumbarton contract. It could be done though, as we are short of men at Faslane."

"Excellent that will get him out of the road and leave the rest of them leaderless. You might just have saved the Prince's life."

McGlashan beamed with delight, "Really?"

"Absolutely without your information we would never have suspected anything. These guys have spotless records. It is clear that Farren is likely to be the brains of the outfit. How quickly could you move him?"

"Give me a couple of days and I should be able to get something arranged."

"Tremendous, I knew you would understand the urgency. We won't take up any more of your valuable time."

Gordon stood up and shook McGlashan's hand. Standing up McGlashan was barely taller than when he was sitting.

"Thank you Inspector, it is good to be doing something positive on this matter. Jean please show the Inspector and his team out."

From the atrium Jean's Iain Paisleyesque tones barked "Follow me gentlemen."

We trooped out behind her. She led us in the opposite direction down some more stairs to what was obviously the tradesman's entrance.

Farrell said "Excuse me we came in through the front door, my car is parked out there."

"Don't worry you just need to cross the car park and turn left into the lane. After about 5 minutes walk you will be back at the front door."

"Why can't we just go back out the way we came in?" said Farrell despairingly.

"That entrance is for major clients only. All our other visitors use this entrance."

"Nice to know the police are valued round here." said Farrell.

Jean simply stared at him then said "Goodbye gentlemen" and turned on her heel closing the door behind her.

Gordon laughed, "That went well didn't it!"

"Why did you start sucking up to McGlashan? Were you afraid he would call the Chief Constable?" I asked.

"Afraid of that wee nyaff? No way. I know just where the likes of him and Snodgrass sit in the lodge hierarchy, he is dreaming if he thinks he has any leverage. I buttered him up to give him something to focus on."

Farrell said "Aye and tae get Farren the sack!"

"What do you mean? He just asked him to transfer him not sack him." I said.

"Aye transfer him where? Faslane Navy base that's where. Farren is heading for the dole queue. He turns up at Faslane, McGlashan passes his Economic League report to the MoD Police. They see Farren's brother is a convicted terrorist and that Farren's burd is a CND member and they tell Herbert-Starr he cannot remain on site because he is a security risk. Herbert-Starr say that Farren didn't disclose this in his application to them and this gives them grounds to sack him."

"Ah! That makes sense, did you plan this?" I asked Gordon.

Gordon looked at me and said "I'm bright but I am not exactly Bobby Fischer. I just wanted to give McGlashan a bone to keep him quiet. I don't believe there is any assassination plot but I do think something is going on at that site. I do feel a wee bit bad if I have lost Farren his job but there is still a chance that he is a wrong un'."

"Aye right! Cut the crap and let's get oota here." said Farrell and he strode up the lane.

Gordon shrugged, "Davie isnae too happy about this but sometimes its omelettes and eggs, you have to break one to enjoy the other."

When we got to the car, Farrell was sitting the driver's seat with a frown on his face.

"See what I mean Davie is in a major huff. He needs to detach himself from the work, you can't get emotionally involved. It doesn't help."

We clambered into the Cortina and Farrell drove off without a word. Gordon broke the tension by telling some impenetrable football jokes. After a few minutes Farrell was back to normal.

"Phil I'll drop you at the hotel now. I'll pop round later and introduce you to Melanie."

"How are you going to do that" asked Gordon?

"Mel's working at the club tonight so we can drop in for a chat."

"Oh aye, just pop in will ye? Phil you are in for a treat."

I was bemused but no-one bothered to explain what the joke was.

Here's the hotel now. "I'll pick you up about 7 ok."

"Davie that would be great, thanks."

"I'll see you at the station in the morning" said Gordon, "About 9.30 eh?"

"Sure" I said and got out of the car. I pulled up the boot lid and took out my case, slammed it shut and waved as the car drove off belching smoke. It was a wreck.

Chapter 11

As I walked in through the marble atrium, a greeter in a blue uniform said hello and waved me towards the reception.

A small attractive woman in an air hostess style blue uniform smiled at me and said in a lively Welsh accent "Hello how can we help you?"

"I have a reservation for tonight in the name of Featherstonehaugh."

She searched the book and I waited for the inevitable question. She looked up and I stared into her liquid brown eyes.

Her Welsh accent deepened, "I am sorry but there is no booking in the name Fanshaw for tonight, have you got the date wrong?"

"No I think you just don't know the correct spelling."

"I do, its F-A-N-S-H-AW."

"That is one version, my name however is spelt F-E-A-T-H-E-R-S-T-O-N-E-H-A-U-G-H and pronounced F'an'shaw. Please have a look for that spelling?"

"Oh I didn't realise, I can see your booking now. Please complete the registration form."

I filled in my name and address and signed the form.

"Thank you, how will you be paying? Cash/Cheque or Credit card?"

"Cash, I will pay for the first three nights now if that is ok."

"Lovely, that will be £96."

I handed over 5 twenties. She gave me £4 change.

"Just hold on and I will get your key. You are in room 120 on the first floor. Breakfast is served from 6.30 to 9 in the restaurant to the left of the lifts. Would you like to eat in the restaurant this evening?"

"No I have another appointment."

"Lovely I hope you enjoy your stay." She paused blushed a little and said "Sorry about your name, first time I have come across that spelling."

"Don't worry about it happens all the time." I looked into her eyes. They were like limpid pools. Her skin was flawless with a slight olive tinge; her black eyebrows contrasting with her blonde bobbed hair. Her lips were full and naturally red.

She looked down at her papers and whispered "Enjoy your stay in Glasgow."

Disarmed, I said I will do my best, picked up my case and headed for the lift. The elevator was mirrored with a polished brass handrail at waist height. Must be a fast lift I thought. I pressed 1 and the doors closed. After a couple of minutes the lift reached the first floor. I stepped out and walked along the plush beige carpet with the repeating fleur de lys motif. The walls were a pale blue and looking a little worn. I reached my room unlocked the door and stepped in.

The bathroom was on the left, all white with a shower over the bath. I had a double bed which was a treat and a portable television in the corner. There was an electric kettle, a couple of cups and some teabags on the dressing table. It was luxury compared to my bedsit. It was 3pm and I was exhausted. I stripped down to my underwear, locked the door and got into bed. The report to Foster could wait a while. The stress of the trip and today's interviews had worn me out. I was unconscious almost as soon as my head hit the pillow.

Chapter 12

I came round in a daze. My heart was thumping. I was drenched in sweat. Someone was shouting nearby. I lay there confused unable to move. I didn't know where I was, I felt paralysed. The white ceiling suggested I wasn't in my bedsit, maybe I was in hospital. No it didn't smell that bad, just a bit smoky. It sounded like a man was growling at a woman who was screaming at him. I couldn't make out a word they were saying, but it sounded German. I couldn't understand how I had ended up in Germany.

I gradually regained control over my limbs. I rubbed my eyes with my left hand. My right hand felt numb. I could feel my toes now. The noise receded and I started to become a sentient human again. I was in Glasgow on a jolly paid for by the department. I had sat through some of the oddest interviews led by an almost schizophrenic Special Branch Inspector. I just couldn't understand what Gordon was up to except wasting his time and winding up bigots and a Polish War veteran. If Foster was here he would have gone home after the session with Snodgrass. There was no evidence against anyone. Plenty of suspicion and lots of people who were behaving in a guilty manner but no crimes committed. I was wasting my time as I had planned but it felt even more fraudulent than I had anticipated. I would have to dress my report up somewhat to prevent a recall message.

Farrell was interesting, I felt he wanted to tell me the truth but never got the chance. Maybe he might open up this evening over a beer, as long as Gordon doesn't appear. I had pretty much had my fill of Chic Gordon, a deeply unsettling individual. His modus operandi was certainly not subtle. He enjoyed conflict, maybe he thought it put the interviewee at a disadvantage. It certainly antagonised Snodgrass and McGlashan. I just couldn't understand why Strathclyde Special Branch's was spending its entire budget on this nonsense. Overnight surveillance on the whole gang was ridiculous and now Gordon was extending it to Zuck as well. Gordon clearly didn't seem to care that we were in the middle of a recession, police funds were just wooden dollars to him.

Still it made no odds to me really. I would make the most of my four nights here. See Glasgow's highlights and maybe meet one of these good looking Scottish women. With a bit of luck I wouldn't have to do too much work.

The curry appeared to have settled now, I didn't feel too bloated. I contemplated getting up but couldn't be bothered. Another hour's rest would do me good. I would call in my report to Foster first thing in the morning. No point in doing it tonight.

I turned on the TV. '*Blue Peter*' was on. Janet Ellis was making a banana cake, her very odd voice rattled in my head. She used to do another kids programme but I couldn't remember which one. My mate Andy reckoned she had been nude in an episode of '*The Sweeney*' but not one I had seen. She was good looking but the voice put me off; that and the sight of Simon Groom and Peter Duncan eating her cake was too much for my delicate sensibilities. I switched over to BBC2 but it was'The Great Egg Race'. I tried ITV, '*Crossroads*' was on, Benny was trying to help Miss Luke tidy up. Adam looked angry and drunk after a lover's tiff with Jill. The sets wobbled and the script was dreadful. Channel 4 had some American comedy. I flicked back to BBC1 but '*Blue Peter*' was still on. I turned the TV off and opened my case. I decided to read '*The Last Parallel*'. It was about a US Marine in the Korean War. I read a couple of chapters then nodded off for ten minutes. I woke at ten to 6. I hopped out of bed and jumped in the shower.

The shower woke me up! I stayed in for about 20 minutes letting the hot water massage my neck and back. It was heavenly unlike the shower in the bedsit which trickled out smelling vaguely of old onions. Feeling spotless I got out of the shower soaped my face and shaved. I put on some fresh clothes and felt great. Beige waffle trousers and a pink shirt. I threw a pale blue v neck over my shoulders. I looked in the mirror and saw a dapper handsome man. Pity no-one else agreed.

I went down to the bar, but not before double checking that my room door was locked. Got to take security seriously especially in hotels. Farrell was already at the bar, he waved to me making a drinking gesture with his other hand. I nodded and walked over to him mouthing lager. I sat down beside him and watched as the barman poured a golden pint with a foamy head.

"Got you a pint of Tennents, that ok?"

"Yes that's fine."

"Room ok?"

"Great, plenty of space, good shower, much better than my flat."

"I don't have a shower, I am a bath man, once a month even if I don't need one!"

I laughed Farrell could be very funny

"How did ye enjoy yerself today?"

"It was interesting.."

"I'm sure it was, what do you really think?"

"The case is paper thin. I don't understand what Gordon is up to. He is spending a fortune for no obvious reason."

"Me neither. Chic seemed to get obsessed with this one as soon as it came in. Mobilised the full squad, day night surveillance; the works! Like you we could see from the start that there was nothing in it."

"Why did he report it to our lot?"

"Don't know, crap reports like this usually go straight into the bucket."

"He doesn't like Snodgrass or Zuck does he?"

"He hates Huns and Zuck gets up his nose."

"What are Huns?"

"Rangers supporters like Snodgrass and McGlashan."

"Oh right is Gordon a Celtic supporter then?"

No really, he supports St Mirren and Aberdeen though really I think he is just a fan of Alex Ferguson who has managed both. I support Celtic and he slags me about them all the time though he does like to see them do well in Europe. He can't stand Rangers though. His mother was Irish and his old man was a true blue shipyard worker so I think he had his fill of sectarianism at the dinner table when he was a kid. I think Snodgrass reminds him of his dad, you know what teen rebellion can be like."

"I suppose if his dad was a bigot who took it out on his mother then you might get soured against it. How does he manage the Masonic stuff then, the handshake with Snodgrass seemed pretty authentic."

"Aye he wus a Mason when he was a young cop in Paisley, his dad got him in and taught him the stuff. It didnae dae any harm in his early days on the force. He seems to have turned against it about ten years ago, left the lodge and become pretty vocal about the danger of Sectarianism in Scotland."

"Interesting, how do you cope with it?"

"I have always hated Huns, but I don't let it affect my professional judgement."

I looked at him and he laughed; only joking Phil, "I am only interested in catching crooks not some kind of Catholic crusade."

"Do want to get something to eat, they do bar meals in here, the menu looks ok. Have a look at it."

I looked at the greasy laminated menu:

Burger and chips
Battered fish and chips
Roast chicken and chips
Gammon steak and chips
Steak pie and chips
Macaroni and chips

I decided to go for Steak pie and chips.

"I'm for the Gammon steak what about you?" asked Davie.

"Steak pie I think."

"Ok I'll order, do you want another pint as well?"

"Yes go on."

Farrell waved at the barman and started ordering. I took a big drink and emptied my glass. A couple of seconds later I belched a wonderful combination of gassy lager and curry. I felt much better.

Farrell paid for the food and the barman poured our pints.

The barman passed me my drink and pointed at an empty table, "Best grab that one it'll get busy soon" he said.

Farrell nodded and set off for the table, I followed sipping my beer. There were a couple of good looking women eating in the corner. I smiled at them but they studiously ignored me.

Farrell laughed, "Don't worry ye'll see plenty of talent later when we meet up wi Mel."

"Oh yes?"

"OOOh yes, just stay calm when you are in there."

I decided not to probe any further; clearly Farrell and Gordon found the prospect of me being in the "Club" extremely funny. I wasn't going to let Farrell wind me up all night. I moved the conversation back to the case.

"So why do you think Gordon is so interested in this case?"

Farrell hesitated, ran his fingers through his hair and sipped his pint. Eventually he spoke. "I think he is after the boy Herrity's dad."

"Why? Surely he is dead?"

"I don't think so; the news on the street as Huggy Bear would say is that ole man Herrity has been roaming the streets of Clydebank and Duntocher with some of his pals from Ireland. I think he is planning to start up a little crime empire."

"Really, is there an IRA link?"

"Only if he plans to sell guns to them, it feels more like a drugs operation."

"Do you have any evidence, photographs of Herrity?"

"No, no cop has seen him."

"A bit flimsy don't you think, no more kosher than the IRA assassination plot."

"True but slightly more possible than a fanny arsed twat like Sean Farren setting up an IRA Active Service Unit to shoot or blow up Prince Charles. Johnny Herrity is a wild man whose days as a mercenary are over. You miss big money when it disappears and crime is the easiest means of getting rich if you are hard enough and clever enough. We know Herrity was both."

"It is still a bit hard to believe he faked his death and has now come back to the same area."

"It's the only place where he has friends and some influence. Ireland is sown up with heavily armed guys that won't be afraid of hasbeens like Herrity but here in Glasgow there just isn't the same volume of tough guys with guns. If Herrity has access to weapons he could be running the city in a matter of months."

Unconvinced I nodded and just to change the subject said, "Where is that food?"

"Calm down they do have to cook it first."

"How far away is this club we are going to?"

"Not far. Just across the road."

"Really? I noticed a few dodgy bed and breakfast places but no club premises."

"Just you wait and see. It's a converted townhouse, very nice inside but subtle not showy. It's not on Sauchiehall Street, it's a couple of streets back from there."

I gave up at that, it was clear he wasn't going to let me in on the joke.

A pleasingly plump waitress with raven black hair brought our meals. Beguiled by her olive skin, strong nose and thick ruby lips, I was sure she was Greek or Italian until she spoke:

"Who's huving the steak pie?"

Farrell pointed at me and said "This handsome man here."

She plopped the plate down in front of me and gave Farrell his Gammon steak.

"Dae ye want ony vinegar or sauce?"

"Vinegar and tomato ketchup please" said Farrell, he watched her walk back to the kitchen and whispered, "She fancies you Phil."

I laughed and said "There might be a language barrier, where is she from Rome?"

"Greenock mair likely" said Farrell. "Film star's body and a docker's voice what a tragedy."

Waitress Aphrodite reappeared with a vinegar bottle and a tomato shaped ketchup dispenser. "Enjoy yer dinner" she said before departing to provide another table with charming service.

Farrell smiled and said "Don't worry ye can chat her up again over the pudding order."

I wolfed down the steak pie without tasting it. The beer had given me a real hunger. I sat back and watched Farrell finish off the strange pink circle of meat that looked as if it had never been near a pig. They must make them from re-constituted bacon or something.

Farrell cleared his plate and took a long draught of beer. "God that stuff makes you thirsty. Go get a round in."

I wandered up to the bar, as I approached the barman threw his towel on the bar and said, "Two Tennents?"

"Yes please."

"That'll be £1.50."

I passed over two pound notes. He rang it up in the till and handed me 50p change. He lifted the pints onto the bar and gave me his Sunday best smile, which was a pretty gruesome view of scarred gums and badly fitted crowns.

"Thanks very much" I said and carried the beers back to our table. I smiled over at the two women but they didn't look up. I narrowly avoided tripped over a chair and only just made it back without spilling the beers down my front. You need your wits about you in these places.

I passed Farrell his beer and sat down. The dark one is not too bad he said nodding his head in the direction of the two women.

I smiled and said "Either would do me."

Farrell laughed, "The prerogative of the single travelling man, any port in a storm, any hole in any port."

"I wouldn't quite put it like that but yes."

"Aye well enjoy it while ye can, marriage soon puts a damper on yer lovelife!"

"I am sure that's not true, how long have you been married?"

"Twelve years, so I know what I am talking about."

Anxious to avoid some horror confidences, I tried to change the subject. "What is the Glasgow nightlife like?"

"If you're young wi a bit of cash its great. There are loads of pubs and discos in the city centre. For old stagers like me, it's ok if you like pubs but ye feel like a pensioner in the discos, they are full of teenagers."

"Maybe I'll get a trip round the pubs before I go home."

"Do you want pudding?"

Remembering the Rum Baba of the other night, I declined.

Farrell seemed slightly disappointed but said "Fair enough. We have had two dinners today. Finish your beer and we'll go and see Mel."

Chapter 13

I swigged back my pint and burped loudly. We stood up and headed to the door. I glanced at the two women. The redhead smiled at me.

Farrell, laughed, "They always smile when you leave, have you noticed that? You are no longer a threat so they feel able to be nice to you."

"Davie you are a bit of a psychologist aren't you?"

"Aye, my theories are based on years of experience and observation not like Freud, who just made it up as he went along."

"There are a few academics that might disagree with you on the subject of Freud."

"Maybe but maist of them are horse's hoof's that don't understand how hard it is to pull a good looking woman."

Anxious to avoid a descent into the horrors of Farrell's psyche I changed the subject. "Where is this club then?"

We were standing outside the hotel on Sauchiehall Street. Traffic was still moving briskly so we would need to be careful if we had to cross the road.

"It's over there" said Farrell pointing to a street about 50 yards away on the other side of the road.

Luckily there was a break in the traffic and we could run across the road. Farrell marched off towards the side street like a man on a mission. I got in step with him as he turned left into the side street which opened into a square with an unkempt garden in the centre. The tenements were large four storey red sandstone affairs with shiny front doors with brass handles. Some had impressive steps up to the entrance. We stopped outside one with a red awning over the entrance. A brass sign proclaimed the Kelvingrove Health Club, members only.

"Here we are" said Farrell and marched up the steps and opened the door. A large bouncer in a black tuxedo sat at a table inside the door.

"Evening Gentlemen how can I help you?" he said in a military accent.

Farrell took out his warrant card and said "I would like to speak to the duty manager."

"Mr Kilrain is not in please call back tomorrow."

"Ok who is in charge then?"

"Miss Simpson is covering for Mr Kilrain."

"Fine let me have a word with Miss Simpson."

The big man looked at Farrell and then picked up the phone on the table and made a call. "Julie, we have a copper at the door looking for Jake, I told him Jake's not here so he's asked to speak to you. Ok I'll tell him to wait for you."

"Please take a seat Miss Simpson will be with you shortly."

We sat down on a bench that wouldn't have looked out of place in Versailles. The entry was very much fin de siècle Paris. Plush red carpet with a gold fleur de lys pattern, mahogany panelling, impressionist style paintings and portraits of wealthy Victorians plus lots of brass fittings and ornaments. A big staircase led off to the left. Behind the bouncer's desk a hallway led to what looked like a bar.

A middle aged man came out of the bar holding on to a gorgeous red head, about 5'4 with long curly hair, wearing a velvet dress of the deepest purple. The dress was strapless revealing an ample cleavage with a hint of freckles.

Farrell and I sat and stared as she led the old boy up the stairs. I was about to explode. Gods knows what the old boy was thinking. At the top of the stair the red head looked down and winked at me. I waved back.

The bouncer shook his head and Farrell whispered in my ear, "She'll be free in an hour if you fancy her that much and have £20 to waste."

I didn't know what to say. Farrell laughed his little laugh and looked at me sardonically. "First time in a knocking shop is it?"

I nodded.

"Thought so. Just stay calm. The girls look great but they are pro's. They are in it for the money and nothing else. They smile and wink at all of us because we are all potential customers to them."

Chastened, I nodded again in a man of the world way

Bouncer smirked and said "Hamburg was my first. After that I couldn't wait until I got a weekend pass so that I could go up the Reeper. What a place, makes this look like a church social."

Farrell chuckled and said "Amsterdam's no bad either."

"Aye they windaes ur crazy! I spent a fortune there. Son don't waste your time wi these dames. Get over to Europe they know how to run a brothel."

By now I was visibly cringing, hoping something would happen before I had to listen to them compare their hooker experiences. Luckily a blonde emerged with a handsome swarthy man in what looked like a pilot's uniform. They ignored us and swaggered up the staircase, the blonde's black dress was low cut at the back and front and split to the thigh on the right, revealing black stocking top and suspenders.

All three of us stared as she climbed the stairs.

"Sandra is something, eh a real film star" said Bouncer.

"Like a young Lana Turner" said Farrell.

"Gorgeous" I said.

We all nodded sharing a manly moment

"She makes a fortune" said Bouncer, "there's a waiting list for her. That Tally pilot comes in twice a week when he overnights here. It's taken him 5 months to hook up wi Sandra."

"Jesus!" exclaimed Farrell "she must be busy."

"Definitely. 4 nights a week she works. 8 hour shifts wi nae free time. Wan efter the other."

"She must be knackered!" said Farrell

"Don't know how she does it."

With that a vision appeared from the bar

"Who does what Jack?"

"Oh! Julie, we were just talking about Mrs Thatcher, survives on 4 hours sleep a night."

"Really!! Are these the policemen?" She said in a voice full of authority.

"Yes Julie this is DS Farrell, they asked for Jake."

I was dumbstruck she was simply the most beautiful woman I had ever seen. About 5'6", with black curly hair and a beautifully made up face that emphasised her dark blue eyes. She wore a black knee length silk dress with a shadow paisley pattern. The dress was demurely cut at the neck but revealed a near perfect figure, a 36 24 36 for sure. Her legs tapered to slim ankles in black patent court shoes. She wore a diamond studded choker round her neck.

Her glossy ruby red lips opened revealing perfect white teeth. Farrell spoke but I had no idea what he said. I was transfixed; it was like meeting a young Elizabeth Taylor in the flesh.

Farrell shook Julie's hand which was small with red nail polish that matched her lips. She pointed to the bar and started to walk away. I felt a crushing disappointment that the vision was leaving. I was jerked awake when Farrell pulled me up by the collar.

"C'mon Phil time for work, follow me."

Bouncer winked at me and whispered "Stunning but hard as nails."

I followed Farrell and Julie into the bar. It was full of well dressed attractive women and older men; a small dark haired waitress in a red basque and suspenders served drinks. A barman with slicked back black hair in a white shirt and a red waistcoat was furiously mixing cocktails.

The décor was all mahogany, brass and red velvet.

Julie ignored everyone and led us to a door to the left of the bar with a brass plate marked Private in Gothic script. Inside was a typical manager's office with ledgers, a typewriter, a brass anglepoise lamp plus a red and a blue telephone. A bookcase to the right of the desk was full of leather bound books. The wall on the left was filled by three green filing cabinets. The wall paper pattern was dark red flowers on a gold background.

Julie sat back in her leather chair, like a beautiful Bond villain. She motioned for us to sit on two red leather chairs in front of the desk.

"Well Davie what brings you here and who is your sidekick?"

I looked at Farrell, unsure how he was going to handle this.

"I thought I should introduce you to the man from the ministry."

I was confused, why was Farrell exposing me to a brothel manager?

"Oh yes, what is the handsome fellow's name?" said Julie with a very sly smile.

"It's Philip Featherstonehaugh, though for some reason he calls himself Fanshaw."

"I like a man who has a bit of mystery about him."

I was getting nervous but angry. My cover was being blown in a very compromising location. I couldn't understand what Farrell was up to but I had the distinct impression I was in danger of being manipulated in some way. Hopefully not physically, the bouncer looked like a dangerous man. Were they going to blackmail me?? Compromising shots with a hooker might not be too bad. What did they hope to gain?

Julie stood up walked round the desk towards me with her hand outstretched. "Hello Philip, I am sure we will enjoy working together."

I stood up and shook her hand. Her grip was warm and strong, her skin felt soft, her hand tiny in mine. I looked into her eyes and fell in love. I was in heaven, she could torture me if she wanted; I would do anything for her.

"Hello Julie I said, very pleased to meet you, but I'm not sure we will be working together." She stepped back a little shocked.

Clearly they didn't expect me to put up any resistance. I smiled at her. What would they do now?

She laughed and looked at Farrell. "You didn't tell him?"

Farrell collapsed into laughter, "No!!"

Julie laughed, sat on the edge of the desk. "Phil, Davie is a tosser. My name is DC Melanie Kerr. I work with Davie at Cranstonhill. I take it that Farrell didn't brief you on what I am doing here?"

A tidal wave of embarrassment swept over me, I flushed bright red, I could feel sweat running down my back. I looked at Farrell who was laughing furiously. He would be no help. I said, "No he didn't tell me anything about you."

"Sit down Phil, and Davie shut up it's not that funny. The force has a close relationship with the owners of this establishment. We let them operate as long as they keep us informed on the customers. Every six months the manager gets to go on holiday whether he likes it or not and a DC like me covers for him. We take copies of the books and the customer contact details, plus the closed circuit footage of the customer rooms. We get to know who has been entertaining who and what they get up to. Plenty of politicians and businessmen have accounts here plus more than a few of the city's gangsters and crooks. If anyone tries to extort the owners, we sort them out before it gets nasty. It works very well for all concerned. Julie Simpson is my cover name."

I relaxed a little. This woman was a very slick operator. No wonder they let her work undercover. "Is it always a woman?"

"Yes because you really couldn't trust a desperate twat like Davie in a place like this. He would try all the merchandise. I can speak to the girls when they aren't busy without being a threat. It's a great way to pick up information. Did you see the bald man in the pin striped suit at the table with three women?"

"Yes I think I did. A small guy with a three strand comb over. What about him?"

"He's a law and order Tory MP who is always banging on about moral values being destroyed now that you can open pubs in the Glasgow suburbs."

"A bit of a hypocrite then" I said trying to sound as blasé as possible.

"A bit of a sex maniac. He's in here two or three times a month and hires three girls at a time and doesn't just talk to them about morals."

"Really? Can you use this stuff?"

"We don't but the tapes get passed to your friends in MI5 for safekeeping."

"Sounds like the kind of thing I joined the department for, rather than spying on a bunch of navvies."

"I don't agree. This job is deadly boring most of the time. That's why I only do one week a year."

"Your station is so close. Isn't there a danger of someone recognising you?"

"No once I take the make-up and the dress off; I look completely different. The customers only have eyes for the working girls; I am just like part of the furniture, a servant to them."

The woman was amazingly modest or completely naïve; nobody would forget a face and a body like hers.

"Anyway I don't think the Dumbarton case is in the least bit boring. We need to do more digging on Zuck, Farren and Herrity. Something is going on there and those three are at the heart of it."

"Do you really think Farren is a terrorist?"

"No, but he is up to something. I have been at some of his CND meetings and a couple of his James Connolly Society gatherings. He is a political activist with some strong views. He is no idiot. Herrity has so many family connections to the IRA, he is practically a member by default. His father was a member in Derry in the forties and was involved in an incident where three students blew themselves up while trying to make a bomb. After that he did a runner to Dumfries and worked as a forester for a while before getting into the building game. He got a job in East Africa in the early Fifties on a dam building project. While he was out there he discovered he could make more money as a para-military hunting the Mau-Mau. After that over the next 15 years he turns up in every colonial war in the Middle East and Africa."

"How do you know all this?"

"We requested a copy of John Herrity's records from the Security Service and they sent us a massive file. This man spent the 50's and 60's killing innocent people."

"And now you think his son is going to follow in his father's footsteps?"

"Possibly" she said with a hint of anger.

"What about Zuck? He is a weird man but what is his connection to these guys?"

"I don't know but there are gaps in his story. I think he may have been in Africa in the 50's and 60's too. He has a son Chris, who is working in Saudi, when Zuck junior applied for a passport, he submitted his birth certificate. It was written in Swahili and was issued in Dar es Salaam, Tanganyika in 1956. I have also contacted an officer in Falkirk who keeps an eye on the Polish ex serviceman's club there."

"Is that near where Zuck lives?"

"It's nearby, more importantly the Free Polish Army was based there in Callendar Park during the war and loads of them settled in Central Scotland after the war. Every now and then they start agitating for Polish freedom so we keep an eye on them to make sure they don't do anything stupid like attack the Polish or Russian consulates, or get up to no good with eastern block ships in Grangemouth harbour."

"Interesting, is Zuck a member of the Falkirk Free Polish Club?"

"Strangely he is not. They know of him but he is not regarded as a Pole."

"What do they think he is?"

"Some say he is a German and others that he is a Ukrainian."

"That kind of fits with what Zuck told us. He grew up in Danzig and his family originally came from Galicia a former Austrian province. They speak German in Austria and Danzig had been a German city before Poland became independent so that explains why he might be considered German and Galicia was, I think, in Eastern Europe so the Ukrainian bit fits as well."

"Very good Philip, you know your geography and your history."

"Thanks I read Modern History at Cambridge."

"Excellent! It's good to have an educated man on the team unlike Mr Woodwork 'O' grade in the corner."

Farrell shrugged and muttered something about the University of Life.

Mel ignored him. "I agree that Zuck's story fits but the funny thing is the Falkirk Poles don't remember him from the war. They say he turned up in the late sixties claiming to have been at Monte Cassino and Arnhem. Nobody remembered him. The unit he said he had been in; had been more or less wiped out in Holland in early 1945. As far as the Poles in Falkirk could tell, Zuck seemed to be the only survivor."

"So our Polish friend is telling some big lies. What about his wife, he claims to have met her in Scotland during the war?"

"Well from what I can find out Mrs Zuck does come from Drymen and was a nurse in the Army Medical Corps during the war. She appears to have married Zuck in Germany in the mid to late 40's. The neighbours in Drymen all say the Zuck's moved back there in the late 60's shortly before Mrs Zuck's parents died. Most say the kids had South African accents when they started school. Nobody is sure where exactly they lived before Drymen. The guy in the local paper shop has heard Mrs Zuck going on about the heat in Africa and how it has gone downhill since independence."

"Have you asked the Security Services if they have a file on Zuck?"

"Yes"

"And?"

"They said it was classified and not available for distribution."

"So they admitted that they had one but said you couldn't have a copy."

"Yes"

"Does this happen often?"

"Only when we try and get files on VIPs like Mr Baldy in the bar!"

Like Gordon the woman seemed to be obsessed with Zuck. I had to try and nip this in the bud. "OK; so Zuck is known to the Security Service; may or may not have been a mercenary chum of John Herrity in the 1950s or 60s. He may have made up his war record but appears to have been a law abiding resident of Drymen for the past 15 years. The local Polish community think he is a German or a Ukrainian. It is suspicious but it doesn't exactly add up to the kind of case we could take any action on. I am here to investigate the threat of a terrorist attack on Prince Charles not investigate old geezers who kid on to be Poles."

"Philip you have a very one dimensional view of the situation. We think we have stumbled on something bigger than a bunch of IRA wannabees fantasising about killing the heir to the British throne."

"What exactly?"

"We can't answer that yet but it has something to do with Herrity senior and Mr Zuck. Gun running, mercenary feud something much more nasty!"

"Why did you ask for assistance from my department, we are a counter terrorism analysis unit not the FBI?"

"Well you have your advantages?"

"Such as?"

"You can legitimately request restricted files like Zuck's and John Herrity's."

"On what grounds?"

"In order to undertake a thorough investigation of the threat to Bonny Prince Charlie. If hardened mercenaries are involved then it becomes a lot more dangerous than if it's a bunch of shit shovellers led by a twat like Sean Farren."

I could see that Simcox what was trying to warn me about. This was a stitch up, they were after Herrity and Zuck and they wanted me to steal them copy of their Security Service files. "I could get sacked for doing what you just suggested."

"Not if you write up your report the correct way. I am sure we can help you." At that she smiled at me exposing beautiful white teeth.

I almost melted. This woman was lethally attractive and she knew it. I was too tired to resist. I changed the subject before she put the heat on me. "Let's discuss this tomorrow, I am too tired tonight."

"Yes you best head out to the bar for a while or Jacko the bouncer will get suspicious."

"Why?"

"Well the staff in here think cops are all corrupt and only come in to shake down the owners for some protection money and freebies. Jack thinks I am handing over some cash as we speak. If you guys don't have a free drink and a lech in the bar, Jack will think something is going on. I'll lead you out. Look mean and miserable; just copy Davie's usual expression."

Mel walked past me and opened the door. "Goodnight Sergeant. Please have a drink before you go."

"That would be lovely Miss Simpson" said Davie as we stepped back into the bar. The baldy MP now had a companion; a small thin faced man with straight black hair. They had a large bottle of champagne in a silver bucket on their table and four very attractive hookers helping them to drink it.

Julie walked over to the bar and told the barman to give us a drink on the house.

Davie asked for a Macallan, I opted for a Gin and Tonic.

The barman poured our drinks and handed them to Julie. He gave us a disdainful look and walked to the end of the bar.

"I take it your man is no lover of the police Miss Simpson?" said Davie.

"On no Sergeant, he just doesn't like to give out free drinks" said Julie as she directed us to a table in the corner. "Drink up and go you are spoiling the ambience" she whispered before leaving us.

I watched her exit the bar with the air of a woman who knew she was the boss.

The other customers carried on trying to impress the hostesses.

I sat back sipping my drink and counting about twenty stunning women in the bar, all dressed in either in low cut gowns or basques and suspenders. It was every man's fantasy.

Davie looked at his watch. "Time we left it's nearly 10 o'clock. You must be knackered". Davie downed his whisky and I slugged back my gin.

"Let's go."

We got up and walked out, admiring the lovelies at each table as we left.

Jack nodded to us as we left.

In the open air I felt shell-shocked. I was suffering woman overload. I had never seen so much female flesh in my life.

Davie looked at me and nodded. "I told ye this place would be an experience."

"Never seen anything like it."

"Only one like that in the city, probably the only other place with one half as good is Aberdeen, lots of money there. Edinburgh has lots of brothels but they are pretty downmarket."

"Mel is some woman!"

"Beautiful, clever and very, very hard! If she was a bloke she would be in the SAS. She could beat the crap out of that bouncer in a couple of minutes."

"I could tell she was not someone to trifle with."

"Aye, I'm for a taxi. See you at the station tomorrow." Davie stepped into the road hailed a cab and hopped in. In flash he was gone with just a brief wave.

Alone I crossed the road and went back into the hotel. I had a look in the bar, it was dead just a young couple and a couple of middle aged men. No nubile women in sight. I trudged up to my room.

Once in the door the tiredness hit me. I brushed my teeth, set the alarm clock for 7am. I took off my clothes and piled them on the chair. I put the chain on the door and made sure it was locked. I pulled on my pyjamas and climbed into bed. For the first few minutes my mind was a kaleidoscope of beautiful women with Julie Simpson at its centre. I was too tired to sustain the dream and promptly fell asleep.

Chapter 14

Julie danced with me on the polished teak floor the jazz band played a very slow version of Moon River. I held her close as the music swept over us. Her hair was a mass of glossy curls. I moved in to kiss her, her eyes were limpid pools. I was alone on the dance floor with the most beautiful woman in the world. On stage Franz Zuck was deep in a saxophone solo and Ruby Snodgrass was pounding on a huge drum. Chic Gordon seemed to be flailing a huge brass bell. The bell was drowning out the music, Julie pushed me away and walked off the floor. Angry I turned to the stage I was going to kill Gordon how could he do this to………

The white ceiling brought me back to reality. The alarm was throbbing and my head was aching, I didn't think I had drunk enough for a hangover. If it wasn't the drink something had done me in. My mouth was like the Kalahari, my eyes were full of grit my limbs felt like they were someone else's. I lay back and shut my eyes, more rest was required. Yesterday felt like the longest day of my life. So much information, so many people and Julie Simpson! I couldn't believe she was real. Even better I was going to see her again today. The end of the dream came back to me, if Gordon was here I would strangle him. I was so close to kissing her.

It was a dream nothing else. A surreal dream; why were Zuck and Snodgrass in it? Was there any significance to the instruments? Probably not Snodgrass was in an Orange band and Zuck had a certain Mittel Europa style exoticism. Just nonsensical ramblings but Julie felt so real.

I sat up and looked at the clock. It was quarter past seven. I decided to get up and spend some time on grooming as Julie or Mel to be precise was not going to be impressed if I turned up a dishevelled wreck.

After showering and shaving I put on a shirt and trousers and went down for breakfast. In the lobby I followed the signs for the dining room. A tall bald man greeted me at the restaurant in a broad Geordie accent

"Moornin sir, can ah have yor room noomber?"

I was non plussed, I couldn't recall the number.

The Geordie looked at me waiting for me to speak. Eventually after an endless silence my brain chugged into life. I pulled the room key out of my pocket and waved it in front of Geordie. I managed to whimper "120."

"Whats the name?"

"Featherstonehaugh."

"That's not the name I have here, sir."

"Yes it is, it's spelt F-e-a-t-h-e-r-s-t-o-n-e-h-a-u-g-h."

"Oh I see, follow me."

Geordie led me to a table in the corner

"Tea or coffee?"

"Coffee please."

"The breakfast is a buffet, hot food on the left and cereals on the right, enjoy your breakfast."

I wandered over to the hot counter, the chef handed me a plate and told me to take my pick. I selected a couple of rashers of bacon, a fried egg, two sausages, some baked beans, mushrooms, a piece of black pudding and something called white pudding. I sat down and found a pot of coffee and a rack of toast on my table. This was heavenly; loads of food and plenty of time to eat it. The breakfast was delicious, the coffee tasted like nectar. I was tempted to go up for seconds but thought I best hold off in case we went for another lunchtime curry. No point in being so full, you can't manage lunch!

I got up and wandered back to my room oblivious to my fellow guests. All I could think of was meeting Julie again. Back in the room I got ready for work. I combed my hair carefully and made sure my tie was knotted perfectly. I looked at my watch it was 8.40 too early to leave. I turned on the television; Frank Bough was leering at Selina Scott as they discussed whether the Secretary of State for Trade and Industry had fathered his secretary's baby. I bet Frank would love to have an affair with Selina, she was a real stunner. Before I knew it, it was ten past nine. I turned off the set, grabbed my briefcase, locked the door and shot off down the stairs.

I came out of the hotel and turned right and then right again. After 10 minutes I was outside the station. I walked into the reception. The old troll was at the counter again. I stood in front of him and said "Please let Inspector Gordon or DS Farrell know I am here."

He looked at me and said "You here again, sit down and I will let them know you are here."

He picked up the phone, after a few minutes someone answered. "Hello Chic Mr Fannybaws or is it Featheryhole is here again. Aye he's come back. I'll send him up."

He put the phone down and said "You can go up." He jerked his thumb towards the door. "On you go don't keep Chic waitin!"

I wandered along the drab corridors to Davie's office but it was empty. I carried on to Gordon's office. I could see Gordon standing gesticulating enthusiastically. Farrell nodded occasionally clearly entranced as Gordon provided some inspirational leadership. I knocked the door and Gordon waved me in.

"Sit down Phil I was just discussing how Aberdeen won the Cup Winners Cup."

"Chic was there you know, he is the only Glaswegian Aberdeen fan I have ever met. Chic do ye follow the Dons just to annoy yer old man?"

"No I follow them because their manager used to live across the road from us in Govan. I've known Alex since I was a kid."

"Did you really go to Gothenburg for the final?" I asked sounding as interested as I could.

"Absolutely, no way I would miss the biggest day in the club's history. It's a great city wi loads of canals and trams, big long avenues and boulevards. The food is great loads of fish and the meatballs, mash and gravy is delicious. The only downside is that you need take out a mortgage to buy a round, the drink is very dear."

"Are the Swedes all blonde giants?"

"Aye especially the women, we had great banter wi a group of Swedish lady cops. They were all like models in police uniforms. Nothing like our lot!"

I refrained from disagreeing with him on the last point. I couldn't believe there were many better looking policewomen than Julie.

"Anyway Phil I think Davie and Mel explained what we need your help with last night."

I looked at Gordon; he smiled and looked straight back at me

I had to say something, be assertive a little voice said, then I heard Simcox' warning rattling around inside my head. "Chic I feel as if I am being ill used, do you really think I am going to pass you classified data based on some hunch or personal vendetta against Polish building workers?"

Gordon rolled his lips; it made his moustache look like a live caterpillar crawling under his nose. He didn't like my response.

"Phil it might look sketchy and flimsy to you but we have been building this case through dedicated surveillance. Mel has got close to Farren at his CND meetings and everything points to something not right with Mr Zuck."

I just couldn't understand how Mel could fit into a bunch of raggedy CND types. A Venus like Mel would look very strange at Greenham Common.

"Has Farren helpfully told you what it is he thinks Zuck is up to?" I asked.

"Not quite but he has alluded to a problem at work that he was going to deal with."

"As does almost every worker, we all have work problems to deal with. I am sure you let off steam with your friends, telling them how you are going to sort out your bosses. I know I do."

Gordon stared hard at me, then said "I would if....."

"He hud a pal!" laughed Farrell, "but as he's a miserable loner he just rants at the telly."

Gordon smiled, "Davie you are so sharp wan day ye'll cut yersel."

"Maybe but I'd say that cutting ma ain throat is mair likely than you huvin a pal that's no in the force."

"True a policeman has to be careful who he mixes with."

I sat there bemused unable to work out if this was another of their jokey set pieces

Gordon snapped back to the point, "Farren is not your average bloke, he is articulate and well read, a bit of a visionary in the CND according to Mel. If you ask me she is kind of fond of our Sean and a bit too sympathetic to the ban the bombers in general. However she is a very good undercover officer."

"How does she manage to switch from Brothel madam to hippy protester?" I asked.

"Skill son, she was born to it I think, one of life's chameleons. You can ask her yourself."

A young woman entered the office wearing a grey suit with a pink blouse. Her black hair pulled back from her pale face. She sat down in the chair beside Gordon and demurely crossed her legs which were very shapely despite her thick black tights and sensible low heeled shoes.

Only then did I realise it was Mel. Only the vaguest trace remained of the beautiful Julie Simpson. I was almost disappointed.

"Hi Philip, nice to meet you in a normal setting."

Her voice was if anything sweeter than before, it lacked the underlying hardness of last night. I could feel the passion rising. I loved this woman.

"The pleasure is all mine Mel, I am amazed at your mastery of the undercover game. How do you do it?"

"I don't know if it's anything special just prepare well and make sure you create a character that you can live with."

"A bit deep that for first thing" muttered Davie.

"Aye" said Gordon, "it's lucky Mel is a workaholic. Anybody else would want a few days off after stint at the knocking shop."

Mel smiled and said "I need to write up my report on that little party. The punters are getting richer and more depraved according to the girls. They spend loads and behave like they have been reading some well dodgy books. Tying up and whipping is all the rage among Glasgow's smart set!"

"Might try that tonight" said Davie, "tell the missus its foreplay!"

"It would be the first time she let you do anything spicy" snapped Gordon. "Yer no even allowed curry in your hoose!"

"True" nodded Farrell, "she nearly threw up when she tried a bridie. Onions and spice don't agree wi her dicky tummy."

"I would throw up if I ate a bridie" said Mel, "God knows what type of meat is in those things, probably horse or badger."

Gordon laughed, "Ah bet its badger or maybe rat if you are really unlucky. The wife's cousin is a health inspector in the East End. He always takes a piece wi him, cos he doesn't trust food cooked in cafes and restaurants, reckons they are all dirty bastards."

"Best no tae think aboot stuff like that" said Farrell "or you woudnae eat anything."

"True, anyway time to cut the crap and start talking work."

"Mel tonight is your CND night, are you up for it? Not too tired after life as Mrs Simpson?"

"No it's a relief to spend time with sensible folk. The Health Club whackos drive me mental; bunch of posing twats just after their hole and a chance to spend money like water. The CND mob at least are people who care about the world and are trying to do something good even if they are a little misguided."

"I sense that you are sympathetic to the CND cause?" I asked trying to sound professional but it came out as pompous and every so slightly right wing.

Mel looked at me with disdain, "Clearing the world of nuclear weapons is pretty worthwhile in my view. Does this bother you?"

"No it is worthwhile but they don't seem to understand the strategic view. The Atomic bomb is about the only thing that has stopped the Soviet Union taking over Europe. Do you really think the troops in Germany would hold the Russians up for long?"

"No but I am also not convinced that there is any threat from Russia or Red China. They can barely feed themselves what good would it do them to invade us?"

I had no answer to that. Mel looked at me waiting for a riposte, when I didn't respond she gave me a warm smile.

"Ah another victory for the people" sneered Gordon, "Phil ye gotta learn that a man like you can never win that kind of argument. Yer too posh and too sensible to debate nuclear weapons wi a hardline pacifist like Mel. Mel what is the plan for tonight?"

"The CND meeting is at 7pm in the Holy Redeemer parish hall. Afterwards Farren and his pals head for the Seven Seas on Kilbowie Road for a drink. I'll go along and see what they say. It's usually a good laugh, nothing heavy."

"Who do they think you are?" I asked

"I'm Avril Nicol from Ralston in Paisley. I work at John Browns as a temp. That's why I started coming to the Clydebank branch of CND; close to work and a chance to get to know folk in Clydebank since I am thinking of getting a flat in Clyde St."

"Sounds plausible" I said.

"It is. I have even spent some time as a temp at John Browns just to fill in my back story."

"Mel's a pro Phil" said Davie

"OK you are going to have drinks with Farren tonight after you save the world. How are you going to get info on his alleged terrorism plans because that is all we are interested in, is it not?"

"Phil, our Sean is a real talker when he gets going; always laying off about any topic under the sun. I will get him to talk with a bit of careful probing. Don't you worry!"

"Aye and our Sean will be in a bit of a mood tonight because his pal Mr McGlashan will no doubt have let him know he is being transferred to Faslane. The sort of place a good CND man has very little chance of getting in to seeing as he will be asked to fill in a security screening questionnaire" said Gordon.

"There might be fireworks at the site today" said Davie

"Yup I have asked Jim to keep an eye on things this morning. Now Phil we need you to request the files on Zuck and Johnny Herrity from your Registry. There is a connection between those two that is the key to sorting out this mystery."

"I still don't see what the mystery is; you don't have any evidence expect the ramblings of a pair of Protestant bigots."

"No hard evidence but lots of circumstantial stuff. There is a bad feeling in the underworld. The neds are worried that some out of town guy is going to try and take over the Glasgow crime scene. At least two guys have been taken out in pseudo military style, with a bullet in the back of the head. We think Herrity is organising the hits."

"What evidence do you have of this? I would have thought I would have been informed if a terror gang was roaming round Scotland shooting people. It is my job to monitor this kind of thing!" I gasped.

"Mel show him the file."

Mel passed me a bundle of pink folders, the first one was entitled Joe Fryar murder 14/08/83. I opened the file and skimmed to the crime scene photographs. A body lay face down its hands tied behind its back with an orange cord, the feet were bound with the same cord. The victim had a dark red hole in the back of his head, the grass surrounding the head was stained a dark reddish brown.

Open the next one said Mel

I put the Fryar file back on Gordon's desk and opened the next one in the pile, Ricky Addison murder. The common modus operandi was unmistakeable down to the use of the same orange cord except this time a piece of cord was used to tie the victim's hand to his feet. They clearly didn't want this guy to get away.

"The other three are similar but not quite the same. Mark O'Neill's hands and feet weren't tied. Willie Gaughan was shot in the face, Ian Haughie must have tried to escape and was shot in the back at a range of 10 yards. They were all killed by an Armalite AR 10 rifle." Gordon added.

"The Armalite is the IRA's weapon of choice is it not? I am starting to see a link." I said

"There is a link but it is not quite that obvious" said Mel, "The Provos use the AR18. The AR10 is an earlier version used by the Portuguese and the Sudanese who strangely enough may have been previous employers of Messrs Herrity and Zuck."

I was beginning to love Mel's intellect as much as her looks. This woman was an immense combination of brains and beauty. I was also stunned that Glasgow could have five fatal shootings without it becoming national news with questions raised in Parliament and troops despatched to patrol the streets. The violence levels in the city must be phenomenal. A stabbing in Cambridge would bring the city to its knees, even in London a murder rate like this using military grade weapons would be big news.

"So why do you think Herrity has decided on a campaign of executing Glaswegians, what do the victims have in common?" I asked

"Drugs, Phil!" Gordon interjected. "Each one was a middle ranking West of Scotland drug dealer. Fryar ran a small gang based in Duntocher, Addison was a big man in the Partick drugs scene, O'Neill was an enforcer for the Anniesland team, Gaughan handed heroin imports at the docks in Greenock and Haughie worked for the Rasta boys in Paisley. These guys were all dangerous, feared in their communities but none of them were known to use firearms. Finger chopping and stabbing was their style not blowing people's brains out with automatic rifles! This is why we need your help, this case is big. I think Herrity may be trying to take over the West of Scotland drug trade in order to fund the Provos. I suspect he has engaged Zuck to help out. I want to see what your department has on these two. They have access to deadly force and are quite happy to use it. I don't want an arms race in this town. The last thing I want is neds carrying tommy guns!!! I can see the headlines now 'Shootout in Sauchiehall St', ;the gunfight at the Argyle arcade'. Are you going to help us?"

"I'll do what I can but if these files are classified I have no more chance than you of getting access to them."

"You can try though" said Mel looking at me intently. "It will be worth it!"

I was un-nerved what did she mean. Did she mean what I hoped she meant. I hoped so. I could understand why she was so good at undercover work; she got under your skin very quickly. I couldn't think of a reason why I wouldn't punch through walls to get Mel anything she asked me for.

Chapter 15

I quickly realised that I was thinking with my groin. I had to keep things rational so I decided to sum up the situation. The story was full of holes.

"These are big allegations but you still don't have any evidence. We have a series of gangland killings which may or may not be linked. We have some odd goings on at a building site that has a spurious link to a dead mercenary who may have been resurrected. You were asked to investigate the ramblings of a pair of loyalist bigots with a long track record of making unfounded allegations against Catholics. What makes this case any more valid than claims that the Pope is a child molester or that Jews eat babies?"

Gordon shrugged, "You are a hard nut to crack Phil. It is flimsy in places but there is something that ties it together."

"Oh yes what would that be?"

"Well Herrity's son works at that site."

"That is rubbish! He is a teenager who probably thinks his dad is dead."

"Ok we agree that there is no hard evidence."

"Why are you wasting your time on it? These guys are not going to attack Prince Charles. Nobody in Dumbarton is roaming round with an assault rifle knocking off drug dealers."

"Yes but I have a hunch that there is a connection and it points to Zuck."

"Phil, Farren has mentioned sorting out Zuck more than once in the pub after CND meetings" said Mel

"That is just the ramblings of an unhappy employee with a grudge against his boss."

"No its not, Farren knows something about Zuck, I don't know what but he thinks it is big. He has alluded to something that could make the papers."

"What is it?"

"I don't know but I plan to ask him tonight."

"What straight out over a pint of lager?"

"No I will be a little more subtle. Sean likes to talk. I just play the devoted follower and listen actively; asking innocent open questions that get him talking a little more openly."

Gordon, snorted, "Mel we don't want a graphic description of your seduction techniques. You will upset Phil's sensibilities."

I was a little discomfited; Gordon had yet again touched a sensitive spot. I was feeling jealous of Farren and his implied closeness with Mel.

Mel laughed; "I thought he was interested because he wanted to learn about undercover information gathering techniques." She looked at me, paused and then said; "Chic you are right. There is no point in taking the mystery out of it. What is the agenda for rest of today?"

"We keep monitoring the building site, maybe we go back for another chat with Zuck. I expect Phil will have to report to his superiors. The question is what does he intend to tell them?"

"All I can do is report the facts, which are pretty slim. I don't have enough evidence to request access to any classified documents on people who are peripheral to the investigation at best."

Gordon looked at me and said "What more do you need? We have a series of murders by suspected terrorists; we have rumours of gun running and drug dealing; we have mercenaries lurking on the edge of everything. We have a commie CND member who has been overheard making threats to the Royal Family. This is solid stuff that just requires some background facts to make a strong case. Your files might provide the clincher."

All three stared at me, I stared back at them. If I went along with it I could have a few days break in Glasgow, hopefully not as intense as yesterday. My mind was replaying it constantly especially the trip to the Health club.

Mel broke the silence, "Phil this is the biggest case I have ever worked on. If we don't take action Herrity's mob could take over the Glasgow crime scene and fund a massive upsurge in IRA violence."

I couldn't resist this woman. "OK I said I will call in a report saying there appears to be a risk of enhanced terrorist activity and put in a request for the Herrity and Zuck files. I won't be able to get them transferred to here but they will be waiting for me when I get back. I may be able to send you copies of any pertinent pages."

"Phil you are a star", said Mel

Gordon smiled and clapped his hands, "With Phil's help we might just solve this one. Davie give Cannon a call and see how things are going in Dumbarton. Mel you best head off home for some kip, we'll see you tonight after the CND meeting. Phil I'm off to a meeting at the City Chambers, use my office to write your report. I'll be back about 2pm."

Gordon picked up his briefcase and left. Mel said "See you later Phil" and followed Gordon out the door. Farrell remained seated.

"That went well" I said

"Aye, ye did whit ye were telt so they are happy."

"I tried to say no but I could see they wouldn't take no for an answer."

"Aye that and Mel is so gorgeous ye cannae think straight when she speaks to ye."

I blushed, "Is it that obvious?"

"Yup but she has that effect on every man she meets, that's why she is a great undercover officer. Nobody can think straight when she gets close to you. Loads of neds have confessed to her and never realised what they were doing. They don't even realise when they go to trial and hear that an undercover officer infiltrated their gang that it was her. Usually they start attacking their mates."

"I can understand that, who would believe a woman like her would betray you."

"Naebody! But that is what she specialises in, Betrayal!! As long as you remember that you will be able to protect yourself. If you don't Mel will chew you up and spit you out like everyone else.

There was a hint of bitterness and/or jealousy in Farrell's tone. I decided not to investigate too deeply.

I'm off to the radio control room to call Cannon. You best get on with your report.

Chapter 16

I dropped some paper into Gordon's typewriter and knocked off a few paragraph's summarising the situation. Highlighting the potential links to former mercenary operatives who were known to be armed and involved in gang violence. This was the kind of golden stuff Foster loved.

I dialled the duty officer's number.

After a couple of rings a West Country accent answered, "Synge & Goodwin furnishings how can I help you?"

"Hello I said this is Peter Flint I ordered a new suite from your Clapham Branch, I would like to arrange delivery."

"Please hold on Mr Flint and I will transfer you to the Despatch department."

After a few clicks and burbles, a female public school voice answered, "Hello Clapham Despatch, is that Mr Flint?"

"Yes Peter A Flint of 21 Clapham Road."

"What is your post code?"

"SW9 0JA."

"What is the purpose of your call?"

"Update."

"Hold on while I put you through."

"Philip, I was wondering what had happened to you" said Foster

"Sorry John, the plod kept me very busy yesterday."

"Well do I need to send in the SAS?"

"Not yet, but there is definitely something amiss here."

I gave Foster a summary of the situation as Gordon seemed to see it; emphasising potential linkage between Farren and Co, Herrity the former mercenary and Zuck the suspicious DP. I covered the gangland killings with

Herrity's MO and a general overview that Prince Charles was in no danger but there was a risk of criminal activity being used to fund arms for the provos.

Foster listened intently then said "What does Mr Zuck look like?"

"Tall heavily built, receding grey hair strong eastern European accent."

"Sounds familiar, be very careful. These Poles were used for a lot of black ops after the war. He may still have contacts in military intelligence. If there are guns involved we need to make sure we are not stepping on military intelligence's toes."

"What do you mean John?"

"If this is the same Zuck I used to know then he may be working for the Army. There is every possibility he is part of an operation to pick up IRA support groups in Scotland. If they have quality firearms then I wouldn't be surprised if the army have supplied them via Zuck."

"Why would they do that?"

"Easiest way to get an idea of the size and efficiency of the network; we did it all the time in the colonies and Germany."

"Did you work with a Mr Zuck on this type of operation?"

"Yes, that is why I think you need to get our flat footed friends to back off this operation. The army boys will not be happy if their operation is blown by a bunch of interfering bobbies! Phil I need you to lay some false trails and generally prevent our Inspector Gordon from making any kind of move against Zuck. I will speak to Brigadier Roy the Intel CO at Craigiehall and see if he will confirm whether or not his people are running this operation. If he won't tell me anything at least we will have warned him that his operation has been rumbled."

"John, do you want me to stay till the end of the week?"

"Yes Phil, I need you to keep a close eye on things. Under no circumstances allow Zuck to be arrested. Army Intel will press the panic button and god knows what might happen."

"What do you mean John?"

"I mean that Army Intel might decide to break Zuck out of custody. Which could mean Army spooks shooting up the police station and retrieving Zuck; Wild West style."

"Really?"

"I am deadly serious; they don't like losing their assets. We don't want Strathclyde police to have a pile of dead coppers to bury so make sure Zuck is kept at arm's length."

"OK John I will call you asap if there are any more developments."

"Please do, bye Phil."

With that the line went dead. I was flabbergasted! I had expected Foster to tell me that Gordon's theories were a load of nonsense and to come straight home before I wasted any more of the department's money. Instead he appeared to accept it all at face value and identified Zuck as a Military Intelligence agent. My instructions were to protect Zuck and hinder/deter Gordon's investigation. It was as if Foster knew what was going on before I had even arrived in Glasgow. In some ways my mission hadn't changed I was consistently sceptical of Gordon's theories but now I knew that the bulk of his theories were very close to the truth. I didn't know how I would be able to hide the fact that I was trying to obstruct rather than help, especially when Mel stared at me with her limpid eyes. I would have even less chance of securing Zuck or Herrity's files now. Foster must have known all about this before he sent me here. A shiver ran down my back; was I being set up too? Simcox's warning before I left came back to me; don't let them make a fool of you! Was he in on the act or just wily enough to spot that a naïve colleague was being used as cannon fodder. I really couldn't tell who was friend or foe.

I folded my report and stuffed it into one of our pre-addressed and stamped envelopes and popped it into the mail tray outside Gordon's office. The mail room guys would just think one of their colleagues was sending a letter to a furnishing company, Synge & Goodwin, 2345 Balthasar Avenue, Cuckoo Hill, Pinner, Middlesex, HA5 1AA. From the street Synge & Goodwin appeared to sell very expensive furniture favoured by survivors of the Raj, the window was full of heavy dark hardwood furniture with rich velvet upholstery. In truth the shop was just the department's post office box. Potential customers who stumbled into the shop were usually deterred by the obscenely expensive prices quoted by the deeply rude shop assistants. As a result Synge & Goodwin rarely sold anything but appeared to receive an inordinate amount of mail. The local postmen reckoned it was a mail order business.

I sat down at Gordon's desk and relaxed. Time to take it easy I thought, the less I did the better. If Foster wanted me to be obstructive I would be obstructive.

Chapter 17

I sat alone cogitating for about an hour before Farrell re-appeared and asked if I fancied heading out for lunch.

I nodded and said, "As long as it is not curry that should be fine."

"Don't worry Phil even I don't have a curry every day. MacKinnons bar round in Finnieston Street does a nice Haggis, Neeps and Tatties, it'll help you get to grips with Scottish culture."

"Haggis is sheep offal isn't it? I don't know that I fancy it much. I hate tripe and stuff like that."

"Don't worry Phil its not tripe, probably more like black pudding than any else. I bet you like black pudding?"

"I do I had some with breakfast."

"C'mon lets get some grub before Chic comes back and sends us on a 24hr stakeout in Zuck's septic tank."

I laughed, gorging myself with Davie, certainly couldn't be construed as aggressively pursuing the case so I was really just following Foster's orders. I was struggling though to work out how I could start laying false trails. At the moment no one asked me for information; they just told me what they knew. Maybe I could claim to have received top secret data from Foster that implicated Snodgrass in the Royal murder plot. Gordon would love to lock the bigot up and through away the key.

"Phil are you coming or not?" squealed the always starving Farrell.

"Yes just let me tidy Chic's desk."

"Leave it he never looks at it, some of those papers have been there since he got the job two years ago."

I followed Davie down the stairs and out of an unmarked side door onto a busy street about 15 yards from the main entrance.

"Cleaners door." said Davie, "Allows the cleaning staff to claim they work for some faceless company rather than the polis. It's essentially a wee safety measure to avoid civilian staff being followed home and intimidated by crooks."

"Sounds sensible" I said

"Ah but nothing compared to your lot I expect."

"Oh yes we enter our office via a disguised washing machine that we climb into; which then drops us into the cellar via an escape slide."

"Really?" Davie said looking shocked.

"Only kidding; it's a shower cubicle that hides the entry door."

"Dae ye get beamed up tae yer desk like in *"Star Trek"*? Ah suppose ye huv a communicator in yer pocket that lets you call your boss at any time."

"Oh yes every agent has his own portable CB radio."

"Dae ye use yer hair as the aerial?"

"No just my pen which can be converted into a sniper's rifle."

"A real James Bond eh! One o' they *'Star Trek'* communicators would be great. Ah hate using radios, can't stand all that Golf 1 calling Golf 6 over, please switch to channel 19 over! It really drives me mad! Give me a phone any day ye can communicate much faster on one."

"Very true but I can't see Radio telephones ever getting as small as *'Star Trek'* communicators. I saw one on *'Tomorrow's World''* that needed a huge battery. Seemingly they have them in Japan and the States but they cost a fortune."

"Aye, way out of our price range and far too big to fit in your jacket pocket. What about computers do ye think they'll take off? My cousin's boy has one that looks like a tape recorder that he connects to his telly to play games. His dad reckons we will all have one in ten years time."

"To do what, control moon missions!"

"Ah dunno, watch the telly maybe or communicate with Klingon battlecruisers like in *'Star Trek'*."

"I can't see it catching on; more people want a good hi-fi than a glorified cassette recorder or a big colour television. I just can't see a use for computers in the real world. The proper ones NASA has are the size of a house and run on giant tapes, God knows how you could shrink one to a size that would be useable in your living room."

"True but when I was a kid televisions were huge wi tiny black and white screens. Now most people have 21 inch colour boxes."

"Yes my parents finally moved to colour last year. Dad prefers the wireless. I don't like it much myself, too much misery. I prefer the cinema."

"You get a few good cowboys on the BBC. I love '*The Searchers*' and '*The Alamo*'."

"John Wayne made a few good ones, I like Clint Eastwood myself."

"They boxing films he made were good."

"Oh you mean the ones with the Chimp?"

"Aye '*Every Which Way but Lose*', I love a good fight. Here we are, MacKinnons Bar centre of the Finnieston universe home of good beer and manky company."

We entered a grimy dark wooden bar adorned with old black and white pictures of the highlands. It smelt of empty beer bottles, stale but sweet. The conversation halted for a moment when we entered but when Farrell headed for the bar everyone dismissed us as being of no interest.

"They know me here, and that I don't shite on my own door step."

"What do you mean?"

"I don't come in here in a professional capacity to lift or question anyone. I send one of the other guys for that. It means folk don't treat me like a plague carrier."

"Two pints of Tennents Davie?"

"Aye Roddie, what's on the menu today?"

"The usual, Haggis or steak pie" said the barman in his sing song accent.

"2 haggises Roddie, it's this man's first time."

"Ooh really will he be having the double whisky as well? It's traditional for a first timer."

"Aye nae point in breaking wi the culture; double Whyte and MacKays for my friend."

"It's a bit early for a short surely?" I gulped

"Not if you are having your first haggis laddie, you need to get your feets wet first."

I looked at Davie and at the fat barman. They smiled benevolently back at me.

"It's for your own good, a dry haggis sits badly on the stomach" said Roddie.

I marvelled at the fat man's jet black hair, paper white skin and red lips. He seemed very trustworthy. So I said "Yes get me the whisky."

"Wise man" said Roddie, poured our drinks and wobbled off into the kitchen behind the bar.

"You'll enjoy this" said Davie as he inhaled a third of his pint. The beer wasn't too bad in a cold gassy kind of way. I looked round the bar and listened there were a few sing song accents like Roddie's."

"Some interesting accents in here" I said.

"Yes it's an islander's pub, lots of folk here from the Hebrides. Used to be the first place you went to when you got off the boat at the Broomielaw. Come in here wi your luggage and somebody fae your island would meet ye and gi ye a bed for the night."

"Sounds romantic, where is the Broomielaw? Is it a ferry terminal?"

"It's just down the road, nothing there now. The Irish ferries come intae Stranraer and the Islanders have to go to Oban and git the train or the bus from there. Shorter boat trip but a longer more expensive journey."

"Progress eh!"

"Yup progress, is slowly destroying this town; not many places like this left. My dad was Irish from Donegal and my mother was from Barra like Roddie so I know this pub well. We used to meet all the Barra relatives here at Christmas. We used to go year about to Ireland or Barra for our holidays."

"Must have been fun as a kid?"

"Aye loads of freedom to play in the country but as you got older you did find the lack of running water and flush toilets a wee bit difficult. Plus the lack of anything to do in the evenings! I used to tell people I went to Blackpool or Scarborough to stop them laughing at me."

"Do you still have relatives on Barra?"

"Aye but I haven't seen them for years. They are too old to travel and my family wouldn't put up with a holiday there. They are only interested in going to Spain and I don't really blame them. I would like to go back to Barra though and see if it has changed. It is a lovely place, huge empty beaches full of shells. Heaven when the sun shines but hell the other 350 days a year when it blows a howling gale and tips it down wi rain."

"A traditional British holiday destination then?"

"Aye Blackpool; without the trams, the lights, the funfairs or the pubs!"

"Sounds fantastic what about your Irish holidays?"

"Much the same, long ferry trip then a draughty bus to the back of beyond. My Granda lived in a wee cottage up a back road not far from a one horse village called Termon which was on the main road to Derry. He drew his water from a rock well by the side of the road, had a bucket in the shed for his toilet, a cow and a goat for milk and grew his potatoes and veg. He worked for the local farmer for about 10p a day and lived till he was ninety. We would stay for three or four weeks and never bother washing unless we were going to mass. It was a real hillbilly lifestyle."

"Was this before the troubles?"

"Oh aye we're talking 1950's through to the early sixties. The IRA was a bit of a joke then, something the Clancy brothers sang about. There were the odd Republican die hards about but most poor folk were too busy trying to make a living to even think of bringing down Stormont or overthrowing the British state. Even now most Donegal people I know here in Glasgow haven't clue why the North is so mental. Back in the 50's Derry was a great town, the place you went to for fun not to experience Europe's leading war zone. Maybe I was sheltered from it because Granda was a Fine Gael supporter; I think he fought against the IRA during the Civil War."

Davie was proving to be a man of hidden depths, Hebridean Irish, his childhood holidays sounded like something out of Tolstoy. Life among the peasants, Glasgow must be like heaven in comparison. Now some social history as well a grandfather who fought in the Irish Civil war on the winning side!

"Did your Grandfather ever tell you any stories about what he did in the Civil War?"

"No, not a word! I only found out at his funeral when my Aunt Bridget starting singing a rebel song at the wake and dad told her to shut up because she knew Granda hated De Valera and his gang of Republican bandits. Apparently he hated them even more after Dr McGinley cut off Granny's leg when she went into Letterkenny hospital to get her piles done."

"What did the Republicans have to do with that?"

"Old McGinley was a Sinn Fein TD back in the 20's."

"That makes sense. Did he cut off her leg deliberately in some kind of revenge against your grandfather?"

"Who knows? According to Dad if you were poor McGinley had two treatments, aspirin or amputation. No national health service in Ireland; if you couldn't pay you were usually a goner."

"Sounds grim, do you ever go back there?"

"Just for funerals, the last one was my aunt about five years ago. After Granda died the old house was left to rot. My cousin says you can hardly see it now, trees have grown up to the front door and the roof has fallen in."

"That's sad who owns it?"

"We all do, all 30 grandchildren, that is why nothing has been done. Nobody is prepared to take responsibility for getting the work done. One cousin lives nearby and still grows veg in the garden but does nothing else."

The fat barman reappeared with two plates of food, "Gentlemen lunch is served please take a seat."

I followed as he led us to an empty table.

I looked at my plate with dismay there were three glutinous splodges, one of mashed potato, an orange dollop of turnip and a grey brown mass of haggis.

"Tuck in" said Davie and started shovelling the food into his mouth.

I picked up a forkful of haggis and mash and gingerly put it in my mouth.

Davie watched me carefully

I started to chew, trying to suppress my subliminal fear of eating sheep's unmentionables. But all I could taste was a fiery, spicy meatiness which was quite pleasurable.

"You love it don't you?" laughed Davie, "You thought it was going to taste like shit I could see it in your face. Then you tasted it and it's good. Superb."

I had to agree, this was real manly comfort food.

"Don't forget your wee nip" said Roddie depositing my double whisky onto the table. "How is he coping?" Roddie asked Davie

"Like a native born Scotsman he loves his haggis."

"Treemendous, another convert" laughed Roddie as he wobbled back to the bar.

"I suppose I best drink this" I said lifting the tumbler to my lips.

"Ye don't have to drink it, you can pour it on your haggis like this" said Davie taking the tumbler from my hand and emptying half the whisky on to my haggis. "It's Roddie's idea of a whisky sauce. It doesn't taste too bad."

He was right in a rough kind of way, it was quite tasty. Soon plate cleared belly full and slightly woozy we sat back. "That was good", I said

"Certainly was" murmured Davie

At that a uniformed officer entered the bar. The whole room froze. He pointed at Davie and said "Chic says tae get yer arse back to the station now."

"Caught!" said Davie sheepishly. He stood waved to Roddie and led me out the door. A muted wave of laughter followed us out the door. "What's the drama Tam?"

"Cannon called in to say that there is a big fight at the building site in Dumbarton. The big Pole banjoed one of the labourers apparently. Chic's waiting for you at the corner in your motor."

"Get a move on ladies!" shouted Gordon as we turned the corner. We climbed in and the car took off like '*The Sweeney*'.

Gordon's face was flushed red; he was fused with a near manic energy. "I knew you pair would sidle off to the boozer the minute my back was turned. At least Cannon knows to keep his mind on the job during working hours. Was our Davie introducing ye to Hebridean hospitality. Ye better watch out they burnt the last innocent copper that went up there. Edward Woodward acted him in the film, burnt him in a giant wicker man so they did. All mad inbreds they islanders!"

"Don't listen to him Phil, he is just winding you up."

"Rubbish, the Wicker Man is a true story. Glesga cop flies up tae Teuchter land and gets done in as a human sacrifice, it was in aw the papers!"

"Bollocks, whit's the story in Dumbarton? Watch where yer going ye nearly killed that old woman! "

The car hurtled down Dumbarton road with Gordon flashing his lights at any vehicle or pedestrian that crossed his path

Gordon slowed down to sixty miles an hour, turned to me and said "I think Stewart told Farren he was getting transferred to Faslane. Farren being the clever boy he is realised that meant he would have to get approved or vetted by the Ministry of defence before he could get in the door which surely meant he would lose his job when they found out about his CND stuff and his looney brother. So he decided that Zuck his worst enemy must be responsible and decided to sort him out.

Cannon says Farren came storming out of the site hut charged Zuck and started ranting at him. Zuck just stared at him. Cannon reckons Farren said something like you lost me my job you bastard, I know all about you too. You'll regret this and punched Zuck in the face. At which point the Polack pretty much melted Farren. Cannon says it was like watching Foreman v Frazier. Zuck lifted Farren off his feet with a right uppercut and left him flat out like a rag doll with a left hook. Nobody had a chance to intervene. Stewart and Snodgrass took Zuck into the site hut and the site clerk guy gave Farren first aid. Everybody else stood around looking shocked. An ambulance came but didn't take Farren away. He is in the workers hut with a cup of tea. I think we will attend the site now and investigate this distressing incident on the premise that a member of the public reported a serious assault."

"You just want the chance to lift auld Zuck don't you!" sneered Davie.

"Not lift just shake him up a bit, it sounds like self defence really. Farren attacked him and then got stiffened so it was his own fault and he got what he deserved by the sounds of it. Maybe he will explain why he hates Zuck when we speak to him."

"Mebbes aye mebbes naw, ah bet he keeps shtuum!" interjected Davie.

"True it must be embarrassing getting splattered by a sixty year old, expect being a Drumchapel ned he will get a team tae sort Zuck out."

"Don't think there is a direct bus fae Drumchapel tae Drymen so I can't see the Drumchapel Young Team making it round to Zuck's hoose tae sort him out."

"To be honest I can't see the Drumchapel young Team huving a doughba like Farren as a member!"

Chapter 18

We sped past the slip road for Old Kilpatrick and the Erskine Bridge. Gordon slipped into tour guide mode. "OK on your left with the mighty bridge spanning the Clyde."

"Very impressive what was it like before the bridge was built?"

"More fun" said Davie, "ye had to queue up at the slip for the ferry and it got pulled across on chains. The engine would be clattering away and you could get out of your car and climb up on deck. I loved it. You'll be on the old ferry this evening when we meet up with Mel in Renfrew."

"That sounds really interesting, I like boats; must have been some chain to pull a boatload of cars."

"Ye'll get a good look at the chain in Renfrew this evening" said Davie.

"What!" Gordon snorted, "Are you clowns here to work or just be fecking tourists. Keep your mind on the job for God's sake, we don't have time to go boat spotting or chain measuring."

"Talking of boat spotting we could always pop down to Bowling Harbour" said Davie pointing at the latest road sign, "There might be an old wreck of a puffer or a fishing boat we could look at."

"Shut it!" growled Gordon.

I settled into an uneasy silence as we passed Dumbarton Rock and turned towards the site. Davie stared straight ahead muttering under his breath.

A panda car was already there with a constable standing beside it. We pulled up beside him and he sprang to attention when he recognised Gordon.

"What's going on McArthur?" asked Gordon.

"Nothing much, Andy has tried to get statements but everybody says it was just a wee falling out. No malice intended, happens all the time. You know the sort of stuff lowlife always come out with."

"What is Bob Stewart saying?"

"Nothing much, like most of the site he didn't see the fight apparently. There seems to be an outbreak of collective blindness."

"Where is Stewart now?"

"He is in his office with Andy."

"What about the hitter and the hittee?"

"Zuck has gone back to work and Farren is still in the canteen."

"Davie, you and Phil have a word with Farren. I'll speak to Stewart."

We walked into the hut that doubled as a canteen/changing room. It had a number of tables down the centre surrounded by those brown plastic chairs with black metal legs that councils and doctors use to fill their waiting rooms. Coats and trousers hung on pegs along the walls with lines of shoes along the floor.

At the back of the cabin a thin man with receding ginger hair sat nursing a grubby white mug with a green shamrock on it. He had a large bruise on his right temple and a massive swelling on his left jaw. Zuck was clearly a heavy puncher and very accurate for a middle aged man.

He looked up, recognised us for police instantly. "Guys you are wasting your time there is nothing to talk about."

"Are you sure Mr Farren?" Davie responded, "We have reports of a serious assault committed at this site and you look like you were the victim."

"Victim, aye right! Mair like an idiot that stuck his chin and asked to be hit!"

"Are you saying you wanted to engage Mr Zuck in a fight?"

"Yes, he has had it in for me from the start. He likes to treat us like slaves, work or die is his motto."

"Is that why he hit you, was he coercing you into work?"

"No I was speaking metaphorically, I started it. I lost my temper when I got some bad news and decided to take it out on Zuck. Unfortunately I forgot that he was he was a Russian bear and got splattered."

"Mr Zuck is Polish and not exactly young, does he have a history of fighting with labourers?"

"He certainly has a history, …… but yes he is handy with the mitts. I was just so angry I forgot myself. Still it doesn't matter he'll get what's coming to him, you can't hide forever."

"Sorry Mr Farren you are not making much sense here."

Davie gave me a sideways grimace, I nodded in agreement. Farren seemed physically ok but he seemed to be rambling; not at all what we expected.

"No I don't suppose I am; no surprise when you don't know the full story. It'll come out soon so no point in making a meal of this nonsense. I told the uniformed guy I don't want to press charges, I started a fight and I lost, end of story. You are wasting your time this wouldn't get near a court."

"Are you sure Mr Farren, maybe you best rest and think about things and make a decision tomorrow after a good night's sleep."

"Look nothing to think about, young guy attacks boss and gets belted. Happens all the time in this trade and nobody bats an eyelid. I don't understand why you guys are so interested."

"A member of the public reported the incident we have to investigate."

"Really? Funny how you are not so keen when it's a fight in the Drum or Possil on a Friday night. Who called you? The Queen?"

"Nobody that important; just a local resident" Davie answered.

"Tell them thanks, but I am fine and don't want to take this any further."

"Ok Mr Farren that is your choice. We will also speak to Mr Zuck, he may wish to make a complaint if you assaulted him first."

"I sincerely doubt it. Our Franz is a little averse to that kind of publicity. He has a lot to hide."

"Mr Farren you have alluded to some mystery surrounding Mr Zuck a couple of times now. Is this something the Police should know about?"

"Oh no, lets just say he is a little morally compromised. You will hear all about it one day."

"Why not tell us now?"

"It has nothing to do with this incident and is nothing that Strathclyde Police is capable of taking action on. If you don't mind I need to get back to work, I have only a few days left before I am back on the dole. I resigned this morning."

With that Farren stood up and left the cabin.

We stared at each other nonplussed. Farren was either, severely concussed and effectively "away with the fairies" or a man convinced he had a very effective means of taking revenge on Zuck.

"Whit dae ye think bonkers or genius?" said Davie?

"Bit of both I think."

"Bonkers I reckon. I suspect Zuck has scrambled his brain; though I found his icy calm a bit off putting."

"Maybe he works on the 'Don't get mad get even' principle".

"If that was true he wouldn't have nutted Zuck. He is just an educated Dumchapel ned. The red mist is never far from the surface."

"That would suggest that he thinks he can get back at Zuck somehow."

"Aye probably thinks he can raise a complaint that Zuck is too hard for him. He can't claim Zuck assaulted him and we know that Zuck had bugger all to do wi getting him transferred tae Faslane. Naw I think Mr Farren is just a tit who lost his rag wi the wrong man and now is desperately trying to save face."

We stepped out of the cabin and went round the corner into Stewart's hut. The site clerk looked up as we entered and said "Your boss is still in with Bob."

"Thanks we'll join them" said Davie.

"Did you get any sense out of Sean?"

"Not really, have you spoken to him?"

"Yes I am the site first aider, when I got there he was coming round. Zuck was standing a few feet away swearing in German or Polish I couldn't tell which but it was definitely Eastern European. I had never heard him speak anything but English before."

"Did Farren say much when he came round?"

"Lots but it made little sense."

"Please tell us everything you remember, it's probably nothing but it might give a clue to his state of mind."

"Well...ok, I feel bad saying this because Sean is a bright guy but he seemed to be wittering on about the war. God knows why."

"In what way? Was he gibbering about D-Day, Dunkirk, Battle of Britain, sinking the Bismarck??"

"No nothing predictable like that. It was more about SS murderers and dying in death camps. Your fault he kept on saying, you killed them. It made no sense."

"Was he directing this at Zuck?"

"He didn't know where he was, Franz knocked him into next week. He had no idea who I was or what had happened. He just kept on mentioning the SS and murdering people. Anyway the Nazi's killed Franz' family so I don't see why Sean would associate Franz with the SS. It was like he was in another world. I was worried in case he was badly hurt."

"Maybe he is concussed after all. I believe Farren was in to see Mr Stewart before he attacked Mr Zuck. Did you see or hear what happened?"

"Well Bob got a call from Mr McGlashan then he came out and asked me to bring Sean in, said he wanted to talk to him."

"Ok and what did you do?"

"I went out and brought Sean back here and he went in to Bob's room. They are pretty pally so he seemed calm and certainly not angry or expecting bad news."

"When did Farren's mood change?"

"After about 5 minutes, Sean shouted "the fucking twisted bastard he has got in for me. He thinks that this will get me out of his hair. I'll sort him!" Bob tried to speak to him but he was already running out of the door."

"Who did you think he was talking about?"

"To be honest I thought he was going after big Ruby."

"Why did you think Farren would get angry with Mr Snodgrass?"

"Well it wouldn't be the first time that Ruby has complained about a labourer or a brickie in an attempt to get them sacked. I was at Inverkip when he almost got killed by those brickies. He is a particularly abrasive and unpleasant man particularly to Catholics."

"So you thought Mr Snodgrass had done something to get Mr Farren into trouble?"

"Yes he has a long history of this kind of thing, which is a bit ridiculous in an industry which is about 50% Irish Catholic. He is just a bigot."

"I see, so your first thought was that Farren was going to confront Snodgrass?"

"Yes."

"How did you feel when it turned out that he was after Zuck?"

"I was amazed, one because Franz is hard but fair generally and two because Franz is as hard as nails; Sean had no chance against him. Franz spent time in a Russian labour camp breaking rocks with a sledgehammer as a result he is still as strong as a bull. He was showing young Herrity how to use the big hammer the other week and I saw him break a half ton boulder in half with one swing. The only man on this site as strong as Franz is Joe Gallagher. Sean is a seven stone weakling in comparison. Snodgrass he could take because Ruby is nothing but a big bully afraid of anyone who fights back but Franz would have him any time of the day or night."

"So our Mr Zuck is the archetypal Russian bear toughened by life in the gulags" said Gordon emerging from Stewart's office.

"Well yes, he was very lucky to survive the war."

"Must have a few tales to tell then."

"He doesn't go into great details just the occasional snatches" said Craig looking slightly embarrassed at being caught telling tales.

"Well maybe we need to get them recorded for posterity why don't you nip out and give Constable McArthur a statement."

"I already have told them everything."

"Really; well tell them again and make sure McArthur writes it down."

Dismissed Craig rose nervously and left the hut.

"Do you need anything more from me?" asked Stewart from door of the office.

"No I think we have everything we need."

"Will you be arresting Franz?"

"No, he committed no crime, he just defended himself."

"What about Sean, is he in trouble for attacking Franz?"

"No he seems to have suffered enough for his misdemeanour. We will just confirm that Mr Zuck does not want to press charges."

"Franz is out on the site, shall I get someone to call him in?"

"Yes please."

Stewart left the hut and headed out into the site.

"Well lads, what Mr Farren say?"

"A load of bollocks to be honest! He won't press charges, says it was just one of those things and kept alluding to some big secret that he knew would sort out Zuck. He appears to have been babbling about the SS when he came to. The site clerk was concerned that he might be concussed."

"Sounds like it, though young Mr Craig is a bit of a gossipy old washerwoman. That type is not always the most reliable of witnesses."

He said "Zuck was swearing in some East European language after he hit Farren."

"Well not really a surprise he is Polish. Davie I am sure that you swear in pure Glesga when you have just lamped somebody. Craig probably added that to make his story interesting. That's why I told him to go and give a written statement. With guys like him it's a different story every time they tell it."

"What about Stewart, what was he saying?"

"Nothing interesting! He got a call from McGlashan saying Farren was to be transferred to Faslane straightaway. Says he queried it because labourers like Farren are generally employed for the duration of a job and only move on when the work winds down. McGlashan said they were desperate for labourers at Faslane and Farren was the only spare man available. Which Stewart thought was strange because Farren isn't exactly 'Superhod'. He called Farren in and gave him the news and couldn't believe it when he went completely mental ranting about "the big bastard having it in for me, I'll show him, he knew I couldn't work there." Then as Stewart was trying to calm him down he stormed out."

"Who did Stewart think Farren was ranting about?"

"Who'd you f'ing think?"

"Zuck?"

"No, Stewart thought Farren was going to confront everyone's favourite Orangeman."

"Snodgrass!"

"Yes which probably explains why they didn't exactly do much to restrain Farren."

"Are you saying that they wanted Farren to attack Snodgrass."

"Definitely, it's clear that they all hate him and you can see why. He is an obnoxious git."

Davie laughed; "They must have been gutted when Farren ran towards Zuck instead. I can just see Craig and Stewart watching hoping to see big Ruby battered and instead Farren sticks the heid on the Polish pensioner. Who promptly knocks him 'senseless'. It sounds like something out of Fawlty Towers."

"Hold on here comes the Polish tank" said Gordon.

Zuck entered the room with his head down. "Mr Stewart said you wanted to speak to me" he said in a low Polish drawl.

"Ah yes Mr Zuck, we just wanted to go over today's incident one more time. Please sit down. Sergeant Farrell will take notes. Don't worry it's nothing serious, just procedure, so that we have a record of the discussion."

"Fine what you want to know?"

"Just tell us what happened."

"OK I was standing by the manhole speaking to Coleman, making joke about the man who was in the woman."

"What?" spluttered Gordon.

"The Government man who got his secretary pregnant it's..... was in all the papers."

"Ah you mean Cecil Parkinson" interjected Davie, "Man in the Woman! Never heard it called that before."

"Thanks Davie glad it tickles your fancy, maybe you might get in your wife one day. Please carry on Mr Zuck."

Davie muttered something under his breath, Gordon casually ignored him.

Zuck stared at both of them, looking bemused.

"Anyway I was talking to Coleman when Farren came running towards us with a beetroot face. He was shouting something but I no really hear him over noise of the HyMac."

"What happened then?"

"He got close to me, called me a fuck bastard or summat like that and butted me. I staggered back and hit out a couple of times just to keep him off you know. I no really try to hurt him but he is pretty weak so he got knocked out. That's about it really."

"So it was purely self defence on your part, you had no idea why Farren was attacking you? And you had no reason to attack him?"

"Yes I no fucking idea why he came at me. Ruby I could understand but why me?"

"When Farren came round he seemed to be babbling about the SS and murderers, does that mean anything to you?"

Zuck paused, smiled and said "You know these young guys they all grow up reading war comics. Anyone with a European accent seems like a Nazi to them. I ran away from the Nazis, I wasn't one of them. It's crazy, all my life this kind of thing happens, foreign voice means Nazi to you British." Zuck shook his head and scanned us disdainfully.

"Mr Zuck I can assure you that not all Britons are zenophobic wazocks who think every European is a closet Nazi. One of the witnesses said you were ranting in a foreign language after the fight. Do you remember this?"

Zuck looked up with a little start. "Did I? It must have been the shock. I was probably saying something like 'Mother of God, what was that about' in Polish. It comes back to me in times of stress you know. Mostly these days I even think in English though it took a while. When I am confused I find myself speaking English with Polish grammar which makes me sound like a bumpkin."

"I see some other witnesses commented on the effectiveness of your response to Mr Farren assault. Have you had a lot of experience in unarmed combat?"

"One guy said it was like Foreman against Frazier" interjected Davie

Zuck laughed,"Just my Army training that kicked in. The sergeant always said, hit fast and hard and be accurate, there are no second chances in battle. I don't know how I moved so fast I am not young you know. I just knew I had to react before he hurt me."

"It stood you in good stead; Farren won't be trying again any time soon I suspect. Do you want to press charges against him?"

"No, I see no benefit in humiliating him, bad enough he gets beaten by an old man like me."

"Thanks Mr Zuck, I think that is all we need for now."

We watched in silence as Zuck rose and left the hut. After we saw his white helmet head out onto the site and safely out of earshot; Gordon sighed and said, "This place stinks! Nobody knows what the truth is. They all peddle their own versions."

"Zuck seemed sincere enough" Davie commented, "Old guy was just bantering then some ned tries to put the heid oan him. Anybody else and we would be nicking Farren for GBH."

"Aye Davie but that wusnae a distressed old geezer that got in a lucky shot, that bam was super calm and in control. He has whacked hundreds of twats like Farren, ye could tell in his eyes. He tries to play the white man but old Zuck has a black, black heart. You can tell he has been through a few interrogations in his day. We have no chance of breaking him without resorting to the third degree."

"Shall we talk to anyone else what about Coleman?"

"Nae point, we'll get no further. Though mark my words Farren hasn't seen the last of Mr Zuck."

"What? Do you think Zuck will have it in for Farren from now on?"

"Definitely!"

"Why would he bother, Farren will get the boot for this or refusing to go to Faslane so he's screwed and no threat to Zuck."

"Aye Davie in the work sense you're right but I think there is something extra going on between Zuck and Farren."

"Like what? Do you really believe that Farren has discovered that Zuck was a Nazi camp guard?"

"No but I reckon Mr Zuck has some other skeletons in his cupboard that Mr Farren might know about. He is almost certainly an ex mercenary and I wouldn't be surprised if he had a few friends in Moscow."

"Chic you have frigging lost it. You have been reading too many Len Deighton books. Nazis, Russian spies what next? I suppose Farren is really a CIA agent!"

"No chance o' that, he is just a patsy."

I watched this exchange non-plussed. At that point a Welsh voice said "Hello Mr Stewart suggested that you might want to have a word regarding the fight."

"Ah Mr Coleman please sit down."

"Coleman was about 5'8" with a shortish dark brown Beatle cut. He seemed to be dressed in shades of blue; dark blue v neck, pale blue shirt, navy blue parka, blue-gray slacks and dark blue wellingtons. His pale blue eyes stared out from a red face that was to be honest a relief from the overwhelming blueness."

"I thought I best make sure everyone knew what happened."

"Well so far it seems pretty cut and dried. Farren got told he was being transferred to Faslane, lost the plot and decided to attack Zuck who promptly blitzed him. Everyone is a bit embarrassed and nobody wants to press charges so not much of a case for us to investigate unless you can add something new."

"Well see I don't think I can add much to the basic facts. It happened just like you said there. But somehow I don't think it was just the Faslane thing that kicked it off. For one thing Franz seemed a little on edge before the incident. He was telling jokes and talking to folks in a way that just wasn't normal. He is a nice fellow but he is not what you would call cheerful or friendly, on the site he is all business always telling the men to get a move on he never tells jokes that is more big Ruby's style. I couldn't understand what he was up to."

Gordon looked disinterested in Coleman's warbling

"Sounds pretty normal to me" said Davie. "Maybe he had a win on the horses or his wife was extra nice to him this morning."

"I don't think either of those things would make Franz outwardly happy. He is a stoic serious man. But this morning he was more jumpy than happy, full of energy."

Gordon yawned "Mr Coleman what bearing does this have on the incident. Is there a point to your story?"

The engineer looked up with a timid expression and said "Yes if you let me finish you will understand."

"Ok make it quick."

"Well see it wasn't just the bad jokes and the... the nervous energy. He was shadow boxing, punching the air."

"Are you sure he wasn't just trying to keep warm?"

"No way man, Franz doesn't feel the cold, he grew up in Poland where they have 10 feet of snow. He was like Ali warming up for a fight. At one point he was play sparring with young Herrity who fancies himself as a boxer. This was nothing like Franz at all."

Gordon looked up quizzically

"Are you suggesting that Mr Zuck looked as if he was getting ready for a fight?" interjected Davie.

"Yes that's exactly what it felt like."

"Did he show any signs of surprise when Farren came charging across the site?"

"No he just watched him coming, stopped fooling around and waited for Sean to arrive."

"Then what? Did they exchange any words?"

"No Franz said nothing. He just waited until Sean hit him and then let his hands go just like when he was shadow boxing. Only difference was that this time the punches landed and turned Sean into jelly. I have never seen anyone hit so hard and so fast before. I played rugby back in Neath but never saw any rugby player capable of doing what Franz did to Sean."

"He is a war veteran so he probably learned to fight during the war, they take no prisoners these old sogers." said Davie.

"Man he is over sixty; you should be past it by that age" said Coleman. "Based on what I saw today Franz is as fit as a 25 year old."

"Lucky man" said Gordon. "Is that all you want to tell us? Did Mr Zuck do anything else unusual?"

"Why yes after he floored Sean he sounded as if he was swearing at him in German."

"Really? What did he say? Do you speak German?"

"I speak a little German, my brother married a German girl when he was stationed in Moenchengladbach. When they came home on leave they used to teach us kids swear words for a laugh."

"Ok what did Mr Zuck say?"

"I am not totally sure but it sounded like: Drecksau! Du Hurensohn, Arschfotze, Blode Fotze!!!! " After the outburst of shouted German Coleman went quiet and a little red with some spittle running down his chin.

"Sounds bad can you translate for us?" said Gordon.

"Well it's pretty nasty."

"Go ahead we are all men of the world" said Gordon.

"Ok then, Shit Pig, son of a whore, asscunt, stupid cunt!"

"Obviously our Mr Zuck was feeling pretty angry. Strange that he ranted in German rather than Polish. Has he mentioned being able to speak German before?"

"No never but he probably learned it during the war."

"Possibly but most men swear in their native tongue when they are under stress. Is that all Mr Coleman?"

"Yes I think so."

"If you think of anything else, ring me at the station. The constable will give you the number."

Coleman stood up mumbled a thanks and left.

Chic waited till Coleman closed the door and walked passed the window. "Well!! A right bunch of charlies we have here. What do you make of that tale?"

"Well I don't know about Phil" said Davie "But it feels to me like Zuck was tipped off that Farren was going to get his transfer notice and put two and two together and reckoned Farren would blame him; something that makes a mockery of his previous claims of having a reasonable relationship with Farren. I don't know that we can believe anything Mr Zuck says."

Chic rested his forehead against his steepled fingers and turned to me. "What do you think?"

"I think Davie is right that Zuck was prepared but I can't understand who would warn him and why. I can't see McGlashan pre-warning Zuck maybe he told Snodgrass and he passed it on to Zuck."

"That would make sense said Chic. Where is the lovely Ruby?"

"McArthur said he left about 20 minutes before the fight."

"Probably told by McGlashan to make himself scarce. What about his sidekick McGregor? Has anybody spoken to him?"

"Dunno ah'll ask McArthur."

"This site stinks I don't think anyone would recognise the truth if it slapped them in the face."

Gordon was obviously finding the situation stressful for some reason. "Why do you say that surely all investigations are full of murky facts?" I asked.

"Yes but usually at least one person you speak to is simply telling the truth. Here not a single one appears able to provide the facts without some kind of embellishment which doesn't sound right."

I didn't know what to say to this so opted for silence which suited Gordon.

Davie reappeared with a short stocky man with greying black hair, a weather beaten face and some very even nondescript features. He was wearing a yellow oilskin suit with a green army jumper underneath. On his feet he had a new pair of wellingtons with green toecaps.

"This is Hughie McGregor" said Davie.

"Hello Mr McGregor please sit down I am Inspector Gordon we would like to ask you a couple of questions about this morning's incident."

"Ok fire away, cannae tell ye much ah reckon."

"Possibly but we just have to make sure everything is covered. Did you see the fight between Mr Zuck and Mr Farren?"

"Aye fae a distance I was filling a barra wi whin dust fae the pile by the road. I heard a shout turned round and saw Farren lay intae Zuck then get flattened. It was pretty funny."

"You don't sound too fond of Mr Farren

Well ah'm no he is a bit o a Fenian smartass tae be polite."

I see said Gordon, "Do you have any idea why he attacked Mr Zuck?"

"Ye wouldn't say that they get oan. Zuck thinks Farren is a bit of a ponce and always makes a point of haeing a laugh when he tries to lift heavy stuff. Farren's a bit o a weakling no very strong, no a surprise they've decided to move him oan."

"How did you know Farren was being transferred to another site?"

"Big Ruby was talking about it all morning; said Wattie had fun him a joab at Faslane that would suit him better."

"interesting, do you know if Zuck had been told this?"

"Oh aye they were laughing about it first thing."

"Who was this?"

"Oh Zuck and Ruby they were standing out at block two haeing a laugh at the thought of Farren going intae Faslane and getting eggs thrown at him by his CND pals. Everybody on the site knew except maybe Stewart, Farren and some of his Fenian pals."

"I see. So Mr Zuck was well aware of Mr Farren's imminent change of circumstances?"

"Oh aye, the GF's always keep aheed o that kind of stuff. Ye never know when a labourer might turn on ye."

"Thanks Mr McGregor you have been very helpful."

McGregor got up and left.

"So now we know Zuck is a lying bastard" said Davie. "Though our Hughie is not the most reliable witness I would say."

"Very true Davie he is a right bluenose just like Snodgrass but I think he was telling the truth. One thing is for sure we have a Polish geriatric who is very much not what he seems. He knew Farren was going to get shunted to Faslane and was pretty sure that Farren would blame him even though he had nothing to do with it. All this despite the fact that he claims to have a good relationship with Farren and had no idea why the ginger twat had a pop at him!! He was so sure that a fight was inevitable he was warming up with some sparring as soon as Farren got called in by Stewart to get the bad news. Not the action of a mild mannered family man especially as when the fight kicks off he was able to pulverise a fit man over 30 years his junior. Pretty impressive from a man of pension age, could your old man take a Drumchapel ned?"

"Naw he's barely able to get out of his chair, due tae the emphysema he got from the 100 fags a day he used tae smoke."

"Exactly old Zuck is still battle hardened, must have been some soldier in his day. In addition the German swearing fits in with Mel's enquiries with the Falkirk Poles, he must be a German by birth. The only bit I don't really understand is what it is that Farren has against him."

"Maybe Farren hates Germans or just anybody that is not British" I suggested.

"Bollocks, Farren is a commie, workers of the world unite and all that shite. He probably loves foreigners. No he hates Zuck for a specific reason and Zuck knows it."

"True Chic" said Davie "But does it really have anything to do with us?"

"Definitely there is something big going on here and we need to stop it."

"What do we do now?" I asked.

"Nothing! Nobody wants to report a crime. We have gone in mob handed so there shouldn't be any other trouble today. Back to the office I think and then rest up for tonight's exercise in Clydebank. Maybe Mel will get something tangible from Farren. Let's head. McArthur can tidy up here."

We left the hut, waved to Stewart and drove off.

The journey back to Glasgow was quiet. No one really spoke except to mention traffic and the weather. At the office Chic suggested that we take a break for the rest of the afternoon and meet back at the station at 6pm in preparation for the CND meeting in Clydebank.

Davie dropped me at Charing Cross and suggested I go for a walk round the City Centre.

Chapter 19

Following Davie's directions I crossed at the lights over the motorway. Even at mid afternoon the there was a loud roar from the traffic. I walked up Sauchiehall Street a wide canyon with black sooty tenement walls.

On a weekday afternoon things were fairly quiet. I passed a succession of pubs and cafes with slightly American names like The Variety Bar and Oceans 11. The epitome of which was 51st State which also looked like an American diner. They fitted in with the large scale architecture which did feel more American than any British city I had been to. I half expected a gang of mobsters in pin striped suits and fedora hats to be in the diner with its leatherette booths discussing a "hit" or a "bank job".

Deciding that it was a little too early for a burger, I wandered on. The scale of the city surprised me, I expected a slightly provincial place like Nottingham or Leicester but no, Glasgow had the feel of a very large city with its high tenements and extremely long streets. Left and right I could see seemingly endless vistas of four and five storey tenements heading up and down the hill. I paused in front of a Victorian style tearoom and admired the strawberry tarts and large meringues packed with cream. They looked lovely. I was seriously tempted to pop in when a very English voice blared in my ear.

"I say what a fine place just like Betty's in Harrogate, what? Hard to believe the jocks could have such a fine example of civilisation in this industrial backwater! Shall we pop in for a cup of tea?"

I turned to find myself face to face with a well dressed man of about six feet. His greying dark hair was well combed with a parting on the left. He wore a grey raincoat over a blue pin stripe suit with a white shirt and a Guards tie. His black Oxford brogues gleamed with an amazing depth of shine; clearly a military man with an over friendly streak.

I smiled and said "I was just having a look and didn't really fancy anything." His next words shook me to the core.

"Come now Philip you can't be that full after your lunchtime haggis. A cup of tea won't do any harm."

Shocked I ran through the training manuals on the appropriate response when approached by a hostile agent. My new friend was standing rather close in a less than friendly manner. I could try the palm strike to the nose and then make a run for it back to the station. As I weighed up the options he spoke again.

"Don't be alarmed John Foster suggested that I make contact with you. If you come in and sit down we can have a private chat. Never know who is following you in this town."

I decided to play a straight bat. "Listen my friend I have no idea what you are talking about and have no interest in going anywhere with you," I said in a reedy voice an octave higher than usual. "I shall move away now please do not follow me or I will have to report you to the police."

He gripped my wrist and calmly twisted it behind my back. "Dear boy I have no time to play games lets go inside." With that he firmly guided me into the tearoom and up the mahogany panelled stairs. On the top floor he selected a table in front of the window with a full view of the street.

"Perfect can't beat a seat with a view. I love to people watch, even if it is plebeian Jocks. Now old boy what would you like? Don't hold back it's my treat."

A middle aged waitress appeared, before she could speak. My new friend said, "Hello my dear please bring us a pot of tea for two, a chocolate éclair and a cream meringue for my colleague."

"Is that all, sir?" She said smiling at my abductor like he was a film star.

"Oh absolutely my dear, we are looking forward to them most dreadfully."

The waitress almost simpered with pleasure as she walked away, practically genuflecting in the presence of my upper class gaoler. I waited until he spoke trying to assess the situation. He was too posh to be the IRA. His shoes were polished enough to be a Mason, maybe I had been targeted by McGlashan's contacts. Judging by the ease with which he overpowered me I didn't have much chance of out-fighting him so for now I would have to bide my time.

"Sorry about dragging you in here old boy but I thought it would be best to speak to you sooner rather than later."

"What about exactly?"

"Don't be obtuse Philip it doesn't suit you. Your plod friends are trampling all over one of my ops and I don't like it. John said your orders are to calm things down and get plod chasing hares. Have you had any luck so far?"

"Listen until I see some identification we are not going to discuss anything," I said feeling quite self righteous.

"Ok, I am Major Zuider-Michel of the Royal Green Jackets. This is my identity card" he said.

It gave his name as Alexander Montgomerie Zuider-Michel, Rank – Major, Regiment – Royal Green Jackets. I looked up and said, "OK Alexander it looks like you are a serving soldier. I still don't see any reason why I should discuss anything with you. What is your role?"

"Call me Monty, I am assigned to Military Intelligence and am currently running an operation in Dumbarton to cut an arms supply line to the Provos which your new plod friends are in the process of fucking up."

"In what way are the police causing you a problem?"

"Our man on the inside is Franz Zuck."

"Why would a Pole like Zuck be involved in running guns for the IRA?"

"Well Franz has had a varied career in the late forties he worked behind the Iron Curtain for us before he got blown and pulled out. We shipped him off to Kenya to work on a tea plantation but he got bored and hooked up with one of the mercenary companies and got involved in some fruity jobs across Africa."

"Interesting but I don't see the connection to Irish gun running."

Monty shrugged and said, "Well in the late fifties he met up with a certain John Herrity in Tanganyika at a training camp. They got on well and did some nasty stuff in the Congo, the Central African Republic and finally Rhodesia. Zuck came back to Scotland in the late 60s and settled in Drymen and joined Herbert Starr. He kept in touch with his pal Herrity up until his untimely demise in Rhodesia in the mid Seventies. All along Zuck continued to provide HMG with regular reports on mercenary activity in Africa. He wasn't on our active list but his stuff was interesting. We hadn't heard anything from him for years until two months ago when I received a message from him asking for an urgent meeting."

"So you agreed to meet him."

"Yes just for old time's sake, I was hoping to have a gossip about the good old days."

"Two old soldiers together, eh? But it didn't turn out that way did it?"

"Philip you are sharp, yes Zuck wasn't in the mood for gossip or telling old war stories. He got straight to the point. He had been working in his garden when John Herrity appeared at the gate. Definitely the same man, a few wrinkles but still John Herrity. Zuck was shocked, not often a dead friend is resurrected. Herrity asked how he was and then asked him to help with a business proposition."

"Not very subtle, surely Zuck could have refused."

"Well not really, old Franz and Herrity had done some bad stuff in Africa. The kind of things you can still get arrested for. There are a couple of international arrest warrants out for these chaps you know. Franz likes his life so he couldn't say no but he could get some protection by telling us what Herrity was up to."

"So Herrity is an IRA gun runner who has asked Zuck to help out; how is he helping?"

"Well the site in Dumbarton is being used as the staging post for the shipments. The guns come in loads of pipes. The drainlayers pick them up when they unload the pipes and load them into their van. Herrity then unloads the van in Rogan's yard overnight and takes them to Ireland on Ferris' Minibus which leaves Clydebank every Saturday morning. Zuck makes sure Rogan's men always unload the pipes and load the guns into their van. That idiot Farren thinks Zuck is exploiting the Paddies by making them work so hard and is always trying to play the shop steward."

"Does Farren know about the guns?"

"No Rogan's men know the score; Herrity would shoot them straightaway if they blabbed to Farren."

"Why? Farren is a Republican too?"

Monty laughed showing his thick horselike teeth. "Farren likes to talk about the IRA but that is a sure fire way of ensuring that they never ask you to do anything. The Provos are a very serious organisation. They know that silence is the best defence. Men on active service are trained to be invisible, focused on the mission not talking about a United Ireland in every pub in town. Loud mouths like Farren are the last thing the IRA wants. An easy rule of thumb when moving in Paddy circles is that anyone who is happy to talk about the IRA in public or even private isn't in it or at the very least anywhere near the sharp end."

"Ok so you think Gordon is treading on your toes. Why don't you tell him to back off?"

"Not that easy old boy, we aren't exactly operating within the law."

I looked straight at him, unsure of how to react.

"It's what you might call a black op. We are watching the guns come in, intercepting them, marking them and then making sure Herrity gets them."

My mouth was hanging open aghast at this latest statement.

"I know it sounds bad!"

"Bad! It's worse than bad; you are colluding in the supply of weapons to the very people you are supposed to be fighting. Gordon would arrest you if he found out."

"But he won't find out will he? The benefit of this operation is that we know what weapons the Provos have and we can trace them back to Herrity. It will help us to understand their supply chain and ultimately neutralise them."

"Or just watch them shoot our people with guns we supplied to them."

"Philip the point of this chat was to make sure you divert Gordon off this particular trail before we have to take action against him. Not debate the merits of my mission."

"You're mad! You can't be seriously threatening to kill a policeman" I said in a hoarse whisper as the waitress brought our tea and cake.

"My dear what exquisite cakes, this will be simply delicious" Monty said staring into her eyes. She stood almost transfixed for a couple of seconds before blushing and turning away.

"Keep people off balance Phil and they never remember what you were talking about" Monty whispered through a mouthful of cake.

"Now I can't continue this conversation" I squeaked, "You are incriminating me by sharing this information."

"Come now old boy we are men of the world. I am sure you didn't join the service to drink tea day in day out with crusty old bores like Simcox said Zuider-Michel. I have simply shared some strategic information with you that you are obliged to keep to yourself under the Official Secrets Act which I know you have signed. You are a field operative on a sensitive mission; the act applies to everything you are involved with."

I stared at him amazed at his casual demeanour and worryingly thorough knowledge about me. "What exactly do you want me to do?"

"That is better; you are starting to think like an agent. Plod are very solid, nice people but they are also devious beggars. Don't imagine for a minute they don't know more than they have told you. They are targeting Zuck because they have something on him, not because he may or may not be nasty to a bunch of Paddy pick and shovel merchants. What I need you to do is find out what it is that they want to pin on Franz."

I hesitated for a moment then decided to be open. "Well at the moment all they have is a pile of circumstantial evidence. They don't know about the guns being smuggled through the site though they suspect John Herrity is alive and involved in smuggling guns possibly for the IRA and also to help him progress a private war against drug dealers."

Zuider-Michel smiled, "Friend Herrity has an eye for an opening. Nobody in the underworld has his experience with weapons or is anyway as ruthless so they will have been easy meat for him."

"Have you let him do this?"

"Let's just say he isn't under constant surveillance, we let him have some free time to entertain himself. What about the other Paddies does Gordon suspect them?"

"No he thinks they are all innocent ordinary working men."

"God he has a lot to learn about the IRA. Ok what do they know about Franz?"

"They suspect his past is dubious. They know he isn't a Pole, more of a German."

"Not a bad performance by our Mr Gordon. That doesn't explain why they are so keen on investigating him."

"Well I think he has not done himself any favours by being a little taciturn and slightly too smug. His life story came out as if he had learned it by heart."

"I warned him about that very thing. More than once I told him to make his story more sketchy; forget bits, embellish others. Don't spout it out. I suspect that is how he got blown back in the 40's too eager to prove his innocence. Never trust a man who is too open or too willing to tell his story, Philip. That is a sure sign of a liar or someone with something to hide. Still it doesn't explain why plod are so interested in Franz. The referral was about Farren and the Paddies, Franz was just peripheral to the whole thing. Why are they focusing on Franz? Philip?"

I almost wilted under Zuider-Michel glare. The man had a very threatening demeanour under his old world charm. "I don't know" I muttered desperate to get some space. "Gordon just doesn't like the man I suspect."

"Nonsense Phil, Special Branch are a serious organisation they don't investigate people because they walk funny or have crooked teeth!" snarled Zuider-Michel. "They only take action when they have a reason to. Look at the knocking shop they took you to. They could shut that down tomorrow if they wanted to but it suits their purpose to run it. They appear to have the management under tight control, eh?"

"Yes it's quite a place."

"That temporary manageress is stunning isn't she?"

"Oh do you mean Julie? I said.

"Rather!! I would love to spend an evening with that little minx. Best looking woman I have seen in years."

"Absolutely" I said, for the first time feeling that my new friend did not know everything. Knowledge is power they say and I now had a little power in this conversation for the first time.

"Anyway enough of that" grinned Zuider-Michel, "We must visit there together some evening when this job is finished. What is Gordon's next move?"

"He will be running surveillance on Farren's CND meeting this evening in Clydebank" I said carefully omitting any mention of Mel's undercover role.

"Good, try and plant the seed that Farren is hooked up with Herrity, possibly expecting a shipment of explosives. That will send them off on a tangent. I will see if we can plant some in Farren's flat."

I looked at him incredulously. "Planting explosives! This is not a game you can play with innocent civilians."

"Rubbish old boy the game is keeping this country safe. Farren going down would just be collateral damage. It won't hurt him, might even get him a job with the Guardian."

"Or he might get banged up for 30 years for a crime he didn't commit."

"Don't be so melodramatic, we will make it look suitably amateurish so that he only gets a couple of years. It won't be too bad. I will get an expert to say it wasn't a sustainable bomb."

I gave up the man was mad. There was no point in reasoning with him. "Ok I will try and do what you ask. Can I go now?"

"Yes, well as soon as you finish your cake. No point in arousing suspicion eh!" he said as he stuffed his éclair into his mouth.

I did as I was told. Zuider-Michel paid the bill and we left the tearoom. Outside he shook my hand, said he would catch up with me tomorrow and headed off up the street. I decided to return to the relative safety of the hotel before anything else went wrong.

Chapter 20

Back at the hotel I skipped up the stairs to my room feeling exhausted. Looking at my watch I realised I just had an hour before I was due to meet up with Gordon and Davie. I lay on the bed and shut my eyes. All I could see was a swirl of faces Zuck, Farren, Snodgrass, McGlashan, Gordon, Zuider-Michel growling out their own peculiar versions of the truth. Who could I believe? Probably no-one except maybe Mel; though I found it very hard to think of her without saying the name Julie! I was brought rudely back to consciousness by a banging at the door. I opened it to Davie's eager face.

"Did ah wake ye?"

"Yes" I said

"Time to head for Clydebank, Chic is waiting outside in the car. We reckoned you must have fallen asleep when you didn't turn up at the station."

"Oh yes I feel like I have jet lag, I have lost track of time."

"Too much drink I think is your problem, let's go."

Gordon was waiting downstairs in a yellow Audi. "Get in ladies we have a job to do." The Audi wafted us to a town dominated by shipyard cranes.

"Clydebank I presume" I asked pointing at the cranes.

"Phil your powers of observation would put Holmes himself to shame" said Chic.

We pulled up across the road from a reddish brown church.

"Our Holy Redeemer" said Davie.

"Watch out Davie, Phil will think you are praying if you keep talking like that" quipped Gordon.

"When is Mel due to arrive?" I asked, carefully refusing to take the bait.

"She gets the 6.35 bus from Yoker" said Davie. "She'll be here by five to at the latest."

"There's Farren going in, he usually arrives early to set up" Chic interjected pointing at Farren as he strolled towards the church. "Like all political twats he likes to get things organised, chairs in a nice circle and the tea made; can't have a meeting without biscuits!"

A green and white bus dropped a crowd of passengers at the bus stop. Mel walked towards the church followed by another familiar figure.

"Well it looks like young Herrity has joined the cause" whispered Chic.

"Can't see him sticking CND for long," said Davie.

"What do we do now?" I asked.

"We wait till they come out and then we follow Farren home."

"Sounds riveting what do you expect will happen?"

"Probably nothing" Gordon responded in a managerial tone.

After 15 minutes of nothing I was practically comatose. Davie nodded in my direction and laughed. Gordon smiled and carried on reading the *Daily Record*.

"How much longer will this take?" I asked.

"About an hour and a quarter" Davie answered.

"How do you guys cope with the boredom?"

"Easy just concentrate on the job, watch everything that happens. Test yourself to make sure you are actually watching what is going on in front of you."

"How do you do that?"

"Easy, tell me what you see in front of us?"

"A church, a car park with a few cars, a bus stop, a main road!"

"Ok how many lights are on in the church, how many windows are lit?"

"3"

"Good make a mental note of that or write it down. How many cars in the car park?"

"5"

"Good write it down plus a note of the make, model, colour and number plate of each one."

"Ok"

"Is there anyone at the bus stop?"

"Yes"

"Describe them"

"Male fiftyish, heavy build wearing a grey plaid suit, short curly red hair slicked back 1940s style, black shiny shoes. Woman around 30 blue skirt, green raincoat crème high heeled shoes, pink chiffon scarf over dark blonde hair in a shampoo and set style."

"Great make a note of that. Can you see any pedestrians?"

"One; an old man in dark suit with white shirt wearing a tweed cap heading towards the bus stop."

"Excellent, now I want you to review your notes every 5 minutes noting any changes. Best way to stay awake in a long surveillance job."

After five minutes a short bald man in an Aran cardigan with leather buttons climbed into a blue Vauxhall Viva and drove off. The old man in the cap stopped to talk to the man at the bus stop. They pointed at the church a few times before the old man wandered off. The woman backed away to the corner of the bus stop possibly trying to avoid being brought into any conversation.

Ten minutes later a gang of youths ran past. They went towards the church and started throwing stones at the windows.

"Little bastards" growled Davie.

"Sit still" said Chic.

The man in the suit shouted at them, when one kid talked back to him he left the bus stop and flattened the kid with a left hook. The gang froze in shock, watching their pal stagger upright before running away when bus stop man started walking towards them.

"Well done!" Davie cheered.

"Looks a hard case" murmured Chic

"Brave and public spirited" said Davie.

The man walked back to the bus stop and climbed on a Green bus. The woman had disappeared.

We turned round to discover the car park had emptied

We drifted back to silent torpor, no cars to count, no-one at the bus stop. Gordon was reading classified adverts in the *Daily Record*. Davie and I stared into space.

To break the monotony I asked Davie about the shipyard behind the church.

"That's John Brown's; loads of big ships came out of there. I had an aunt that lodged in Clyde Street. The living room window looked directly into the yard. When a ship was nearly finished it towered over the buildings, practically blotting out the sun."

"That must have been some sight."

"Oh yes when they were building the QE2 crowds of people would just come down to look at it. Clydebank used to be buzzing then day and night, loads of young folk working in the shipyards, Singers and umpteen other factories. Dancehalls open every night, pubs packed. Now look at it, empty like a Wild West ghost town, surprised we haven't seen tumbleweed blowing down the street."

Gordon snorted and started humming like a bad violin. "Davie you'll make me greet if you carry on wi that sob story."

"Well it's a crime the way all the jobs in this country huv disappeared. Maggie Thatcher and her pals want us all on the dole."

"Calm down ye sound like Tony Benn."

"I think the meeting is over," I said pointing at a group emerging from the church hall.

Farren, Mel, Herrity and two other women walked up to the bus stop and hailed a passing Green and White bus.

"Where are they going?" I asked.

"The Seven Seas I expect" said Gordon.

Nonplussed I said, "They are going sailing at this time of night??"

"Naw they usually go tae the Seven Seas pub on Kilbowie Road for a pint after the meeting."

Gordon started the engine and started to follow the bus.

After five minutes we pulled up about fifty yards past the Seven Seas pub. Mel and her companions walked in. "What happens now?" I asked, thinking we might go inside.

"We wait till they come out" said Gordon.

"Is there any point to us being here?" I moaned. "An evening spent in car with you two is not exactly fun!"

"Getting frustrated are you? Davie the master-spy doesn't enjoy the bread and butter surveillance activity."

"Who does" growled Davie

"But shouldn't we be in there at least watching Farren, he could be speaking to anyone. It looks like the sort of place the IRA frequent, Mel could be in danger."

"Listen Mel can look after herself. She is our eyes and ears in this operation. We are just back-up. If she needs help she will let us know."

"How exactly?"

"The barman in there is guy called Paul Connolly, he's one of our guys. Any trouble, Mel will tip him the wink and he will give us a shout. Not that trouble is likely the only people in there tonight will be hard core bevy merchants who have come straight from work and retired or unemployed old geezers who make a pint last two or three hours. No international hit men or Russian special forces."

"They won't be long anyway" interjected Davie, "Seeing as they have work in the morning and Mel and Herrity have to get back to Paisley. It's already half past eight."

Half an hour later they exited. Mel, Farren and Herrity walked past us towards the bus stop. The other two women crossed the road to the bus stop opposite the pub.

"That's odd" said Davie, "Mel and Herrity should be getting the bus back to the Ferry."

"Aye" said Chic: "We better stick close to them."

"There are those two old boys from the church as well" said Davie, pointing at the two men who we saw speaking at the bus stop outside the Holy Redeemer.

"Aye Phil that proves ma point about the type of clientele the Seven Seas attracts, they're probably a pair of has been from MacApline's Fusiliers" said Chic. "Not exactly 'Blofelt' or the 'Man wi the Golden Gun'."

I watched as the two men walked past the bus stop and climbed into a Blue Morris Minor van. They pulled away just as the bus arrived.

"They're going to Drumchapel" said Davie. "Farren must have invited them back tae see his etchings."

"The only etchings that twat has come fae his fleas" said Chic earnestly following the bus.

Chapter 21

We followed the bus until Farren, Mel and Herrity got off. They walked up Walter Scott Crescent a grim street of four storey tenements.

"Farren's on the fourth floor of number 72" whispered Davie, "that's about six houses up on the left. McLintock should be outside ready for the nightshift. Shall we wait Chic? Or leave it to McLintock."

"Let's wait Davie I want to find out what brought them here tonight. They are unlikely to stay long; they need to get back to Paisley tonight."

Two mind numbing hour's later Davie shook me awake. "They're coming out."

I looked up to see Mel and Herrity getting into a taxi outside Farren's house.

"Thank God for that ah thought they were there for the night!" said Chic.

We followed the cab to a ferry crossing where Mel and Herrity got out.

"The Renfrew Ferry" whispered Davie, "It runs twenty four hours a day to get the workers to Clydebank."

"Only problem now is there are hardly any workers" snarled Chic.

"Does Mel live on the other side of the river?" I asked.

"Aye about 5 miles away in Paisley so does Herrity, lucky for them a Western bus should be on the other side in about 10 minutes" said Davie. "Though when Patons ran that route there was always a bus waiting for the ferry."

"Aye Patons was a great bus company" said Chic.

"What do we do now?" I asked sounding a bit like the annoyed child in the back seat.

"We let them get on the ferry then we drive on it as well" said Chic.

"Isn't there a risk Herrity will spot us?"

"No we'll stay in the car they have to go into the passenger compartments."

At that moment a huge dredger sailed down the river dripping water from her row of buckets. Five minutes later the ferry clanked up the slipway.

"She's chain driven" whispered Davie, "a lovely wee boat. You can look in at the engine. It clanks away like yer on a tramp steamer somewhere in the China Seas She used to be the Erskine Ferry until they built the bridge. The old Renfrew Ferry is tied up along the river there."

"For Gods sake no more history please!" groaned Chic. "It's a smelly oily auld tub that carries grimy guys in boiler suits tae work nothing at all special about that."

He waited until Mel and Herrity had boarded and then drove onto the ferry. The red faced deckhand took our tickets and refrained from making conversation after a hard stare from Chic.

At the other side we drove past the bus stop and waited in a gateway about 50 yards further on. A Red bus turned up and Mel and Herrity got on. We followed the bus on its glacially slow progress to Paisley. Herrity got off in the town centre and walked off into the night. We continued to follow the bus.

Eventually Mel got off at the start of a 1960s housing estate, Gordon drove past her and stopped, opened the window and shouted "Hey doll dae ye need a lift?"

Mel looked up prepared to give this weirdo driver a piece of her mind then smiled when she saw us looking at her. She opened the door and climbed into the back seat beside me. Even in dungarees and a bad jumper she looked fantastic to me.

"Hi Phil you look knackered" she said

"It's been a long day" I whispered.

"Right Mel what was so exciting that you felt the need to go to see Farren's cave?"

"Well nice to see you too, Chic" sighed Mel. "Sean was pretty het up about the big fight with Zuck. He couldn't stop talking about it. Jennie and Denise left because he was boring them. He was convinced he had Zuck just where he wanted him. Had all the evidence he needed to send the old geezer down."

"What evidence?" said Chic.

"Well he has documentary proof that Mr Zuck was Standartenfuhrer Hansi Tusk of the SS; a man responsible for the systematic murder of hundreds of Polish Army officers during the Katyn Wood massacre in 1941."

"Really!" exclaimed Chic. "I knew Zuck was a major liar."

"Oh yes Farren has pictures of Zuck in Nazi uniform and letters from Polish veterans identifying him as Tusk."

"How has he stayed free for so long?" asked Davie.

"Well for one he didn't kill many Jews so the Israelis haven't been looking for him. Secondly the old Poles reckon he joined them as a spy in the Russian labour camp. Some accounts claim he assumed the Zuck identity when he was captured by the Russians. Seems he hoped to get better treatment by kidding on to be a Pole. So as we suspected he is a man with some big secrets. A couple of the old Poles reckon Zuck became a British agent after the war and that is why he never got prosecuted for War Crimes back in the 40s."

"That's a lot of evidence" I said.

"Aye but not enough for us to arrest him; It's one for the People or the News of the World" said Davie. "Nae real crime in this country, the war is over and done wi forty years ago. The fiscal would laugh at us if we tried tae lift Zuck fur being a Nazi murderer."

"Very true" said Chic; "The papers however would love it and ruin old Zuck's cosy life in Drymen."

I felt myself redden, thank god it was dark. Zuider-Michel had lied to me or at the very least told me some half truths. Farren was the one who had uncovered some of Zuck's murky past. Chic clearly suspected him of something but didn't know what. Davie's right I thought. Maybe we should drop this investigation and let Farren get on with it. If I could manoeuvre the conversation in that general direction I would keep Zuider-Michel off my back and get this investigation shut down.

"I agree with Davie" I said "We gave up hunting Nazis years ago. This investigation is starting to feel like a waste of time. There is no IRA threat or link to Farren and Zuck. Farren is an anti Nazi who is clearly unable to forget the war. What point is there in continuing?"

Chic, stared at me

Mel didn't look too happy but nodded in agreement

"Don't mention the war!" chanted Davie.

"You might be right Phil" Gordon retorted "But I think there is something behind our man Farren that doesn't make sense. Where did he get all this intelligence on Zuck? You told us yourself it was almost impossible to access his MI5 file. How does a wazock from Drumchapel suddenly uncover the secret life of Franz

Zuck. Farren was fed that info and I want to know who spooned it in. What do you think Mel?"

"Well Chic to be honest you underestimate Sean. He is well educated, charismatic and very articulate. He has plenty of Uni pals who have done well for themselves and loads of contacts in CND and the Anti Nazi league so I am not surprised that he is well informed. From my enquiries in Falkirk, there were more than a few hints that Zuck was not a kosher Pole."

"So you think one of his Anti Nazi League pals has put him up to this?"

"Yes, he has a dossier containing details of Zuck's SS records and pictures of him in uniform plus witness statements putting him in Katyn Wood during the massacre. It is a quality document."

"What is he going to do with it?"

"He is going to take it to the papers tomorrow, the Record, the Herald and the Scotsman. If they don't bite he will go to the London papers."

"Hell hath no fury like a chinned labourer!" said Davie.

"Ok, well all we can do is monitor the situation. As Phil says it is hard to justify the major surveillance operation any longer. I will call off the watchers tomorrow. We can then just focus on Farren and Zuck. We're just wasting money on the Paddies. Mel its time for your bed, shall we drop you at the door."

We pulled up outside 24 Cedarwood Drive. Mel jumped out and waved us off.

"I can't believe she still lives at home wi her ma and da" said Davie. "Woman like that should be married."

"Definitely" grunted Chic.

"Not married you say?" I asked nonchalantly.

"Aye Phil, Mel is young free and single just like you. Though to be honest she is probably out of your league."

"Aw Chic the boy can dream."

I settled for a sheepish smile. This was one discussion I wanted to avoid.

Twenty minutes later I was back at the hotel. Exhausted I was considering going to bed when I noticed that the bar had a few solo women in it.

Chapter 22

I ordered a Gin and Tonic and stood at the bar. The barman served me and walked away without any attempt at conversation. A plump dark haired woman came up to the bar and ordered a Southern Comfort and Lemonade.

I smiled at her and she smiled back. "On your own?" I said.

"Yes I just fancied something before bed. What about you, have you been out on the town?"

"No I just finished work."

"At 11pm! You must be busy."

"Yes lots of reports to write, I am here on a sales trip. What do you do?"

"I'm self employed, public relations, interpersonal services you know the kind of thing."

"Sounds interesting, bet you get a better class of customer than me."

"Sometimes and sometimes you get a monster. What are you? Nice guy or monster?"

"Hopefully a nice guy; I don't have the energy to be a monster. What's your name?"

"Fiona and you?"

"Phil"

Fiona yawned, her cardigan stretched taut across her breasts. "I'm tired!" she said. "I think I will drink this and head up to bed. What about you?"

"Bed is probably a good idea" I said and drank my gin down. Fiona virtually inhaled her Southern Comfort and said "Let's go." In the lift she pressed the third floor button. I reached across to press button one for my floor but she caught my wrist. "No rush Phil the night is young."

At the third floor we turned left and stopped outside 316. Fiona pulled my head down and kissed me. I kissed her back. When we came up for air Fiona opened the room door and pulled me in.

Her room was identical to mine. We carried on kissing for what seemed like an age. I felt my clothes waft off. Her dress slid to the floor. God knows who opened the zip. I unhooked her red bra and began kissing her huge soft breasts. I pushed her onto the bed.

"Come on big boy time to climb on" she whispered. I slid inside her and began to thrust gently.

"Harder" came the instruction

I went faster

"Harder really do it"

I was like a piston

"Keep going"

I could barely breathe, my lungs were burning

"Don't stop"

My stomach muscles felt like they were going to cramp

"Come on keep it up"

Her nails were tearing my back apart

I exploded with a final furious thrust

She laughed

"Keep going" she whispered

I struggled on for another minute before the pain and exhaustion overwhelmed me

I rolled off.

"Well done, you nearly had me!"

She pushed my head down between her legs

I started to kiss her gently and felt her hips start to roll. I licked harder and she started to whimper. She came with an almighty scream.

"Calm down, someone will think you are being murdered!"

"Calm down yourself lover boy, you made me do it."

We hugged for a while, had some less vigorous sex then lay in silence.

"Are you in Glasgow for long?" she asked.

"A couple more days, what about you?"

"I am heading back to London the day after tomorrow. Maybe we can have a repeat in your room tomorrow night."

"Definitely!" I said eagerly, no point in missing out on the opportunity for a bit of loving after my recent dry spell.

"You best go or I won't get any sleep tonight" said Fiona. "I need to get up at seven. See you in the bar tomorrow night after 8. That way you can at least buy me dinner before corrupting me."

I got out of bed and scrambled around searching for my clothes while Fiona watched me with a slightly mocking smile. Once I was decent I said "I'll be off then."

She drew back the bedcovers and gave me a full frontal view of her Reubensesque figure. I almost jumped back in with her. I bent down and kissed her while my left hand caressed her wonderful breasts.

She gently slapped me and said "Time to go naughty boy." She stood up and walked me to the door we kissed again before she pushed me out into the night.

I walked back to my room feeling like I had won the pools. This trip to Glasgow just couldn't get any better.

Chapter 23

I woke at 8.30 feeling extremely refreshed. I showered and shaved and popped down for breakfast. The breakfast room was almost empty no sign of Fiona, the very thought of her made me smile. I ate my breakfast quickly and headed out to the station. Tie up some loose ends today, write my reports followed by a night of passion with Fiona then get a train home tomorrow. No more interminable interviews with Gordon or pointless stakeouts. This case had been a real waste of time from my perspective. Obviously Zuider-Michel had a lot to hide but as long as there was no real threat of terrorism on the streets of Glasgow, there was no point in me being here.

The desk troll waved me in without comment. I walked up to Chic's office and found Davie reading the paper.

"Any exciting news?" I asked.

"Nope, apart from the usual threat of nuclear Armageddon, life is fine and dandy. You look rather pleased with yourself. What's up?"

"Nothing, I am just looking forwards to heading home. After last night it looks like there is nothing to keep me here. The assassination plot was a load of nonsense and Farren hates Zuck because he thinks he was in the SS. Not really my territory. I will write my reports today then head home tomorrow morning."

"Aye Ah suppose so. Never quite understood why Chic took it so seriously myself."

"Is there a typewriter I can use?"

"Aye, try the one on my desk."

I typed up my rather dry report on the investigation over the next two hours. Davie sat in Chic's office updating files. Around 11am Davie started making some tea and opened a packet of biscuits.

"No sign of Chic or Mel?" I asked.

"Oh he's at a management meeting and Mel isn't due in until about 12" said Davie, enjoy the peace.

We were interrupted by Chic's phone. "Ah better get that" said Davie.

I continued eating my chocolate digestive.

Davie re-appeared looking shocked. "Best saddle up there's been a development."

"What, has Zuck fled to Buenos Aires to live in Martin Bormann's house?"

"No, Farren's deid!"

"How? Did he have an accident?"

"Aye he broke his neck or to be more accurately somebody broke his neck?"

"When?"

"Dunno his ma found him this morning when she came round tae pick up his washing. He was lying face down on the living room floor heid practically twisted aff."

"Did McLintock see anything?"

"Dunno, he just called me to say he saw Mrs Farren going in then heard loads of screaming. He ran into the close and went up to Farren's flat. The door was open and Mrs Farren was standing screaming beside the body. He called the local cops, an ambulance and he wants us down there straight away. I've asked the Deputy Chief's secretary to let Chic know. Let's go."

I followed Davie as he strode to the garage. Inside I was shuddering. I was certain Zuider-Michel was behind this latest development. Far from being over; the case had sprung back into life. I was terrified that Zuider-Michel had killed Farren when he found out he had evidence against Zuck. Where did that leave me? I knew about Zuider-Michel but I hadn't told Gordon. Would I be in danger of being charged with withholding evidence? I needed to keep Foster informed to make sure he would support me if Gordon found out anything. He had warned me about the Military interest but I really hadn't had time to do anything.

When we arrived in Farren's street it was blocked off by a panda car and an ambulance. We climbed up the dank stairs to the green door of Farren's flat. Davie flashed his warrant card at the young PC at the door and he let us enter.

McLintock was talking to Jim Cannon. "Hi Davie" the big man shouted, "Look at the poor sod. Somebody didnae like him!"

We walked over and looked at Farren's lifeless body spreadeagled in front of his mantelpiece. His head was practically facing backwards. I felt scared and sick.

"Broken neck the cause of death; Jim? "

"Aye Davie that's what the medics say, though we cannae be sure until they do a post mortem."

"We were outside until about half 10" I said, "What was the time of death?"

"No sure yet but probably between midnight and four am the doc reckoned."

"McLintock did you fall asleep?"

"Davie, no way, it was a long night but I didnae miss anything. Though there wasn't much to miss; nothing happens round here after 11.30 except maybe the odd burglary.

The street was dead; Farren's light went out about midnight. There were no cars or anything until the milkfloat at six. One guy went to work at about 5 but he does that every day."

Davie nodded and McLintock continued.

"Jim was late relieving me so I was still here at ten o'clock when Mrs Farren turned up like she does every week to pick up his washing. The next thing I heard loads of screaming coming fae the close. I ran up and realised it was coming from Farren's place. When I got there he was on the floor and his ma was screaming at the top of her voice 'he's dead, help he's dead'. I called it in and calmed her down and called you. Jim turned up about 15 minutes later."

"Where is she now?"

"One of the uniform boys took her home. The poor old soul is completely broken. Naebody should find their son like that."

Davie nodded, "Who is running the case?"

"Tommy Swaggart, the Drum murder guy."

"Where is he now?"

"Oh he's going door to door in the close just in case anybody heard or saw anything. He knows we were watching Farren and that my car was here all night and that Chic was here for a couple of hours before midnight. He doesnae know about Mel being in the flat."

"Well we won't mention her unless we are asked directly" said Davie, "Understood?"

"Yes Davie!" said Cannon and McLintock in unison.

"Phil did you get that?"

"Yes don't mention Mel."

"Good' no point in blowing an undercover op."

"Farrell ya tosser, what was going on here?" said a harsh Glaswegian voice.

We turned to see a squat grey haired man in positively geriatric tweed jacket standing in the door way.

"Tommy" said Davie "Good to see you too."

"Pleasure, anyway why were you watching this poor bastard?"

"C'mon Tommy; need to know and all that! He was a person of interest to us in an ongoing investigation."

"Would that hae something tae dae wi a fight at a building site in Dumbarton that left our friend comatose?"

"Possibly, why do you ask?"

"Well being a simple kind o guy I asked Ma Farren if her boy hud ony enemies like. Of course he hud none being a lovely big teddy bear o a son. However she did mention that the Polish foreman had pummelled oor Joseph at work yesterday and thet they didnae really see eye tae eye. More interestingly Mrs Farren, a lovely wumin ye know, said Joe wus investigating this Pole's war record cos he reckons he's a Nazi. Apparently Joey had a big book full of information on said Pole that strangely enough seems tae be missing. It used tae sit ower there next tae the telly, Mrs F a'ways hud tae move it when she did the dusting. But it wusnae there when she fun poor Joe deid on the flair."

"Interesting stuff Tommy" said Davie noncommittally.

"Aye well lucky Mrs F is pretty nosey and read her boy's masterpiece. Seems this Pole Zuck was a overfurher or sommat in the SS and had been living a lie here in the UK for years kidding on to be a Pole. Wise really when you're responsible for ordering the murder of a load of Polish POWs. Based on this lead ah sent a couple of boys doon tae Dumbarton tae bring Mr Zuck in fur a chat and some fingerprinting. Jist in case he maybe decided tae huv a wee read o Joey's wee dossier. Ye know whit it's like wi these authors. They don't like their subjects reading their work. Joey might've got arsey an asked him politely of course tae go fuck himself. Naturally offended, maybe Mr Zuck got carried away like he did yesterday except maybe this time he didnae stop until he sorted Joe out permanently."

"Have you any supporting evidence Tommy, cos McLintock was outside all night and he didnae see any sign of Mr Zuck or anyone else pulling up outside here."

"Well call me an auld fusspot but maybe our murderer came in the back door without being visible fae the street. Nipped up tae Farren's weighed the shit oot o him and did a runner wi his dossier, exiting by the same door he came in. Cross they gairdens and ye come out on Kilbowie Road. Stay calm and ye can walk away without being noticed. So ma prime suspect is this Polish bastard until somebody tells me otherwise. Or is he wan o yer need tae know cases as weel?"

"No nothing to say about Zuck other than he's a bit of an oddball who lives up in Drymen. Jim has his address."

"Well ye better gie me that address as we will be popping up there for a search and a chat wi Mrs Zuck."

"Are you seriously going to arrest Zuck?"

"Aye but only if his finger prints match! The place is full of prints but our Joseph disnae appear to have put up much o a fight. Nae skin unner the finger nails or blood on his hauns. It feels like the murderer jist came up behind him and snapped his neck. The kind o thing they teach ye in the army I suspect. Nae doot the auld SS trained its boys well. There is however some lovely prints where the dossier used tae be. Ah wouldnae be surprised if they belang to a certain Polish gentleman wi large hauns."

"Getting carried away Tommy, remember the old innocent til proven guilty stuff. You cannae just decide a man is guilty based on a conversation wi the victim's Maw."

I was bewildered by the turn of events. Scottish cops seemed to take great pleasure in the prospect of arresting Mr Zuck. I couldn't understand why they seemed to hate Poles so much. On the other hand Zuck was clearly a man with a past worth hiding. Zuider-Michel had acknowledged that he was not Polish but carefully neglected to mention he was ex SS. My gut instinct was that Zuck was innocent of Farren's murder. I suspected that Zuider-Michel broke into his flat and tried to plant something incriminating as he had threatened. Farren interrupted him and Zuider-Michel took the opportunity to kill him. I had felt his strength when he accosted me earlier. I had no doubt he was capable of breaking a man's neck with his bare hands. The only problem was I couldn't tell anyone what I suspected. Gordon would laugh in my face if I tried to convince him that Snodgrass and McGlashan were half right. The Paddies on the building site were IRA, fortunately gun runners rather than potential Royal assassins. Zuck is a British agent and his handler killed Farren. Not forgetting that John Herrity is not dead.

"Davie jist you crawl back into that dark Special Branch crevice and leave us real cops tae investigate real crimes. Remember motive and opportunity make people do strange things. Zuck wus under pressure; the fight proved that. Seems like he was struggling tae control himself, maybe Farren has been threatening him with exposure or maybe he was blackmailing him. A guy in that state will do anything tae protect his family and stay oot o the papers."

"Fine Tommy if that is the basis of your case you should just carry on. Let us know how you get on wi Zuck."

"Tommy come and see this" said a voice from the bedroom

We followed Swaggart into the sparsely furnished room. Just a double bed with a red, black and grey striped duvet cover and pillow, an old brown wardrobe, a white chest of drawers and a small dressing table.

The Forensics man had found a plastic bag under the pillow. Inside it was a Browning automatic pistol.

Swaggart carefully lifted the bag with his pen. Sniffed it then put back down on the bed. "Weel Davie would this piece o ironmongery happen tae hae summat tae dae wi your need tae know case?"

"Possibly" said Davie "Though we did not suspect that Farren had a firearm. We will need a copy of the forensic report when it comes in."

"Aye ye'll get it. So yer still keeping stum aboot why ye were so interested in puir deid Joe?"

"Yes Tommy, Chic will update you if he deems it appropriate."

"Ah'll hey a word aboot that, young Chas will soon realise ah cannae be fobbed aff fur ever specially when ah'm investigating a murder."

"Good luck Tommy, Chic will be impressed I'm sure. We better go and let you get on."

"By the way Mrs McGlinchey fae next door says Farren had a visitor late last night. A big, broad, foreign looking man in a grey suit. She said he had a guid tan. Does that sound like Mr Zuck?"

"It could be" said Davie. "McLintock will bring over one of our pictures of Zuck and you can see if she identifies Zuck."

Chapter 24

Back in the car we sat in stunned silence. Farren was dead and Swaggart was moving with unseemly haste to arrest Zuck. Davie sent McLintock back to the station to pick up some pictures of Zuck for Swaggart's team.

"Tommy's on form the day" said Cannon. "Gie him a lead and he's like a shark that's scented blood. Zuck will be in the cells and charged before teatime."

"Aye whether he's innocent or not!" Davie snapped "I can't believe Zuck would kill Farren in such an obvious manner. After yesterday he would be the prime suspect for any murder team. Did your son have any enemies? None he was lovely but his boss is a nutter who beat him up yesterday. Cops like Swaggart like easy solutions, closes cases as quickly as possible."

"Even if innocent men go down!" said Cannon. "Where the hell did that frigging gun come fae?"

"Ah don't know but we have searched Farren's place a couple of times while he was out and naebody reported finding a gun."

"Come tae think aboot it Davie ah don't remember any folder full of Nazi shite either. Ah like a war film but I can't understand the attraction o digging into folks pasts like Farren must've been doing."

"Yes so we can assume that Mr Farren acquired a gun in the past 5 days. Not sure where he was hiding the dossier but we turned the place upside down last week and didn't find anything of interest. We have also been following him everywhere so as far as we can tell he didn't have a post office box or shed or garage to hide things in. Something stinks about this."

"If Zuck didn't do it, who do you think did it?" I asked weakly.

"Phil if I knew that I would be a genius" snorted Davie. "The thing is Frank Thompson was watching Zuck's place last night so unless he fell asleep like McLintock he will be able to confirm whether or not Zuck went out for a wee birl in his car last night. Jim get Mel to contact Thompson he will probably be home by now."

Cannon jumped out of the car and waddled towards the phone box.

"Is there any chance of this being IRA related Davie?"

"Somebody is certainly trying to make it look that way but if the IRA wanted to kill Farren they would have just shot him or disappeared him. Leaving somebody with a broken neck is just not their style. If anything it is more like a sojers murder like Tommy suggested. Could've been an ex squaddie trying out his unarmed combat training for real."

"Maybe it was Snodgrass!" I laughed. "He is an old jungle fighter, probably broke a few necks in his time."

"Aye, but he is a gutless twat. He is certainly capable of killing with his bare hands but like a lot of his kind he likes to threaten rather actual perpetrate violence. Too feart o getting hit back."

Cannon climbed back into the car looking pale. "Mel says Thompson's wife has been on wanting to know when Frank is off shift. Hasnae heard fae him since he left yesterday evening. Chic wants us to pop up tae Drymen and check if Frank is ok."

"Surely he is big enough to fix his ain punctures" said Davie. "Probably away wi another woman."

"That's whit ah said but Frank isnae the kind o guy to go awol. Chic said we wur to get up there asap."

Davie slipped the car into gear and shot off like a grand prix driver. It was a quiet journey on some very picturesque country roads. I had no idea where I was or indeed where Drymen was. After about 20 minutes we pulled up outside a row of substantial bungalows all with very well kept gardens and a shiny second car in the drive.

Cannon pointed to a blue Sierra parked about 50 feet away, "That's Frank's motor."

I got a worried feeling as we approached the car. The driver seemed to be intently reading his paper. Worryingly he didn't move when we stopped beside his window. Davie banged on the window but still no movement.

"Fuck he's deid!" gasped Cannon.

"As the proverbial dodo" said Davie. "Jim call Dumbarton CID and get Chic up here as well. This is turning into a major situation. Find out if Swaggart has picked up Zuck. I hope to fuck the mad Polack hasn't gone crazy or he might have knocked off the boys Tommy sent tae bring him in."

"He might have died of natural causes" I said.

"Natural death caused by knife in the throat!" Davie exclaimed.

"What???"

"Look at his shirt, it's covered in blood."

I looked down and realised that Thompson was not wearing a rusty brown shirt. His chest was covered in blood. Before this morning I had never seen a corpse now I had seen 2 within hours. I tried desperately to suppress a retch.

"If you are going to heave, do it over by the grass well away from the crime scene" whispered Davie. A couple of local ladies walked towards the car. Davie pulled out his warrant cards and asked them to stay back.

"What has happened officer?"

"I'm afraid this gentleman has taken a funny turn. We are waiting for the ambulance now."

"Oh dear, I noticed him late last night when I was walking the dog around 11. He was sitting in the dark reading the paper which seemed odd."

"Did he move or acknowledge you when you walked past?"

"Nothing just like now"; suddenly the woman realised the significance of her words. She put her hand over her mouth and began to sob. "He's dead isn't he?!!! I feel so guilty if I had reported him last night maybe he could've been saved!!!"!

Davie clasped her hand and said "Don't worry missus in cases like this death is virtually instant."

The woman began sobbing hysterically, her companion began hugging her. Davie quietly ushered them away from the car. I stood guard over Thompson as Davie helped the woman back to her house. A couple of other neighbours watched from their windows. I felt very alone and isolated. Thompson must have stuck out like a sore thumb sitting in a parked car in an area like this.

I was extremely glad when Cannon re-appeared.

"Chic's on his way. We've tae stay here and keep things under control. A dead undercover cop in a quiet Stirlingshire village has the making of a TV news headline, especially if they find oot he wus Special Branch. You awright?"

"No"

"Don't worry we all get affected by dead bodies, no matter how many ye see. I'm sad aboot Frank he was a good laugh loved his bevy and his fitba. Played for Clydebank in the sixties you know."

"Really" I said, just to speak.

"Aye, before they joined the league but they were a great side then. Where's Davie?"

"Consoling a resident who appears to have saw Frank last night sitting in the same position."

"About what time?"

"Around 11."

"Bollocks that certainly fits with Zuck making a nocturnal trip to Clydebank. He had obviously clocked the surveillance and decided that it would be best to stop Frank following him."

"How do you think they were able to get close enough to stab Frank?"

"Looks like somebody was in the back seat waiting for Frank; he would have arrived parked and went for a walk like a normal visitor. I suspect the killer climbed into the back seat while he was away. When Frank got into the driver's seat and started reading his *Glasgow Herald*. The killer would have grabbed Frank from behind and stabbed him."

"Is it that easy to kill someone?"

"Fraid so especially if you have the right training. Make no mistake the guy who killed Frank had some serious training. An average Ned would never be able to kill so neatly. This was done in a calm and controlled manner. Like Farren this feels like a sojer's killing."

"Do you think it was Zuck?"

"Could be or maybe there is another potential murder suspect living in this street. Once Davie comes back I'll go door to door and see if anyone saw something from 10pm onwards last night and try and find out when Frank started reading his paper. Who would believe that an experienced Special Branch officer could be killed in a wee posh street like this without somebody noticing?"

"Doesn't seem possible" I said.

"Aye, expect Chic will huv tae tell Frank's wife. I couldn't face that...where the fuck's the Drymen murder team? I bet Davie's haeing a cup of tea with that auld granny. Tea's good sometimes takes yer mind aff the horrible stuff."

I then realised that Cannon was as shaken as I was by the turn of events. I think if he had known me better he might have cried. "Did you know Frank well?"

"Oh aye he wus old school very thorough, took plenty of notes. Kept active, didn't just sit in the car, moved around made himself look like part of the furniture. A surveillance professional. Whoever killed him was very sharp. Frank wasnae the kind of guy yer average ned could just sneak up on. No this killer was well trained."

Davie wandered back to us. "Alright you two? Mrs Quinn definitely saw Frank sitting like this about 10.30 last night. Apparently Zuck went out in his car when she went to bed around 11.30. Something he did often apparently."

"So the fucking bastard Polack kilt Frank and then went doon tae Clydebank and kilt Farren. The guy's a fucking psycho!" growled Cannon.

"Possibly but it is all theory until we get some evidence linking him to the murders. Looks like the murder team have arrived."

A group of tall well dressed men emerged from a series of dark coloured Vauxhalls. A couple of panda cars blocked the entrances to the street. A van disgorged a group of scruffy technicians. The tall men joined us, the youngest looking one spoke.

"Hi I'm DI Neil Stevenson, this is DS Joe Russell and DC Colin Stoner. I presume you are DS Farrell?" he said offering me his hand.

"No I'm Davie Farrell!" interjected Davie taking Stevenson's hand. "This is DC Phillips seconded to us from the Met and DS Jim Cannon."

"You found the body?"

"Yes he was one of our guys working a surveillance job on one of the residents in this street. He didn't come home at the end of his shift or contact his missus to say he was delayed, so we were sent up to check on him?"

"Very caring" sneered Stevenson, "Do you babysit all your men?"

"No but this was part of a multi site surveillance operation. One of the other subjects was found dead this morning and the prime suspect is the guy who lives in this street so we were more concerned than usual when Frank Thompson didn't report in this morning."

"I see" said Stevenson, "cause of death?"

"Almost certainly stabbing but your guys should be able to confirm."

Stevenson stared in the car window at Thompson's lifeless corpse like a man looking at the mannequins in Selfridges window on Oxford Street.

"Aye he's deid, bled a fair bit first fae yon cut in his throat. It's like something fae the Wild Geese, did ye see that film?"

"No" said Davie

"Ye should it's the best thing Burton did for years. He shoots Richard Harris in it. Must huv been fun shooting that tosser. Joe get the cordon set up. Naebody opens the motor til the Doc and the forensics guys arrive. Colin, you start going door tae door; nae way that this happened in Drymen without somebody seeing it. You guys come wi me?"

We followed Stevenson to the street corner as his forensics guys began recording the crime scene. An ambulance appeared at the end of the street. Russell told them to park up and wait. Once we were alone Stevenson exploded.

"What the fuck is going on here? A Special Branch officer has been murdered in cold blood in a wee village street. What are you cunts up tae? Mair importantly why weren't we informed of a high risk operation like this?"

"You know the rules Stevenson, Special Branch work is strictly need to know. We don't need local approval for surveillance. This was strictly hands off no intervention stuff. Frank was working here a couple of times a week without incident for the past month. We had no reason to suspect last night would be any different. However something has changed and two men are now dead; one in Drumchapel and Frank."

"Who are ye dealing wi? The fucking Russians! The last time I saw something like that it was in a James Bond film. There's nae ned in Scotland capable o killing a man like that I reckon."

"Stevenson calm down, this isnae a Harry Palmer film. There is no Soviet master-spy living in Drymen, it's all a wee bit more ordinary."

Stevenson stared at Davie clearly convinced he was lying.

At that point a pale blue Skoda appeared driven by Mel with Gordon in the passenger seat.

Chic leapt out and joined us. "Hi Inspector Chic Gordon, Cranstonhill Special Branch, who are you?"

"DI Neil Stevenson, Dumbarton CID."

"Right then Neil I need you to get this crime scene secured and make sure there is no leak to the media until the Chief Constable gives the ok."

"Listen Gordon I am the Senior Investigating Officer in this case so I think you can climb down off your high horse and wait until I am ready to interview you and your men."

"Listen you twat, Douglas Linnet will be here in ten minutes I have already briefed him on the phone and we spoke on the radio two minutes ago. He said you were to give me all possible assistance."

"Really I'll wait until I hear that from the horse's mouth, in the meantime stay off my crime scene!" said Stevenson and stomped back to the car.

"That cock is going tae get his baws toed when Linnet arrives, Dougie said he was a prick."

I looked at Davie and mouthed who's Linnet?

"Linnet's Chic's pal the local Chief Constable and currently head of Special Branch in Scotland."

"Ah" I said

"Yup Mr Stevenson is going to be in real trouble when Linnet arrives, he's a right angry bastard" said Cannon.

"Chic, any news from Swaggart?"

"Davie they picked up Zuck at the site and he came pretty quietly. Denies everything. Never been near Farren's house and didn't see anything strange out side his house this morning when he went to work. If he's lying Swaggart will beat it out of him like a southern preacher casting out demons. I almost feel sorry for Zuck trapped in an interview room wi sweaty Tommy for hours. Has anybody spoken tae Mrs Zuck? "

"Not yet" said Davie.

"Ok we'll go in when Dougie arrives. His house is the white one wi the big dormers."

A huge Rover appeared driven by a uniformed PC. Two men in high ranking uniforms stepped out. One was about 6'7" whereas his companion was about six feet but looked tiny in comparison.

Chic shouted at the giant, "Dougie yer boy Stevenson is being a wee bit un-co-operative."

"Don't worry he'll soon change his ways. Stevenson here, now!" bellowed the giant

Chic stood beside Linnet as Stevenson walked towards them. The conversation was brief; Stevenson's contribution was a series of nods as the giant told him who was in charge.

Linnet then strode off towards the crime scene with Stevenson and his assistant trailing behind him. Chic waved us over and said "Dougie will get Benny Moran his bagman to put Stevenson on toilet cleaning duties if he fucks this up. Follow me, its time we let Mrs Zuck know where her beloved husband is."

We walked along Zuck's drive conscious of curtains twitching in every house in the street. Chic rang the doorbell. After a short delay a tall reddish haired woman opened the door.

"Hello", said Gordon politely "Mrs Zuck?"

"Yes"

"Hi Mrs Zuck I am Inspector Gordon I have some information for you, can we come in?"

"I don't know, what is this about? Is it related to that car over there?"

"Possibly, but it would be best if we sat down and had a chat."

"Can't you wait 'til my husband gets home, he deals with this sort of thing."

"What sort of thing would that be Mrs Zuck?"

"Official stuff, Franz is the expert on that sort of thing."

"Actually we want to speak to you not your husband. Can we come in, it'll be more private?"

She stood to the side and pulled the door fully open. "Please go into the lounge, it's the first on the left."

"Jim go back and keep an eye on the Forensics" said Chic before entering. Davie and I followed him in.

The hall was decorated with floral wallpaper, very feminine and middle aged. The lounge was entirely different more like an East African hunting lodge with lots of timber panelling and teak statuettes of antelopes, elephants and giraffes. On the walls lots of photographs of big game and the Zucks in full safari gear. Over the mantelpiece was a collection of African spears and hunting knives. The perfect tools for cutting a man's throat I thought as I sat down on the brown leather sofa. I looked at Davie and he nodded. Clearly he had also made the connection.

Mrs Zuck sat down in a leather armchair directly opposite Chic. "Please tell me what this is about Inspector?"

"I am afraid I have some bad news. At 2pm your husband was arrested by West Dunbartonshire CID on suspicion of murder."

Mrs Zuck whimpered her hand covering her mouth, all pretence at self control disappeared in an instant. "Franz didn't murder anyone, he is a good man!!!! You are lying!!!" she screamed.

"No I am not Mrs Zuck. We believe that your husband murdered one of the labourers based at the site in Dumbarton sometime after 11.30pm last night. Please tell us whether or not your husband was at home last night?"

"Of course he was. He came home about half five and ate his dinner. We watched some TV and went to bed around 10. Franz was up again at five am and left for work around 5.30."

"Are you able to confirm that your husband stayed in bed from 10pm?"

"Of course other than his usual trip to the toilet around 3, he always wakes me up regular as clockwork searching for his slippers. He never turns on the light see, tries to avoid waking me but he always does."

"Ok so your husband was at home all night and went to work as normal this morning?"

"Yes."

"Did your husband leave the house at any point before he went to bed last night?"

"No, in the summer he usually goes out to the garden after tea but at this time of year its too cold and it gets dark too early. Africa was different, it would get dark at six every day but it was so warm you could sit out on the verandah to midnight every day. I never really wanted to come back you know but Franz' work was drying up."

"Very interesting, so Mr Zuck didn't leave the house last night? Didn't go for a walk past where the police van is parked?"

"No, what is going on over there?"

"One of my men was found murdered in the blue Sierra parked beside the van."

"Oh my God, that's terrible."

"What is more interesting is that the victim was running surveillance on your husband."

"Why? Franz is just a working man nothing else."

"Was Franz behaving normally? Or was he showing signs of being stressed or under pressure?"

"No we are ordinary people, we don't have a cross word from one week's end to the next."

"Your husband didn't spend any time looking out the window at the blue car or make any reference to it?"

"No why should he! Why was the man watching Franz?"

"Your husband was a person of interest in an ongoing investigation. Did he mention being involved in a fight yesterday?"

"No not really, just mentioned he had some argy bargy with a stupid Mick labourer, he never mentioned a fight, it just sounded like an argument. It was the sort of thing foremen always have to deal with."

"It was more than that I'm afraid he knocked Mr Farren unconscious. Mr Farren chose not to press charges against your husband and sadly was then found dead this morning at his house in Drumchapel. A neighbour described a man fitting your husband's description banging on Mr Farren's door late last night. In addition Mr Farren's family believe that the argument with your husband was related to Mr Farren's suspicion that your husband was a member of the SS during the war."

Mrs Zuck sat there dumbstruck

"Is there anything you want to say on this?"

"It's lies! Fucking lies! Every time people in this country hear a Polish accent they assume it is German. Obsessed with the fucking war you people. Franz lived through hell and fought for this country. The fucking Germans killed his family but just because some ignorant bastard fantasises that Franz is some Nazi Stormtrooper you think Franz murdered him and a policeman. You read too many comics."

"At the moment all of the evidence leads to your husband I'm afraid."

"Well he didn't do anything, he came home had his tea, watched some telly and went to bed at ten o'clock like he does every day. He didn't nip out to kill a policeman on his doorstep or make a 30 mile round trip in the middle of the night to kill somebody and go back to bed only to get up again at 5am. You seem to think Franz is some kind of James Bond."

I shared a wry smile with Davie, if Mrs Zuck was telling the truth then old Franz was not our murderer. My money was on Zuider-Michel, he had the men with the resources and skills. Of course there was no way I could mention this to Chic or Davie. God knows what Zuider-Michel would do if he was cornered. Farren I could understand but there seemed no point in killing Thompson.

"Mrs Zuck did your husband have any visitors last night?" I asked in a very reedy voice. All this excitement had made my mouth feel like the Sahara.

"Yes, a man from the company came round."

"What was his name?" asked Chic

"Mr Mr ...er ..Satchwell or Honeywell I think."

"What did he look like? Had you met him before?" interjected Davie.

"Maybe, he reminded me of one of the young soldiers Franz dealt with in Africa."

"Unlikely, too much of a coincidence" said Chic.

Mrs Zuck looked up at Chic confused, "Why do you say that?"

"It doesn't sound plausible Mrs Zuck that your husband would have a mystery visitor on the same night that a policeman is murdered while watching your house."

"He did, it was a tall middle aged man, tanned military looking. We knew lots like that in Africa."

"Did they provide security for building projects your husband worked on?"

"Oh no Franz never worked in construction until we came home in the late sixties."

"What type of work did he do in Africa?"

"He was a military security advisor to lots of governments. He worked all over the continent. Kenya, Tanganyika, Somaliland, Sudan, Congo, Nigeria, Rhodesia, South Africa, Zambia, Malawi, Angola though mostly me and the kids lived in Kenya then Cape Town. We had a lovely house on Lake Naivasha, a great life until that man Kenyatta ruined things."

Chic smiled. "So your husband is a very experienced soldier then?"

"Oh yes, he has trained thousands of young lads. People like Franz gave their lives to stop the communists taking over Africa. What thanks did he get when we came home. Nothing! Just a job standing in the rain watching navvies shovel muck!"

"So this visitor last night, did you speak to him?" asked Davie.

"Only to say hello then I went back into the kitchen. He only stayed about ten minutes."

"Did Franz say why he called round?"

"Just something about new workers," Franz said. "Paperwork to sign."

"I see. Does this happen often?"

"Every now and then; especially if Franz is moving site."

"What time was this?"

"After eight I think."

"How long did he stay?"

"About 10 minutes as I just said."

"Did Franz seem concerned by the visit?"

"No he said it was nothing, just a bit of administration."

"What happened then?"

"I have already told you, we watched television and went to bed."

"At 10pm?"

"Yes we watched the nine o'clock news and then shut things down for the night. All sockets off, curtains closed, doors locked. It's a bit like being in the army. I often joke that Franz should get a bugle so that he can play the Retreat at 9.45. Once I had taken my sleeping pill and brushed my teeth I was straight into bed and so was Franz."

"Sleeping pill? Do you take one every night?"

"Oh yes I struggled to sleep for the first few years after we came home. Finally the doctor prescribed me some wonderful pills and I sleep like a log every night."

"What are your pills called?" Asked Chic

"Valium, they're great."

"Can you let me have a look at the bottle? Just to ensure that my colleague gets the right spelling in his notebook."

"Ok"

As Mrs Zuck left the room Chic gave us a wry smile.

"Must be in outer space most nights" said Davie. Chic nodded.

"No idea what happens after she goes to bed I suspect" said Chic.

Davie gave a slightly disgusted grimace. "We are not all like you Charlie!"

Mrs Zuck re-appeared with her medicine bottle. Davie made great play of writing down the medical name and dosage.

"Mrs Zuck I am afraid your husband is unlikely to be home tonight. He has been arrested under suspicion of murdering Joseph Farren in Drumchapel and we will want to talk to him about the murder of DC Frank Thompson. I must warn you that we will be looking for a warrant to search this house please do not make any attempt to conceal any evidence that could have an impact on the investigation as this would have serious implications for you. You are not currently a suspect and as a result I will not formally caution you, however we will be looking to interview you again in more detail as the case progresses."

Mrs Zuck nodded, "There is nothing to find!! Search to your heart's content" she snarled. "You are just like the kaffirs in Kenya that drove us out of our lovely home accusing Franz of all sorts of trumped up charges. They were wrong and so are you."

"Let's hope so Mrs Zuck" said Chic quietly. "Gentlemen I think its time for us to go. We left Mrs Zuck in the living room staring at the African pictures."

"That was tense" I said when we got outside.

"Aye but strangely predictable. That poor woman has no idea what is going on beyond the end of her nose. Seen a lot of that eh Davie?"

"Definitely they Valium knock them spaced and then they cannae function without them. At wan time almost 50% o' the housewives in the city were spaced on valium every day. Taking 'shelter wi mammas little helpers'. I expect she saw some horrors in Africa and that set her aff now it's just a habit. Probably can't cope wi the peace round here. It's usually so quiet ye can hear the grass growing."

"Yes, so unfortunately for Franz; his wife is a pretty flimsy alibi. A half decent prosecutor would tear her tae bits in court. Let's see how the forensics boys are getting on" he said and strode off towards the crime scene.

"This is hellish" I said to Davie "Two men dead as a result of this bullshit operation."

"Well yes I agree it makes no sense really. Why go rogue now, Farren was getting punted to Faslane and almost certainly the dole. After that his Nazi dossier would just be the ramblings of a ned, not that it had much more value if he was working. I couldn't see a paper printing it without some extremely strong supporting evidence."

I wished I could tell Davie about Zuider-Michel but I valued my life and career to much to end up dead like Farren or Thompson.

Chapter 25

Up ahead Chic appeared to be giving Stevenson a dressing down.

"Let's stay away from that" whispered Davie

We stopped at the nearest lamppost.

"Phil its bollocks the way this case has exploded. It makes no sense to me. We know the bomb plot was a load of guff Snodgrass invented. Chic has a hard-on for Zuck as a villain and today's events make it feel like he was right, almost too right if you ask me. I just don't see an old boy like Zuck killing two fit men in a night. I especially can't understand any reason why he would murder Frank. If he went in the back door to Farren's flat then why bother killing the surveillance man here, just leave by the back door or just drive off and lose him on the road. It's crazy."

"What if Zuck is not working alone" I said.

"Oh so this mysterious guy from the company murders Frank because Zuck doesn't like being watched then they drive down to Drumchapel as soon as Mrs Zuck is comatose. One big hole in that theory; what's the fucking motive Phil? Keeping Zuck's Nazi past secret is only worthwhile if he is the guy who nicked all the Nazi gold. If he is just another semi retired SS man then there isn't much in this for anyone else."

I was desperate to tell Davie about how Zuck was a military agent informing on the IRA but I knew deep down he wouldn't believe me. The more I thought about it the harder it was to believe that Zuider-Michel would have killed Farren and Thompson.

"The thing ah really don't understand Phil, is the gun in Farren's house, that is as likely as a hen growing a set of teeth. We have searched that place umpteen times and found no trace of any firearms or explosives. Then he gets done in when he has a Browning automatic under his pillow. Bullshit, if he had a gun why the fuck did he open the door without it last night? If Farren had a gun for his own protection then we would be investigating the shooting of a geriatric SS man! Whoever killed Farren wants us tae think he wus a budding terrorist like his brother. The problem is I don't understand who would benefit from that? Certainly not Zuck! That man is in danger of going down for double murder unless he has a decent alibi."

"I agree it doesn't make much sense" I said.

"No it doesn't and to make matters worse poor Frank is lying in that motor, deid for God knows what reason. Whoever killed Frank was mad. Unless of course Frank recognised them but what's the chances of a Glasgow cop spotting a real bad ned out here. Pretty slim, especially one who is a homicidal maniac."

"Are there any gangsters on the run that Frank might have recognised or been recognised by?"

"Doubt it. Frank hasn't done direct criminal work for years. He was killed by a cold blooded psychopath."

"Aye Davie is that you doing some dispassionate analysis?" interjected Chic

"Naw, just telling the truth."

"Well according to the forensic guys and the doctor Frank was hit from behind and then had his throat cut."

"Eh!!!"

"Aye he must have been out of the car doing a scout round the area, when somebody came up behind him and cracked his skull with something very heavy. They then forced him back into the car and cut his throat with something very sharp like an open razor."

"How did they work that out without an autopsy?"

"Well his legs were just stuffed in; no way could he have sat in the car with his legs in that position."

"Why did they cut his throat?" I asked.

"The Doc reckons that was just tae make sure he was dead."

"Evil bastards!" Davie scowled.

"Maybe or just efficient, making him look like he was reading the paper made sure nobody took much notice of him."

"Dae you think it was Zuck?"

"Could be. We need to call Drumchapel and find out how Swaggart is getting on with questioning the old Nazi."

"What about Frank, are we going tae lead this?"

"Naw Dougie's got it under control the local boys will tidy up and dae the door tae door stuff. Dougie'll front up tae the press tomorrow, for today this will be reported an unexplained homicide there will be no names or any hint Frank was a cop. Ah need tae head back and let Frank's wife know what happened. You two best get back to Drumchapel and find out if Swaggart has sweated a confession out of Zuck."

"Wouldn't be the first time Swaggart put an innocent man down" said Davie. "What about Cannon?"

"He can come wi me, he knew Frank and his missus. You guys best head off now."

The drive back was sobering. We talked over the day's events but neither of us could make any sense of it. Zuck the crazed Nazi who cracked and killed everyone in his path just didn't ring true but it was hard to imagine a string of coincidences that could result in two separate murders in the same night of people associated with one individual. Lone mad men don't tend to stalk villages like Drymen. Frank's murder had to be Zuck related unless he was murdered by a jealous husband who had been tailing him. Again not that likely according to Davie.

At Drumchapel station we were waved in by a big dark haired desk sergeant with the same accent as Davie's barman pal.

"Another relation?" I asked.

"Yup that's Donnie MacKinnon; I think we're third cousins. His family have a croft near the airport on Barra. We used to collect seashells and try fishing off the rocks when we were about seven. His granny was a lovely woman, always gave us fairy cakes and tea any time we went to her house."

We were interrupted by Swaggart's loud hailer voice, "Farrell ower here now."

The shabby man looked jaded but happy. "The auld Polack pit up a guid strong fight but noo he's singing"

"What he's confessed?" said Davie.

"Oh aye, Farren threatened tae expose him, he went round tae his hoose tae reason wi him. Farren showed him his dossier. Zuck realized the game was up and lost his rag. Next thing Farren wus deid."

"Seriously? He admitted all that?"

"No at furst but efter a while he started tae get the jist o it."

"Did you beat that out of him Tommy?"

"Oh God; no! Nain o' that just careful questioning, using open questions to elucidate a broad response. Standard interrogation technique; as you well know Davie."

Davie stepped very close to Swaggart staring deeply into the shabby man's eyes, "If that old boy is a mass of bruises Tommy I will make sure you go down. Do you understand me?"

"Och Davie come on don't be like that. Ye know ah'm above board and kosher."

"Listen you smelly fat fucker, I know all about you and your careful interrogation techniques and so does the fiscal. Mair of your 'confessions' never make trial than any cop in the country."

"That fiscal is an arse you know that, I am a good cop. All I want is tae keep the streets safe."

"Aye round here your interview room sees mair assaults than anywhere else!"

"Davie son you better step back or you'll regret it."

"Fat man you listen to me. We just found Frank Thompson dead possibly killed by the same guy that kilt Farren. There is no way we are going to let a fuckwit like you destroy any chance we have of getting the man who did it. THIS is your last chance. DID YOU BEAT THAT CONFESSION OUT OF ZUCK?"

By now everyone in the station was staring at them as they stood head to head like a pair of stags.

"C'mon Davie calm done yer making a tit of yersel."

"Listen fuckface Dougie Linnet is leading on this case, ye'll answer tae him if ye've fucked up the investigation before we've even started!"

Shabby man stepped back, Linnet's name scared him. "Aw right look I don't think there has been ony herm done."

"Take us to Zuck now Tommy!"

"Ok he is way the doc just now."

I stepped in and grabbed Davie's arm before he punched Swaggart.

"Tommy he better not have a face full of bruises or a busted kidney."

Swaggart blushed, "He is alright, don't worry. He's fine, just a bit tired like."

We went into the interview room. Zuck was sitting with his head in his hands. The doctor was packing his briefcase. "He needs rest; I don't think he is fit to undergo any further questioning today."

"Ok Doc we just need a few more minutes with him then we will make sure he gets bedded down."

"Five minutes, no more" said the doctor.

Davie raised his hands palms facing the Doctor, "Ok five minutes."

The doctor left the room and we looked at Zuck, he had light bruising around the face but nothing serious. He looked old and tired.

He looked at us but said nothing.

"Well Mr Zuck" said Davie as he sat down. "What have you been up to? My friend Mr Swaggart thinks you have confessed to a murder!"

"Yes" said Zuck

"Yes what? Yes I am a murderer or yes I just said anything to make it stop."

"Yes I am a murderer" said Zuck in a very flat tone.

We stared at him feeling slightly shocked.

"Are you confessing to the murder of Sean Farren?"

"Yes, who do you think I am supposed to have killed?"

"Mm well is there anything you want to say about the crime, like what was your motivation?"

"Motivation! I tell you what my motivation was. A dumb fuck bastard push me too hard making up stories about Nazis. Think he know everything when he know fuck all!!"

"What did you do?"

"I already tell the old fucker, I went to his house, told him to fucking shut up and then beat the shit out of him. I didn't realise he would die."

Davie cast me a quizzical look

"So Mr Zuck, when did you decide to visit the unfortunate Mr Farren? After your wife went to bed?"

"Yes she retired early and I set off for Drumchapel."

"Did anyone see you leave?"

"No they all go to bed early in my street."

"Did you notice a man in a blue Sierra parked in your street last night?"

"Yes the policeman or maybe the dole inspector. Every night one of them is there, probably to watch old bastard McIntosh at 23. He claims invalidity benefit for arthritis yet he is more active than me. Always building gardens walls; fuck all wrong with his back I say."

"Did you speak to the man in the blue Sierra?"

"No, why would I do that. Fuck all to do with me. I leave well alone. I no some nosey bastard like Ruby Snodgrass; he would be there asking questions any time he see something he no like. Me I leave well alone. If man want to freeze his balls sitting in car reading paper all night is his problem. No point in me speaking to him!"

I looked sideways at Davie. He shook his head.

"So you did not speak to the man in the blue Sierra or approach the blue Sierra or have any contact with the man in the blue Sierra?"

"Fuck no! Why I fucking want to do that. I left house to sort out fuck basstard Farren not speak to surveillance man. He nothing to do with me!"

"Ok so you left your house at what time?"

"About 10 o'clock."

"Why?"

"I.... I decided to sort bastard Farren out."

"What time did you reach Drumchapel?"

"Around 10.30, I tell this to the... the other fuck bastard!"

"Yes and now you are going to tell me. How did you know Farren's address?"

"I just look up his contact details in Stewart's personnel folder, he keeps it in the filing cabinet."

"When you got to Farren's house what door did you enter through?"

"The back door of course! I parked on the back road watched Farren's window until the light went out and then came through a hole in the fence. Not much chance of being spotted you see. I bang on Farren's door and he open up like the asshole he is. Not surprised I come. He walked into his room and I followed him asking for the papers."

"What papers?"

"His fucking secret papers that say I am a German Nazi?"

"Are you a German?"

Fuck no I am Polish!!

"What happened when you entered Farren's house? Did you argue?"

"Not at first, I ask for the papers and for him to stop. But he laugh at me saying crap about me not listening to my victims. I grabbed him and shook him. He struggled then I lost it and beat crap out of him. Before I know it he was not moving; I couldn't find a pulse so I dropped him. I picked up up a big folder with my name on it and ran out of the house. "

"Was Mr Farren alive when you left?"

"NO I said he no moving I know a dead man when I see one."

"What did you do with the papers?"

"I stopped on the way home and burned them."

"Where did you burn them?"

"In a lay-by near Gartocharn."

"If you are lying we will find out. Do you understand that we will search the lay-bys on that road?"

"Yes and you will find nothing but ashes."

Davie stared at Zuck.

Zuck met his gaze unblinking and said "I am guilty, responsible for the fucking basstard dying, all my stupid fault I no lying."

Davie shook his head and said quietly "Do you wish to say anything else?"

"No"

"Fine, interview terminated."

Chapter 26

Outside the interview Davie leant against the wall and sighed. "This is fucking insane the old bastard has no idea how Farren died but its clear from his confessions that he had something to do with it. He seems to want to go to jail."

I was tempted to blurt out my suspicions about Zuider-Michel but I was afraid it would make things more complicated not less.

"Ah the dynamic detecting duo! The Holmes and Watson of 1980s Glesga! What's the story boys?" said Chic as he ambled towards us.

"Fuck knows!" said Davie.

"Well if Fuck's name is Swaggert then you might be right. It sounds like the smelly old bastard has Zuck tied up like a headless chicken. Nae wunner he has such a good arrest rate."

"Aye battering confessions oot o innocent men and wummin always improves yer conviction rate" answered Davie.

"You a bleedin heart liberal again Davie?"

"Naw; just a polisman that tries tae stay inside the law."

"Bollocks tae that, the auld cunts confessed, case closed as far I am concerned."

We both stared at Gordon as if he had lost his mind

"How can you say that without even interviewing the man?" I snorted.

"Listen son, if it looks like shite and smells like shite I don't need tae taste it tae know its shite. Zuck's guilty; always has been. He is going down for killing Farren and our Frank."

"He says he never did anything tae Frank."

"Aye well who else would've done it bar him, wan o his pensioner neighbours?"

"Ah don't know but I don't think he killed anybody last night."

"Well he's doomed now. Time tae go hame for a sleep you two, it's been a hell of a day. I'll see you in the morning."

I waited for Davie to protest but he just nodded and said "Phil I'll give you a lift to the hotel."

In the car I said "Davie what just happened?"

"Phil I don't know but Chic has decided that Zuck is going down regardless of the evidence. I don't know why he hates him so much."

"It doesn't make sense to me; nothing about today makes any sense."

"Aye two men deid for no good reason, wonder how they'll say Frank died? Cannae see them admitting he was murdered while on surveillance, it might encourage Ned Copycats."

"What will they say?"

"Car crash probably, skidded on patch of diesel, killed instantly, good cop, husband and father. You know the drill."

I began to long for my old boring life.

Davie dropped me at the hotel after 10pm.

I slipped into the bar for a drink before going to bed.

I ordered a lager and drank it down like water and asked for another. The barman looked at me for a second and then decided to I was fit to be served.

"So you decided to turn up after all" said a voice behind me.

I turned to find Fiona staring at me. A little the worse for wear but still very attractive.

"I am so sorry" I mumbled "I had a very hard day, I have just finished work."

"Wow! They do work you bank boys hard."

"Bank boy!" I exclaimed. "I don't remember saying I worked in a bank."

"Oh must have been someone else, anyway I had to eat alone after I spent an hour waiting for you to turn up."

"Look I'm very sorry" I said, "Can I buy you a drink?"

"Yes a double gin and tonic."

I waved to the barman and mouthed double gin and tonic

"So what made your day so long?"

"Oh, just a lot of drama; stuff going wrong in various locations."

"Really? What is it you do again?"

"Oh, furniture sales."

"Drama and furniture sales don't go together in my mind."

"Well you may think that but if deliveries are late, people get angry and refuse to pay, all tough stuff."

"I think you are winding me up, you're no furniture salesman. Are you a spy?"

"No chance, I'm more Basildon Bond than James Bond can you really see me wrestling some Russian hitman?"

"Oh well Mr Bond play your cards right and you can wrestle me, lets have a seat once he brings my drink."

At the table she whispered in my ear, "The barman fancies me. He offered to take me out if you didn't turn up."

"That explained his expression when I arrived."

"Watch his face when I kiss you", before I could speak she was kissing me all the while making sure my eyes faced the barman. He didn't look happy.

We finished our drinks and retired upstairs. I got off at my floor and Fiona followed me. "Do I get a home game tonight?" I asked.

"Oh yes big boy."

Chapter 27

We slid into bed and I remember having fun before nodding off into a very troubled sleep.

Dead men everywhere, Farren, Thompson in various states of decay! Swaggert's braying voice! Chic roaming around like a schizophrenic demon one minute a dedicated cop the next minute a mad Pole hater! Davie standing bemused, wailing I don't understand. Zuck and his wife sitting in a safari lodge drinking gin slings and talking about wildebeest. Occasionally I sensed Fiona's presence sometimes in the bed often outside of it. Sometimes I tried to speak but no words came out, she just carried on reading. Eventually things went black.

I awoke with a dry mouth and a splitting headache. Fiona was looking down at me smiling whimsically.

"Time to get up I'm afraid" she whispered "Its 7.30 and I have a train to catch."

I sat up and kissed her, "Sorry about last night."

"No problem you were tired."

"Will I see you again?"

"Maybe, but not here I am off home today."

"I could phone you when I get back to London."

"That would be nice"

After a rather long pause I wrote my office number on the hotel notepad and passed it to her. "This is my work number I don't have a phone in my flat. Call me next week if you want to."

"Maybe I will big boy" she said before leaving.

I sat on the bed feeling dejected. Yesterday was a terrible day punctuated by what felt like a polite dumping. Obviously she found men who fell asleep during sex rather unattractive. I couldn't understand why she bothered waiting until I woke up. The phone number thing began to feel extremely cringing, the desperate act of a desperate man. It had been a long time since I had even kissed a woman and it felt like the drought would continue after this brief interlude.

My notebook was on the table. I would need to write a report for Foster today. I wasn't sure where to start or what to leave out. I hoped I hadn't blabbed anything to Fiona, if I did it would further explain her keen departure.

I showered and went down to breakfast. I ate mechanically and barely noticed if there was anyone else in the dining room, the coffee was dreadful. Ahmed's Arab muck was better.

After 8.30 I headed round to the police station again. A young PC standing sentry outside, looked at me closely before stepping aside to let me in. I nodded at the Desk Sergeant and made to go through to the back office.

"Haud oan where are you going sonny?"

"I am still working with Chic and Davie" I said. "There wasn't a problem yesterday."

"Aye well we're in the middle o' a major incident so haud yer horses and sit doon until ah confirm that Inspector Gordon wants tae see ye."

Fuming I sat down reluctant to give the troll the satisfaction of an argument.

"Hello Chic, sorry tae bother ye. Mr Fannybaws is at reception asking tae see ye. Send him up. Ok Chic nae bother, jist didn't know if he was in oan the current situation. Ok Ok... will do."

"You can go up noo", he growled at me.

I tried not to smile as I walked past.

The back office was full of people typing and telephoning furiously. There must have been a riot I thought. As I approached Chic's office I saw Mel sitting at a desk writing a report of some kind. I said hello but she barely acknowledged me. I knocked Chic's door and walked in. Davie was sitting in the corner nursing a mug of tea. Chic was at his desk, just hanging up the phone.

"Phil how are you?"

"Fine thanks, what's the big panic today?"

They both laughed

I stood there bemused

"You don't know do you? Have you listened to the radio this morning?"

"No, why?"

"Well our case blew up completely last night."

"Blew up how? You said Zuck was going to get done for Farren's murder."

"Well yes until some guy from Military Intelligence turned up quoting the Official Secrets Act and flashing an order from the Scottish Secretary saying Zuck was to be released immediately."

"Who was this?" I said already knowing the answer.

"Oh a Major Zuider-Michel, big guy looked like he had spent too much time in the sun."

"Strange what happened then?"

"Well Swaggart fought it but the Scottish Secretary called the Chief Constable and that was that, Zuck walked."

"I don't know what to say."

"Well that would have been weird enough but at seven this morning Zuider-Michel's men plus our armed response guys ambushed the Paddies from the Herbert Starr site near Bowling."

"What do you mean ambushed?"

"They set up a roadblock, stopped the van and then opened fire when they thought one of the Paddies was reaching for a gun. Killed all five of them Gallagher, Flood, Walker, O'Brien and Wilson. When they looked in the van it was full of assault rifles."

I felt faint, seven deaths in 24 hours what the fuck was going on. Zuider-Michel was either insane or playing a very hard game.

"Sit doon son it was a shock tae us as well. Noo it looks like that fanny Snodgrass was right and the press is going insane for information. Every spare copper is next door answering calls from journalists and television stations. Dougie Linnett is presenting it a great success fur Special Branch's intelligence gathering and co-operation with the Security Services."

"What about Thompson, do we know who killed him?"

"Well Mr Zuider-Michel thinks the Paddies killed him."

"Why?"

"Ye''ll like this, apparently Frank spotted them going tae kill Zuck and tried tae stop them, then they kilt him and did a runner."

"What about Farren?"

"Oh that's easy they kilt him tae, because they thought he had exposed them."

"Very convenient."

"It is isn't it. Major lah de dah Zuider-Michel seems tae be the greatest detective since Sherlock Holmes."

"It's all a bag of shite!" shouted Davie. "They murdered those Paddies."

"Calm doon Davie, Dougie's happy wi the story so nae point in rocking the boat. We come oot looking good. Lots of investigating and appearances at the site in Dumbarton, probably made the Paddies crack and try tae move their guns and tie up loose ends like Farren and Zuck. Frank was just a casualty of war."

"Fuck off Chic you don't believe that for a minute. This is biggest cover up I have ever seen."

"Davie, shut it!! Its done and ye cannae change it. Everybody's dead except Zuck and he is being protected by Zuider-Michel so he must have been working for the army all along. I don't understand why we were so wrong. The trouble definitely seemed to be between Zuck and Farren. Those poor old boys just didn't seem the type."

"Innocent men murdered, the provos will make this another Bloody Sunday!" said Davie.

"Maybe Zuider-Michel was right, and the Paddies were undercover terrorists."

"Phil don't be stupid, them old boys just didn't huv it in them."

"Well the Guildford Four and the Birmingham Six didn't look like terrorists either and they went down."

"Aye but nain of them really admitted anything and they huv been appealing ever since."

"Well nae appeals this time, they're aw brown bread."

"Aye but they've all got families, Sinn Fein will be sending them all the names of good lawyers. No way this ends good."

"Don't be such an auld wummin Davie, it wusnae you, this was an army cum MI5 op. Fuck knows what the real reasons fur it were. All we can be sure of is that they were using us. Bet they planted the story on Snodgrass."

I was getting confused now. Gordon seemed to be re-writing history. He was the one who was obsessed with the investigation and pushed it forwards. Zuider-Michel said he wanted it to stop to protect his operation. Now Gordon was claiming he had been duped into the whole thing.

"If you were so suspicious of the investigation why did you get so involved why did you get me involved?" I asked unable to stay silent any longer.

Gordon stared at me as if I had appeared from no-where. "Phil there was a case here but it had fuck all to do with the Paddies and any terrorism."

"What was it about then?"

"Zuck!"

"What about Zuck? He is a near geriatric central European who may or may not have been a Nazi and a Mercenary according to the recently deceased Sean Farren. Not a lot there to go on."

"We had information that suggested that Zuck had been involved in war crimes during the war and later in Africa when he was operating as a mercenary. We investigated and lots about Zuck simply didn't stack up. None of the Polish veterans associations had any record of him serving with their units. In fact no-one remembered meeting Zuck before he returned from Africa."

"Wow, Polish guy invents fantasy past, did you think he was a Russian spy?"

"Yes and we asked your mob to run a check on him. Only then we got told a file existed but it was restricted and we were told to politely piss off."

A light bulb flashed on in my head. "So when Snodgrass started reporting IRA activity on the same site that Zuck was working at, you used that to try and get access to Zuck's record by the back door. You were just using me."

"Yes but how were we to know that the IRA pish would blow up like this."

"Phil," Davie said. "We honestly thought Zuck was the villain, all the surveillance on the Irish guys was just to get you guys on board."

"Well it worked but it seems to have backfired dramatically. There are more bodies than at the end of the Godfather and Zuck is free."

"Well I don't think anybody could have predicted the amount of killing in the last 24 hours. Farren maybe but Thompson and all those Paddies is almost unbelievable. I think we must have spooked the military boys by stumbling on to the truth about the guns. Fuck knows what the Paddies were going to do."

"Was Farren working for you?" I asked.

Gordon frowned.

"He was, wasn't he?"

Gordon shook his head.

Davie filled the silence, "Phil, no he wasn't working for us but we may have helped him compile his dossier."

How did you do that?

"Easy really," Gordon responded "Once we realised he was a CND member we sent Mel in to find out what he was like. It didn't take long for the fanny to blab that she reckoned Zuck was a former Nazi. He had contacted the Weisenthal mob in Vienna with pictures of Zuck and they reckoned he could be one of a number of on the run Krauts. Once Mel had joined the circle it was easy for us to feed in our info disguised as her research."

"Not disguised, it was her research" added Davie

Ok so Mel did the hard work as well as the undercover stuff, was there no limit to the woman's talents?

"I still don't understand what you hoped to achieve. We pretty much stopped hunting Nazis in 1946 when the Russians kicked off the Cold War. You don't really believe any UK court would have convicted him of war crimes, do you? Especially the stuff about Katyn Wood, that wasn't even the Germans it was the Russians."

Gordon looked sheepish, "No I don't think we could have got him for that stuff but there are warrants for his arrest in Zimbabwe, Zambia, Congo, Cameroon and the Central African Republic."

"Very commendable but again I can't see any British court sending an old white guy back to some tin pot African dictatorship to get executed. What were you really up to?"

"Philip we were doing the right thing, Zuck is a mass murderer."

I looked round to see Mel standing in the doorway. "Hi Mel" I stammered.

"Philip you don't seem to care that Zuck has got away with murder for nearly 40 years."

I couldn't take much more of this nonsense. "You have all read too many Commando Comics. Not every man with a Central European accent is a runaway Nazi war criminal."

"Well Philip your friend Mr Zuck is the exception that proves the rule. He was in command of a unit that chased the troops carrying the Polish National Bank's reserves to Romania. The farmers who had sheltered their own troops were lined up and shot by Zuck's unit."

"That's war for you its brutal!"

"Zuck's unit was one of the original Einsatzgruppen, Zuck trained the Selbstschutz himself. There are loads of pictures of him in the Stroop Report"

I looked blankly at Mel as she spouted the blizzard of German phrases

"The Selbstschutz were volunteer executioners, by 1945 they had murdered 45,000 Poles and your Mr Zuck was a leading light! Not only that, he was heavily involved in the liquidation of the Warsaw Ghetto. You are right about Katyn Wood but as a pseudo Commie Sean was attracted by the prospect of proving the Soviets were innocent so we pulled together some stuff that implicated Zuck."

"Interesting but still ancient history, I still can't see what justification you have for pursuing him now. The wars over and we have new threats to our existence that are far more pressing than raking up old time Nazi stories."

"Listen he's a war criminal who carried on killing for another thirty years after Berlin fell. Israel have a long standing warrant for his arrest."

"Really? He is hardly Eichmann or Mengele" I snorted.

"No but he harboured plenty of their friends and former colleagues over the years. He wasn't alone in Africa; he employed many on the run SS men and former camp guards."

"Oh for god's sake 'The Odessa File' was just a film, there is no giant conspiracy to protect runaway Nazis. Even if there was I am not convinced it is your job to hunt them down. Have Israel formally asked for Zuck to be extradited?"

"No"

"Ok I don't know what has been going on here but it has to stop. Seven men have been murdered for reasons we don't understand but it doesn't look like Zuck killed any of them."

"Well on the surface it looks like that" said Chic, "However despite the fact that he was sprung last night by his military chum, we investigated the statement he gave Davie and you. Interestingly some of what he told you when he was confessing seems to be true."

The room was silent all of us listening intently.

"Cannon checked out the lay-by where Zuck said he burned Farren's dossier and guess what he found?"

"A pile of litter" sniggered Davie.

"Aye that and something else, namely a partially burned set of documents that look suspiciously like the missing file from Farren's house. He is bringing them in now. So I think old Zuck is still in the frame for the Farren murder or is at least an accessory to it."

"What about Thompson are you saying he killed Thompson too?"

"Well I wouldn't put it past him or his boss Mr Zuider-Michel."

"Why?"

"Well I suspect it was because they thought Frank saw something he shouldn't have," said Davie.

"What exactly would make killing a policeman worthwhile?" I snapped back.

"I suspect it was Zuider-Michel and his boys picking up Zuck to go and murder Farren" said Mel.

"You can't prove it though."

"No but Chic is going to speak to Linnett now and let him know the facts."

Chic stood up with the full dossier under his arm and whistled 'Wish me Luck as you wave me goodbye', as he left the room.

We then sat in silence.

"So how did you miss the news Phil?" Davie asked mischieviously. "It's been on the radio since 8am."

I smiled and said "I was so tired this morning I didn't bother turning the radio on."

"Oh aye, yesterday was a tiring day. Did you have a tiring night too? Young man alone in a hotel, nobody to disturb him, eh?"

I blushed and said "Rubbish! I had a report to write then fell asleep."

"Leave him alone Davie not everybody is a desperado like you." said Mel.

I neatly changed the subject by asking for access to a typewriter.

"Use mine" said Davie and I left them in Chic's office.

Chapter 28

After two and a half hours I had completed a masterpiece and posted it to Foster. It covered all the key events and my analysis that Zuider-Michel had liquidated the IRA cell to protect Zuck. I called him from Davie's phone to give him a summary.

"Foster here," the old country voice as clear as ever.

"Hi it's Phil Featherstonehaugh."

"My God it's my top agent, terrific job up there in Jockoland. I have had a pile of good reports on you from our military chums. Old Zuider-Michel thinks you did a cracking number on the plods."

"Well I ah er.."

"Don't be bashful lad, this kind of operation doesn't come along too often these days and they rarely turn out so well. Paddy gun runners eliminated without any need for a messy trial. Local plod tied in to the operation so that they can't call foul. The Army boys keep their agent out of jail, it's excellent. The only downside being that Herrity wasn't one of the casualties."

I was shocked at the depth of his knowledge and the rather vehement reference to Herrity who after all was essentially an innocent teenaged by-stander.

"John Herrity is a very dangerous man and one day we will catch him."

"I thought he was dead," I said, relieved that Foster was discussing Herrity senior.

"Is he hell!" said Foster. "That murdering provo is still on the loose but one day we will get him. Anyway well done, are you heading back to London tonight?"

"Yes I think so, just waiting for Gordon to come back and I will say my farewells."

"Good keep up a front of supportiveness; teach the beggars a lesson for trying to start messing around on our patch. See you tomorrow, bye lad."

With that he put the phone down. I called British Rail and booked a bunk on tonight's sleeper. I wandered back into Gordon's room where Davie sat fielding calls and drinking tea.

"This is mental the papers are loving it. Think the Record is going to have a 'Bomb plot thwarted by hero cops' headline. Dougie Linnett will be on all the telly news programmes bumping his gums and explaining how he broke the case. He thinks he is Superman, probably solved the Kennedy assassination when he was in New York last year on his holidays."

I laughed

"Chic'll bring him down to earth wi our evidence against Zuck though."

"Fingers crossed" I said.

A couple of minutes later Chic walked in and subsided into his desk.

"Well?" Davie queried.

"Well what?"

"Did Dougie gie the go ahead tae lift Zuck?"

"No"

"Why not?"

"Because according to our esteemed leader Zuck is a valuable military intelligence agent who almost had his cover blown by our investigation. We have been given an unequivocal message to steer well clear of the old Polish Nazi from now on."

"So??"

"So Davie are you fucking stupid? You did hear what I just said?"

"Aye but..."

"Nae buts, just say Aye Chic and shut up! I am well pissed off but Linnett told me to drop it in no uncertain terms. You can carry on hunting Zuck if you want tae end up directing traffic in Gairloch or chasing grouse rustlers in Uist. If you want tae keep your job however you best forget you ever saw head or tail of our Polish pal."

Davie looked at the floor

"It's a shitey cover up!" Mel added from the doorway

"So what! We just need to back off and get on with the day job. We tried; it didnae work now we need to move on."

Mel shook her head in disgust.

I tried to lighten the mood, "The good news is I am heading home on this evening's sleeper so I best check out of the hotel and get out of your hair."

"Oh Phil we'll miss you" said Mel affectionately.

I almost blushed.

"Aye well pity we dragged you through this fracas, we thought we had some real evidence against old Zuck but hey shit happens" said Chic offering me his hand. "All the best maybe our paths will cross again someday."

"You never know" I said.

Mel gave me a hug then returned to her desk. I walked out with Davie. "I have hours to kill before the train at 10pm."

"True, I'll meet you for a pint in the Horseshoe Bar by the station after work if you want. Say sevenish."

"Sounds like a plan" I said and took a note of Davie's extensive directions.

I left the station buzzing with activity and strolled back to the hotel. On the bedside table I found a bra, presumably Fiona's the cleaner must have found it when she made the bed. I slipped it into my suitcase and headed down to reception.

As I paid my bill I asked the receptionist if the lady in 316 had checked out as I had a message for her. The receptionist looked at the register and then looked at me oddly. "Sorry sir room 316 has been empty all week; your friend must have been in another room." I restrained my self from arguing with her and assumed she had made a mistake or was reluctant to release details of another guest.

I wandered over to the bar and ordered a lager. The barman nodded to my case and said "Checking out?"

"Yes, back to London tonight."

"Did you enjoy Glasgow?"

"Oh yes, pretty wild place you have here."

"Yeah, if you don't mind me saying so, that bird you pulled was a strange one."

I felt myself blushing, "She was alright" I managed to squeak

"Aye but it was a bit strange the way she hung round the bar of an evening."

"Well she probably didn't know anyone in Glasgow to go out with. Its difficult staying in hotels on business trips, especially for women."

"Well I don't know where she was staying but it wasn't here."

"She was definitely a guest here" I said.

"No way, I checked, I was concerned that she might be a working girl. The hotel doesn't let them operate on the premises. She wasn't a guest. She came in about seven the last two evenings with an army type, a big guy with over shiny shoes, a tan and a straight back. Your classic English officer! He stayed for one drink and left then she hung around like a bad smell until you appeared each night. Did you check your wallet each morning?"

I tried to speak but couldn't think of anything to say. I had that sinking feeling you get when you have been had. Zuider-Michel had played me like a violin even down to running a honey trap to see what I had learned.

"Shakes ye up when you find out ye spent the night wi a brass, eh! Never mind mate; yer on yer way hame and it doesn't sound like she robbed you!" He moved off to serve another customer while I subsided into a chair and sat staring at my glass.

After half an hour of feeling very sorry for myself, I staggered out of the hotel and hailed a taxi for Central Station. Recriminations and horrors swept through my mind. Zuider-Michel probably knew everything I did this week and probably had pictures of me in bed with Fiona. I was mortified I had seen plenty of horror in the past two days and now I had exposed myself to a major risk of blackmail. I couldn't tell the truth to Gordon and I would need to be very careful around Foster in case Zuider-Michel gave him a detailed update on my night-time activities. Simply put it felt like I had been screwed royally.

From Central Station I wandered around until I found a café restaurant beside a sports shop where I had an expensive burger and chips. Afterwards I strolled down Buchanan Street a pedestrianised shopping street packed with rushing commuters. I meandered round the city for another hour becoming increasing bored as the shops closed and the people disappeared home for their dinners presumably. I circled back towards the station following Davie's directions to the Horseshoe Bar. It was an impressive warm room full of men conversing in the loud angry voices of three pint drunkenness. I ordered a pint and found an empty table and sat down.

It was hard to settle, partly because of the location. Strange bars are never relaxing when you are a solitary stranger. I was still disturbed by the Fiona discovery and a general sense that something really bad had happened. There was a gnawing guilt that I may have missed something that could have prevented the previous day's orgy of violence. For the life of me I couldn't understand what I could have done differently.

Suddenly a hand slapped onto my table. Shocked I looked up in to Davie's laughing face.

"Fair scared the shite out of you there," he said. "I'll hey a heavy if you're buying" he sniggered as he sat down. I got up and walked to the bar glad of the chance to compose myself. I felt quite shaken from my reverie, almost disorientated.

Back at the table we drank in silence for a few minutes before Davie spoke. "Don't worry if you are feeling disturbed by what's happened it's a normal reaction" he said not looking at me. "Most coppers have nightmares after seeing their first corpse, so you will take a while to get over what you saw in the last couple of days. Thank fuck we didn't have to go to Bowling apparently it was a blood bath with bits of the Paddies lying everywhere. They Army SLRs are mair like cannons than rifles, they blow bits aff ye. They old bastards didnae deserve that. Mark my words it'll cause loads of trouble. The Irish love a martyr and old Captain Zuiderman made five this morning."

"You really think so?" I said. "Loads of IRA men have died and they are not all martyrs."

"Aye but this stinks, once the likes of the Guardian start sniffing around all the backslapping will look pretty silly. We watched those old boys closely for weeks and they did fuck all except work and drink. I can't believe we missed their gun running sideline."

I said nothing, unsure whether or not Davie was right. Terrified that Zuider – Michel was lying. Conscious that if I had spoken up maybe Chic could have interviewed them and possibly deterred them from further gun running. I had the overwhelming feeling that they were murdered for no good reason.

"Aye you were right earlier we should never have pursued Zuck so hard. It was madness but Chic and Mel thought it was the right thing to do."

"And you didn't?"

"Well I didnae say that, but It was speculative at best."

"Doesn't matter now, eh?"

"Naw for you anyway. Glesca will be a war zone for a while particularly at the next Old Firm game but it will calm down. What time is your train?"

"I can board from 10."

"Oh well time for another four or five pints then" laughed Davie.

An hour and a half later we were both quite merry.

I was getting up to leave when Chic strode in.

"Awright ya pair o steamers. Ah'm here tae make sure Fannybaws makes his train. Hud a good night?"

"Oh yes" I said.

"He's pissed" said Davie.

"An you're no far away" said Chic picking up my case. I only swayed a little as Chic led us to Platform 10. I was just about to give my name to the steward when Chic turned round and whistled.

Mel appeared from nowhere, the woman was a chameleon. She was dressed in her Julie Simpson outfit and looked simply fabulous. I smiled at her and she smiled back.

"Smitten!" said Davie.

"Aye just as we suspected" drawled Chic.

I thought I saw the slightest hint of a blush under Mel's makeup. "Shut it you old gits leave him alone" snapped Mel, very much in her Julie Simpson persona.

She took my hand and said very softly "Goodbye Phil, thanks for your help. We are all sorry it turned out the way it did."

"It's not your fault" I said trying to stay calm. I was feeling surprisingly touched by the way they had all turned up to see me off. "Despite it all I have had a pretty good time" I said "You all made me very welcome. I don't think I will be able to cope with going back to my boring job."

Davie sniggered, "Yes Mr Bond we all believe you are just a Civil Servant who spends his days paper pushing."

I shrugged unsure how to respond.

Chic broke the silence by shaking my hand. "Good luck Phil, don't forget us when you are back in the Big Smoke. Keep in touch; you've got Davie's number."

"Thanks Chic" I said feeling slightly more emotional.

"Aye, I might look you up when I come down for the Scotland v England game at Wembley" laughed Davie. "Aw ra best Phil, safe journey."

Thanks guys I said and turned to get on the train.

I felt a tug at my arm and before I knew it Mel kissed me on the lips and whispered in my ear "See you again soon."

I smiled at her completely shocked and she smiled up at me and winked in a very salacious way. I nearly fainted with a combination of fear, lust and excitement. Davie and Chic's laughter brought me back to reality.

"C'mon you've got work to do, poor Phil will be throbbing all the way hame. Any mair and he might need tae change his breeks!"

"Shut it Chic" giggled Mel, "Bye Phil" she cried and then walked off with Chic arm in arm like a couple.

"Gie's a phone later in the week" said Davie as he followed them.

Chapter 29

I found myself sharing a cabin with a plastics man from the IBM plant in Greenock. It's a strange experience to share sleeping quarters with a complete stranger. We talked about Glasgow and London and our respective jobs I could see my cover as a hardwood furniture salesman bored him rigid almost as quickly as I glazed over when he described the intricacies of plastics moulding in the computing industry.

I mentioned the Glasgow shootings, he shrugged and said "It served the bloody Fenians right, the cheek of them trying to plan terrorist attacks in Scotland." I could see it was not a subject he was keen on and suggested we adjourn to the bar. After a couple of drinks I retired to the cabin and slept like a log and awoke at 6.30 in Euston. The steward brought us tea and toast and we got ready to get off the train. My companion wandered off heading for a train to Reading. I decided to head home and change before going to work.

At Rubberwood Road everything seemed the same but felt like it belonged to another world, like returning to your childhood bedroom after being away at boarding school. It smelt strange, not homely. The underlying stench of curry and sweat always made me queasy when I climbed the stairs. I opened my door and had a clear sense that someone had been in the room since I left. There was a definite scent, more soap and Old Spice than the sour aroma of my housemates. The bed was too tidy and when I looked in my wardrobe and drawers things simply did not appear to be in order. Some of the jacket pockets had been turned inside out; my socks were in the top drawer not in their usual bottom drawer location. My room had been searched by someone who wanted me to know it.

This was a classic intimidation tactic, the sort of thing that was covered on Day two of my initial department training. Let an agent know his cover is blown and nine times out of ten he will run. I could only assume my friend Mr Zuider-Michel arranged it to keep me on my toes. I resolved to stay calm, the worst case scenario was that they had bugged the room but as I had no phone there didn't seem much point.

After unpacking, showering and popping on fresh clothes I headed off to work.

The office was its glum self, people ignored me as usual. I felt like I had been away for a hundred years rather than a few days. Admittedly the most disturbing days of my life; that appeared to be replying in vivid colour every time I shut my eyes. Last night's beer had anesthetised me but the horror was starting to really hit home. By the time I reached my desk I felt decidedly shaky.

Simcox looked up and said "You're back. Looks like you need a drink."

Before I could speak a mug of tea was on my desk and Simcox was towering over me. "So pretty rough up there by all accounts?"

I nodded.

"Yes we saw the news and read the reports. The Army boys went over the top didn't they. I told you to be careful with those plods; they only call us in if they are up their necks in the smelly stuff. Foster is very happy though, said you played a blinder and kept plod on the hop. He reckons we will get lots of kudos from the Army boys for our help on this one. Pity Herrity got away. I almost had him in Zambia in the 60's but him and his mercenary pals broke out before we could finish them."

I couldn't believe it they were all obsessed with the allegedly dead John Herrity. "Yes I said it was a tough week."

"Well yes, all the training in the world doesn't prepare you for casualties. Hard to simulate mutilated bodies that only comes with experience. How was old Zuck?"

"Fine if a little strange, do you know him?"

"Oh yes worked with him in Kenya, Burundi and Zambia in the 50s and 60s. They bred those old SS men tough."

"The Glasgow cops wanted to arrest him for his SS crimes."

"Typical, their job is to catch crooks and would be terrorists not re-fight the war. There is no way the British Government would risk Zuck being arrested for that. He knows where a great deal of our skeletons are buried. He was a master agent. Anyway drink your tea and go and see John. He is waiting for you."

Stunned by the extent of Simcox, the office bore's, knowledge. I swallowed my tea in silence and wandered off to see Foster.

The interview/de-brief was long and friendly. Four hours later I left the office having recounted the full facts of my trip only excluding my nights with the mysterious Fiona. Foster and the secretary scribing the session found the tales of Mel and her undercover activities fascinating, especially the brothel.

"Amazing Phil I had no idea Linnett had things so well sewn up. That girl should work for us." After some ill-deserved praise I returned to my office read some of my outstanding in-tray items and went home at my usual time.

From there my day time life returned to normal work was back to the dull routine. My relationship with Simcox was more relaxed. Foster sent me on some rather energetic training courses in weapons, undercover work and field exercises with Sandhurst Officer cadets.

Davie called occasionally often about work as Glasgow became increasingly tense. The City Council in a rare moment of genius staved off the risk of major sectarian trouble by offering to pay for the Bowling dead to be buried in their home villages in Donegal. Gallagher had a massive funeral in Dunfanaghy where he was a well known figure. Martin McGuinness and Gerry Adams attended all of the funerals but Gallagher's was the only one where they carried the coffin to the graveside. Wilson had a smaller funeral in Newtoncunningham where he had only a smattering of relatives still living. A man in a Black beret and balaclava played the last post as his coffin was lowered. In Gorthahork O'Brien was waked for days before the unsteady mourners gave him a traditional funeral with no obvious Republican trappings. In Moville Flood was laid to rest quietly, his coffin carried through the town on a horse drawn hearse covered by the Irish Tricolour. Walker's funeral in the tiny village of Drumoghill was attended by young Herrity and his McGill relations. Walker was the only one to be buried with military honours. An honour guard in uniform appeared at the graveside and fired shots over the grave in full view of camera crews and police.

At each funeral the Sinn Fein leadership proclaimed the men as martyrs; victims of the British government's ruthless policy of murdering and maltreating Irish Catholics. The British press generally toed the official line and took the Sinn Fein presence and the strong Republican tone of the funerals as clear evidence of the men's guilt.

In Glasgow Davie reported that they were disarming sectarian thugs from both sides on a daily basis. Thankfully the automatic rifles had disappeared and the executions of drug dealers had ceased. The mysterious undead Mr Herrity had disappeared into thin air.

About six months later after strong campaigns by Nationalists; a number of enquiries were set up to look into the British Government's shoot to kill policy in Northern Ireland. One journalist Denis Jordan from the Morning Star began investigating the Bowling Massacre as it was called by Sinn Fein. A local priest in Old Kilpatrick had organised Vigil masses at the site every month and campaigned strongly from the pulpit for the investigation to be re-opened. Sean Farren and his five colleagues were slowly becoming a cause celebre. A major demonstration was being planned for the first anniversary of Bowling Ambush on 12th October 1984.

Jordan was extremely efficient in gathering facts, greatly helped by Rueben Snodgrass selling his story to the *Daily Record* and describing in great detail how he identified the terror gang and was laughed at by the police.

To my chagrin he recounted in graphic detail his interviews with Chic and Davie and a mysterious man from the ministry (ex SAS by the looks of him). The man was a lying toad but describing me as ex SAS was quite entertaining and made me a bit of an office hero. In Snodgrass' account the cops were dim witted numbskulls who only woke up when the SAS man got involved. I didn't realise I had made such an impression on Snodgrass.

Jordan interviewed Snodgrass and numerous others from the Herbert Star site and pulled together a story that reeked of cover up. He didn't find out about much new on the Frank Thompson murder but he raised many questions about Sean Farren's death and the tenuous link between the five Bowling victims and either murder or indeed gun running. Someone from the Drumchapel station fed him information that suggested that the five men were never suspected of Farren's murder whereas another man had confessed to it and been mysteriously released hours before the Bowling Massacre. At first his stories in the Morning Star got ignored by the mainstream media but he persisted and started suggesting that he now knew who the man from the Ministry was and also the identity of the man who confessed to the Farren murder.

When Foster read this he was furious. I was told to keep a low profile, which was pretty easy now that I had resumed my humdrum existence in bedsitter land. Foster presumably spoke to Zuider-Michel or someone similar. Within hours an injunction had been imposed on Jordan forbidding him to publish any of the names or indeed write any more about the Bowling Massacre. Jordan refused to reveal his sources and tried to release the names. His home was raided and his notes and records confiscated. Jordan was arrested for breaching the injunction and was remanded to Barlinnie prison.

Jordan's arrest sparked an outcry in Republican circles and among the liberal media. John Pilger began investigating the case for World in Action. In Glasgow there was three nights of rioting after Rueben Snodgrass was shot dead as his Orange Band marched past a Catholic church in Coatbridge. The combination of an assault on an Orange parade and the death of a man who had closely associated himself with the Bowling Massacre unleashed a wave of sectarian violence across the city, bars were burnt out in a number of locations and Catholic and Protestants gangs fought pitched battles in a number of housing estates. Rioting in the predominately Catholic Royston Road area was particularly fierce with the locals declaring it Free Glasgow after a wild night which ended with the police withdrawing from the area. Pleas by the Pope for calm and the government's threat to deploy the army brought an uneasy peace to the city. Burnt out buses littered the main arteries to the city centre. The news reports depicted a war zone.

Provost Kennedy oversaw a tacit de-escalation by the Police and intense negotiations with leaders of the main Catholic and Protestant gangs which brought an end to the violence. Davie gave me daily reports plus a running total on his overtime which he reckoned would pay for a new car and a holiday in the

States. He said Chic almost cheered when he heard Snodgrass had been shot. He told me not to worry about Jordan as they had found "fuck all in his papers" that could identify me.

World in Action loved the riots and produced a lurid programme outlining how the Bowling victims and Sean Farren had been ruthlessly killed by the British state on the say so of an Orange zealot(Snodgrass). Much claptrap was trotted out about the Economic League and its stranglehold on Scottish society. Snodgrass was presented as a man with connections to the Scottish establishment and Loyalist terror groups in Northern Ireland. The mysterious man from the ministry was recorded as being present at all of the crime scenes. The description of me was getting closer but was still more muscular SAS tough than weedy Civil Servant in a bad jacket.

Foster began to get worried that my cover would be blown. I was called into his office on the 8th October 1984. "Phil you need a change, you need the challenge of field work not wasting away with old fogeys like us. Our game is simply too tame for a fellow like you. Its time you moved to a department where your undercover skills will be most useful. The most dynamic theatre in British Intelligence where every day is a battle to protect our way of life!"

At this point my chest swelled with proud anticipation, I was being transferred to Berlin the dream posting for any serious Intelligence officer. I couldn't believe it.

"Yes the most dangerous place to work in Britain. I have arranged for you to report to St Lucia as a liaison officer to the Army."

St Lucia! Amazing even better than Berlin I would be in the Caribbean up against the Colombian Drug cartels and the Cubans.

It's a short flight so you should be there by mid-morning tomorrow.

"A short flight, arrive by mid morning is that possible?" I spluttered.

"Oh yes lad you are only in the air about forty minutes."

Was the old fool going senile?

"Yes in the air forty minutes and then about an hour's drive to Omagh."

Omagh they were sending me to Northern Ireland, a fucking death sentence. If the Provos don't get me boredom would.

"What do you think Phil? Are you up for the challenge? There is no tougher place to operate in than Army West."

"John is it the right place for me, especially after last year in Glasgow."

"Son you are perfect for this operation, if you can integrate with Glasgow Special Branch you will love the RUC guys."

"What if someone recognises me, or I get named by journalists writing about Bowling. I wouldn't want to become a liability."

"Don't worry about that old boy. You are getting a new identity with a full cover story. We'll 'disappear' you from London. No-one will be able to track you down as long as you keep your lips sealed. Just tell the family you are working in Europe, let them think you are selling furniture in Brussels or somewhere. I take it they don't know what you really do."

"No, of course not!"

"Good well, pop down to Jilly and get your new papers. Say goodbye to Phil, from now on you are Edwin Coulter, a Ventilation duct salesman. You will be our liaison man between the Army and the RUC. Between you and me it's like an acronym convention, there is the MRF, the FRU, SPG, E4A, E4B, SSU all of them running their own agents and operations. I need you to get them under control or at least allow us to track what they are up to. There are more than a few of the strong characters you handled so well in Jockoland. This is a big job so make sure you read the briefing pack."

"Thanks John I won't let you down."

"Oh don't worry you won't. By the way we are bringing Linnett's floozy on board from next week."

"Who?"

"Oh that wonder-woman you met up in Glasgow, DS Kerr. After your report we checked her out and liked what we saw. She is one of the best undercover operatives I've seen for years."

I couldn't believe it, Mel joining the team, it was a dream come true. "Will DS Kerr be working in Ulster too?"

"Oh God no! We have some special jobs for that lady; she won't wandering around the Bogside chasing PIRA. Not her bag my boy. Anyway time you got going. Once you pick up your papers head home and pack, don't worry about anything you can't get in your suitcase as Polkemmet with be round tomorrow morning to give the place a deep clean and pay off your landlord. To be on the safe side he will tell them you died in a tube accident. No bloody journalist will be able to trace you. We will make sure your flatmates know you have gone off to the bedsit in the sky like a good faceless commuter. We've planted a small piece in tomorrow's Standard about you falling onto the tracks at East Finchley.

So its good luck Edwin, wave goodbye to Phil for a while." With that he patted me on the back and pointed me to the door.

Chapter 30

The following morning I picked up a hire car from Aldergrove Airport and drove through a succession of semi-fortified towns and villages to Omagh. The sectarian divide was all to obvious in the abundance of tricolours, Republican grafitti and police stations covered in barbed wire in the Catholic areas and the Union Jacks, red, white and blue kerb stones and murals of King Billy in the Loyalist districts. I was halted at numerous checkpoints by soldiers and RUC officers. The routine was the same each time but it was clear that some found Edwin Coulter an odd fish.

A few times I was asked to leave the car while it was searched and subjected to a round of probing questioning on who I was, the purpose of my visit and where I was going. My bundle of TyRaVent brochure's was just about convincing especially as my cover said I had just started the job after being made redundant from the furniture trade. One para sergeant was particularly unimpressed and questioned me rather aggressively, trying all the old tricks to see if I was a closet Republican such as asking who I knew in Derry. To which I replied I have never been to Londonderry. Eventually he gave up after getting a RUC man to take my fingerprints and my photograph.

When I finally reached Omagh I checked into the rather optimistically named Gortin Castle Hotel and called my contact at the barracks a Major Crichton.

"Hello" said a familiar voice.

"Hello Edwin Coulter here from TyRaVent, I would like to call round and give you a demonstration of our latest ventilation systems."

"Ah yes Coulter we've been expecting you, how was the journey? No trouble on the road?"

"No the flight was quick and I didn't have too many issues apart from these dashed checkpoints."

"True the squaddies can be a real pain, jumped up little buggers. Where are you now?"

"I am at the Gortin Castle Hotel."

"Excellent I will meet you there in an hour."

I put the phone down and had the clear sense that I had spoken to Crichton before but I couldn't remember when. I assumed he may have been on one of the courses at Sandhurst or that as the provos used to joke all Brit Officers had the same British Army accent.

The hotel had lots of wartime pictures taken when it was an American Army billet. One picture suggested that Montgomery and Eisenhower had met there. Back in my I room I unpacked and mused on Major Crichton, the voice seeming increasingly familiar.

I sat at the window and read *The Last Parallel*, a book I had become increasingly fond of after Glasgow. I found I had to keep my mind occupied these days or my thoughts wandered too quickly back to Farren and his hideously broken neck, Thompson's blood soaked shirt and worst of all Zuider-Michel's sinister presence. My daydreaming had virtually stopped as had my libido. I rarely lusted after women on trains or waitresses these days whereas before I had been obsessed. It was like my innocence ended in Glasgow.

Every day since I had tried desperately to suppress a sense that I was somehow responsible for the bloodbath! Any waking hour not filled with work or some form of activity brought forth a stream of guilt and recrimination. I had become one of the desperately sociable, always available for a trip to the pub after work, even on occasion with Simcox. My name was first on any group outings, skiing, hill walking, football, rugby you name it and I was there playing furiously. Anything to avoid being alone with my thoughts.

I skimmed the *Belfast Telegraph* and found on page 5 yet another journalist investigating the Bowling Massacre. This guy was claiming there had been a loyalist cover-up after Snodgrass was shot. Apparently Snodgrass was a leading UVF man who led the team that killed the Bowling Five. The Glasgow cops apparently claimed responsibility to avoid a massive wave of Catholic v Protestant rioting.

It seemed that Snodgrass was upset that his superb operation was denied the worldwide recognition for taking out an IRA ASU. Apparently he was killed before he could sell his full story to the papers to prevent a UK backlash against the loyalist community. The story was dreadfully written by a typical hack journalist, full of assumptions and no evidence and naturally enough the brawny ex SAS man who sat in on Chic's interviews with Snodgrass was the driving force behind Snodgrass' murder. The worrying thing was that this fellow seemed to believe he knew what the SAS type's name was. At least he thought Bill Fanbeau was the mysterious man from the ministry's name. At that point I realised that the source of the man from the ministry's name was the old troll of a desk sergeant in Cranstonhill who was supplementing his pension by selling snippets to the papers. I could understand how Philip Fannybaws as he used to call me could be converted to Bill Fanbeau by a journalist unfamiliar with the Glasgow accent. At least there would be no one in Omagh who could connect me to the Bowling massacre.

Printed in Great Britain
by Amazon